I0762042

In Manchester, vigilantes are setting traps online to expose sexual predators and once they have a suspect in their sights they're taking the law into their own hands, acting as judge, jury and executioner.

When the suicide of a troubled woman near to Hanging Lees Reservoir implicates an old friend, reporter Danny Johnston has no choice but to investigate.

As more bodies are discovered Danny finds himself being pulled deeper and deeper into a case whose roots date back decades, and as he tries to uncover the truth he begins to be haunted by horrifying dreams of his own.

A terrible secret, kept for than 40 years is about to change everything.

In the final act of David Nolan's Manc Noir trilogy, *The Ballad of Hanging Lees* will play us out... then fade to black.

"The King Of Manc Noir." – Altricham Word Festival

"A dark but compelling novel very much rooted in fact." – I Love Manchester

"Manchester is a location that's been underused in fiction but David Nolan is keen to claim it - this is Manc Noir." - Northern Soul Magazine

This edition first published 2022 by Fahrenheit Press

ISBN: 978-1-914475-38-2

10 9 8 7 6 5 4 3 2 1

www.Fahrenheit-Press.com

F 4 E

The Ballad Of Hanging Lees

By

David Nolan

Fahrenheit Press

Books in the Manc Noir series…

- *Black Moss*
- *The Mermaid's Pool*
- *The Ballad of Hanging Lees*

For Katherine, Jake, Scott and Bonnie…

And the other love of my life, United Utilities, looking after reservoirs in the North West of England.

Manc Noir: A Glossary of Terms

Any road:	*Anyway.*
Chuffed:	*Pleased.*
Cordial:	*Dilutable juice, often orange or blackcurrant.*
Dead:	*Really. Eg: 'I'm dead chuffed.'*
Effing & Jeffing:	*Swearing.*
Ginnel:	*An alley between or behind houses.*
Mam:	*Mother.*
Mard arse:	*Someone who is overly sensitive and easily upset. Not to be confused with the Yorkshire 'mard' which means moody.*
Mucky:	*Dirty.*
Mither:	*To bother or cause trouble.*
Nora:	*A woman's name often attached to a swear word. Eg: 'Bloody Nora.'*
Nowt:	*Nothing.*
Odd:	*Added to other words when approximating something. Eg: 'It's worth fifteen-odd quid, no more than that.'*
On the knocker:	*Turning up unannounced at someone's front door.*
Owt:	*Anything.*
Piffy on a rock bun:	*To waste time or be of no use. Eg: 'Stop standing there like Piffy on a rock bun.' Yes, it is a very odd expression.*

Proper: *Really.*

Right: *Very. Eg: 'That's right tasty.'*

Ta: *Thanks.*

Tea: *Evening meal. Teatime is rarely much later than six pm.*

Tight: *Mean, miserly, unwilling to share.*

Un: *One. Eg: 'You're a wrong un, you are.'*

Vimto: *Mysterious Mancunian fruit cordial (see above). No one knows what's actually in it*

MAP OF MANC NOIR

1 Pennine Way Footbridge
2 Windy Hill Transmitter
3 Bull's Head Pub
4 Maggie Ormrod's House
5 Hanging Lees Reservoir
6 Hunter's Hollow School
7 John Smithdown's House
8 Black Moss Reservoir
9 Royal Oldham Hospital
10 Oldham Athletic F.C.
11 Oldham Police Station
12 Kate Smithdown's House
13 Danny Johnston's House
14 Alexandra Park

The Ballad Of Hanging Lees

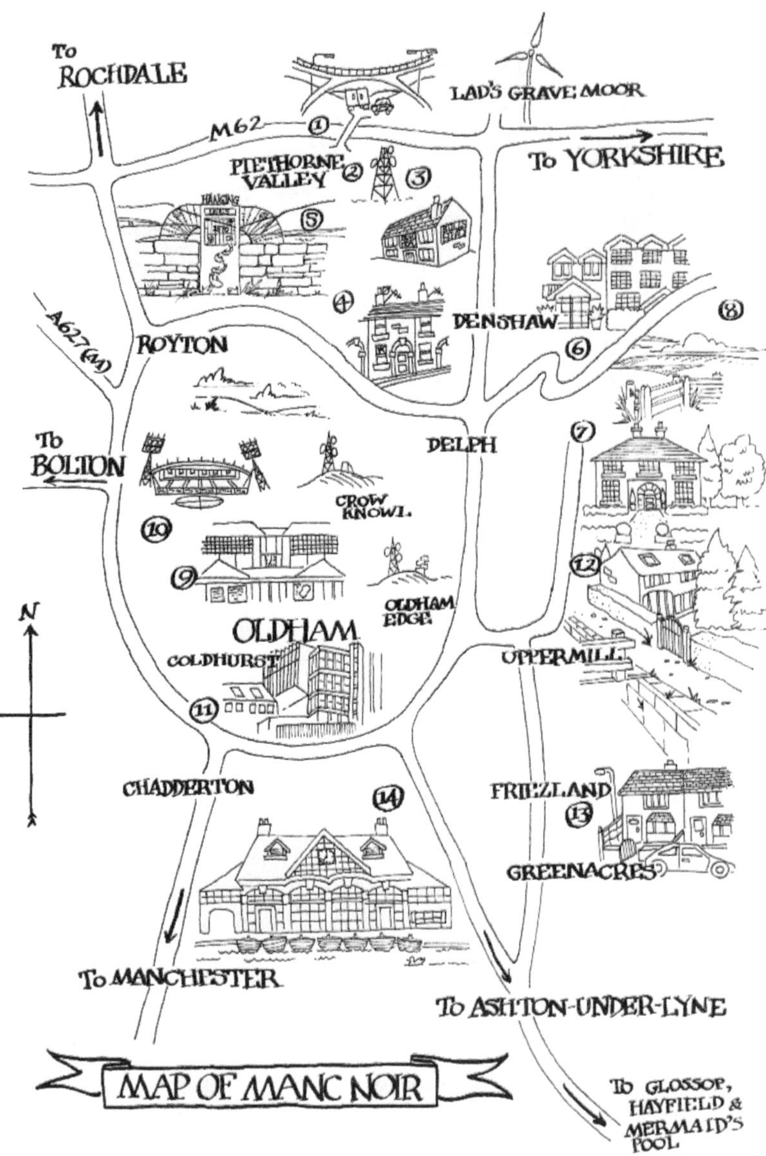

The following is an extract from the book *Twisted Sisters - The Inside Story of Manchester's Most Notorious Child Killers Since the Moors Murderers* by Danny Johnston.

I first came across the terrible handiwork of Beth Hall and Jan Cave at Black Moss Reservoir on the outskirts of Oldham in April 1990. I saw the body of a little boy face down in the sand, weights taped to his tiny chest in a failed attempt to sink his body into the dark waters of the reservoir. The child had been tortured and killed by the two women, one a journalist, the other a police officer. The press later dubbed them the 'Twisted Sisters'.

He was their first victim. But not their last.

At the time, it seemed like no one cared about this poor little boy. A few miles away, rioters had taken over Strangeways Jail, occupying the roof of the prison for 25 days. They provided a show that the whole world seemed very keen to watch.

Thanks to the media, it was the only story that people were offered at the time. The commercial radio station I worked for in 1990 - Manchester Radio - very quickly worked out which side their broadcasting bread was buttered. Strangeways was a listener magnet, and more listeners meant you could charge more for advertisements. Therefore, the more Strangeways we give them, the more money we'll make.

That boy at Black Moss was never identified. To this day I still think about him. I feel ashamed that I didn't try harder to get people interested in his story. But in 1990 every journalist in Manchester saw Strangeways as their ticket to glory. Me included.

Maybe if we had given more airtime to that boy, then Beth Hall and Jan Cave wouldn't have been able to carry on with a killing spree that lasted until 2016. Twelve children died at their hands. *Twelve.*

The two-pronged trick they used to commit then cover up their crimes was ghoulishly simple: wait until the attention of the police and the media was diverted elsewhere by a riot, a bomb or a political scandal… and then strike. Plus, they made sure they targeted kids that had no one to speak on their behalf: care home kids.

They'd worked out that the best way to steal something and not get caught is to steal something nobody really wants. They took children that no one missed - what dreadful words they are to write - while everyone was looking in the other direction.

As well as killing all those poor children, Beth Hall and Jan Cave drugged and kidnapped the son of my friend Kate Smithdown. They attacked and nearly killed her father, former Detective Inspector John Smithdown. They murdered my friend and former colleague at Manchester Radio, Gary Keenan. And they tried to kill me.

But why did they do it?

Because they wanted to. And because society let them.

What they did was evil.

But shame on us for letting it happen right under our noses.

PROLOGUE

Before tonight, Barry Mortimer had never heard Deathrone's 'Fuck Off and Die'. He was more of a Simply Red man. But now 'Fuck Off and Die' was being sung - *screamed* - right into his bruised and bleeding face by his captors as they cranked the song up to a teeth-rattling level. It must have been the twentieth time they'd played it in a row. Maybe the fiftieth. Hard to tell.

Every time it got to the chorus, the gang members crowded round him and bellowed the words directly at him: 'FUCKOFFANDDIE! FUCKOFFANDDIE!' Even through the skull face bandanas that covered their faces, he could smell the sour, acidic blast of super strength cider on their breaths. Several of the gang even pulled down their masks as they screamed the song into his face, as if removing the thin strip of material would mean that Barry would be able to hear them more clearly.

'FUCKOFFANDDIE! FUCKOFFANDDIE!'

Some of them aren't even bothering to hide their faces now, he thought. *Shitting hell.*

Barry moved a little. The plastic back of the old car seat he was tied to stuck to his sweaty, bare skin. His wrists, attached with plastic ties to the metalwork underneath the seat, were purple and raw. One of his eyes was swollen shut and the other wasn't far behind.

The song came to an end. Barry waited for the grinding, metallic introduction to start again. This time it didn't. Two of the group - something about the way they carried themselves made it clear they were in charge - had called for quiet.

One of the leaders produced a claw hammer and then squatted down, pointing the head of the tool at Barry's face. It touched his skin just above the eyes. Leader Number One pulled a sponge - the kind you'd use to wash your car - from Barry's mouth. Leader Number Two also came down to Barry's level; in his hand was Barry's phone. He waggled it close to the captive man's eyes: 'Passcode,' Number Two said. 'Now.'

There was a pause. Only a few beats but the hesitation caused the hammer to be brought down sharply onto Barry's nose. The cartilage made a cracking sound and blood came spilling down his chest and onto his trousers. 'Passcode. Now.'

Barry was crying now. 'One, eight, one, two,' he said. 'Please. Leave me be. I'm sorry. Really, I am. I've been stupid. I know I have. It won't happen again. But, no more. Please.'

Leader Number Two unlocked the phone, opened the Facebook Messenger app and scrolled through the messages. 'Dear oh dear, Barry,' he said. 'This is properly disappointing. It really is.'

Number Two showed the phone to his compatriot. They both shook their heads. 'Not nice, Barry,' Leader One offered. 'Not nice at all. You haven't just let us down; you've let yourself down.'

Number One produced a marker pen, pulled the top off with their teeth and spat it out. 'What was that number again? One… eight… one… two? That was it.' Each number was written on Barry's forehead in the largest letters that the space could accommodate. 'There you go. Lovely.'

Number Two then pulled a roll of gaffer tape from his pocket and strapped the phone to Barry's chest. He smoothed the tape down, so it stuck to the injured man's clammy skin.

Leader One stood up, turned to the rest of the gang and handed one of them the hammer. 'Hands only, okay?' Number One stated. 'Elbows and arms if you must. Leave his legs. I mean it. We'll need him to walk up to the farm. I'm not carrying this cunt. When we get there, feel free to do his feet and shins. We'll save the head to last.' 'Shall we gag him?' one of the gang asked. The others stood perfectly still; their concentration was fixed firmly on Leader Number One. 'Nah,' said Number One. 'Let the fucker scream.'

ONE

Maggie Ormrod stepped out of the Bull's Head pub and into the warm moorland breeze that swept up the sandstone hills of Piethorne Valley on the border between Oldham and Rochdale. To her right, the lights of Denshaw village; to her left, the ever-present low hum of the M62 motorway that crossed the divide between Greater Manchester and Yorkshire.

Last orders had been called some time ago, but she'd been even more reluctant to leave the pub than usual. Everyone knew Maggie. And everyone knew she preferred the low-ceilinged friendliness of the Bull's Head to her tiny, terraced cottage just a few hundred yards down the Ripponden Road.

That Sunday night though, her requests for one last pint had been more insistent, the need to tell just one more tall tale more pressing. The eventual goodbye hugs were firmer, more flamboyant than ever, and they lasted a few seconds longer than usual. *I wouldn't mind,* the landlord thought, *but she'll be back in tomorrow. You can set your watch by Maggie.*

Outside the pub she undid the plum-coloured jumper that had been wrapped around her waist since she'd arrived at teatime and pulled it over her head. It took a while for her to find the arms and complete the task; she was drunk, but no more drunk than usual.

'Bye Maggie,' the other regulars shouted. 'Mind the road, you're pissed! See you tomorrow.'

She waved to them then dug her hands deep into the pockets of her combat trousers and tipped her face into the wind. She felt it brushing and caressing her face and it made her smile. Maggie sat on a nearby wall out of sight and waited until the last of the pub-goers had left. Then, instead of walking down the A872 towards her house, she turned and took the path that ran behind the pub. In front of her the moonlight bounced off the series of reservoirs that ran through the valley below the road. In the far distance was Ogden Reservoir. Before that, Kitcliffe. Just off to Maggie's right, Piethorne Reservoir. To the left, Rooden. Then up above her to the right, was Norman Hill Reservoir. But she wasn't interested in any of them; Maggie headed to the reservoir that was dead ahead of her: Hanging Lees.

The path down to the triangular reservoir wasn't designed to be walked in the dark by someone who had spent all evening drinking, but Maggie knew every pothole and rock it had to offer and got to the outer wall of Hanging Lees without so much as a stumble. She looked at the ornate metal gate that stopped the public getting access to the cold, grey water. She touched the butterflies and dragonflies that adorned the gate and ran her fingers over the letters and numbers that had been welded into it. She sounded them out as she touched them:

H. A. N. G. I. N. G. L. E. E. S. 1. 8. 7. 0.

Maggie used a large rock to step up to the top of the wall next to the gate, pushed herself upwards, rolled and over and slid down the other side.

Easy.

She walked towards the water. Of all the Piethorne Valley reservoirs, Hanging Lees was her favourite. People didn't notice it, it was tucked away to one side and had no path around the back to tempt walkers, so most people just passed it by. Not Maggie. She often came here at night to watch the surface ripple and sway. And to think.

And cry.

Maggie sat down by the water's edge and listened to the sounds of the moors; the hissing of the grass as the wind pushed against it, the left to right arc of bird calls above her, and even the drone of the motorway traffic to the north. She listened to the sounds of the night, and she loved them all.

After a few minutes she took an envelope from the buttoned-up thigh pocket of her combat trousers. She'd wrapped the envelope in a plastic bag, the thin kind you get fruit in at a greengrocer. It fluttered and crackled in the breeze as she rummaged in her other pocket. Maggie lay back on the grass so she could get right to the bottom. Finally, she produced a safety pin and attached the bag with the envelope inside to the front of her jumper. *Just in case it rains. It's forecast. That's thinking ahead, that is.*

It took several goes before she was satisfied with the way it was pinned. She spread it flat with both hands, nodded her approval, then rolled up both sleeves of her jumper. She took out her favourite knife – the one she'd bought at the Army and Navy shop in town - and, with a series of upward strokes, opened up the veins in both arms. Then Maggie lay back in the mossy grass and closed her eyes.

The following morning Maggie's rain-soaked body was found by two walkers, a married couple from Slaithwaite. They'd argued about whether they should look at the envelope pinned to her jumper or leave it to the police. He said leave it. She said they should look, as the poor woman might be from nearby. If the letter had her details, they could contact her family, she pointed out.

After some debate they agreed to leave the envelope where it was. There was no mobile signal out there by the reservoir, so the husband headed off to find the phone box which their map said was up near the pub. 'Which service do I require?' the man had asked when his 999 call was connected. 'Police, I suppose,' he said. 'And ambulance. Bit late for the second one through.'

While her husband was away, the woman carefully released the safety pin and read the note attached to Maggie Ormrod's jumper. Then she wept.

First up, can I say sorry to the person what found me. It can't have been nice for you at all. I have tried to do things neat so as not to terrify you too much. Don't have no nightmares, please.

Sorry also to the ambulance staff what will have been called out. I know its your job and that but no one would want to see a thing like this. You do a great job + I love the NHS.

Any road. Here we are.

My name is Maggie. Everyone who knows me would think I were just fine. Always been happy on the outside me. Inside, I was totally NOT + haven't been right for years.

When I was a kid I was in care. Look up my name. I was at a kids home in Greenacres. The things what were done to me weren't right. Sexual abuse + worse. I was messed with when I were young, just a kiddie. It fucked up my head + I hate them all for letting I happen.

But there's one person who were the worst. I hate him the most.

He should have helped us but he never. His name is John Smithdown and he were a detective with Oldham Police. He abused me/ raped me. Said he would kill me if I said owt.

Well he cant kill me now can he?
Sorry again to the ambulance people + the person what found me.
MAGGIE

TWO

<There's a dead body next to Hanging Lees Reservoir. Cops are there now. Looks like a suicide.>

'Body found near reservoir,' muttered Danny Johnston, peering over the top of his glasses to read the Twitter direct message he'd been sent from an anonymous account. 'Absolutely my four favourite words in the whole world, no question about it.'

Danny Googled Hanging Lees Reservoir, then he messaged back:

<technically over the border into Rochdale, that is.>

Danny was a stickler for borders. Always had been.

<Could take a look though. Any pix?>

The reply came within seconds:

<There's a note pinned to her jumper that fingers one of your Oldham cop mates as a paedo. Stick that on your fucking website.>

Charming. Danny took a screenshot of the message just in case the sender had second thoughts, deleted their account and the words were lost forever.

It was a good thing he did, because a few seconds later @rambo536448 was no more, taking their faceless account and their zero number of followers with them.

Danny's DMs were always open - as editor of news website *Oldham Now* he got his stories any way that he could. Most of the tip offs he received centred on traffic problems, illegal dumping of rubbish and local charity events, so this one stood out a little. He did a quick social media search to see if there were any photos or video clips of the scene. Nothing. *Way too specific to be a prank, it must have just happened.*

He got the directions to Hanging Lees - *24 minutes despite heavier than usual traffic* - and headed out of his tiny, rented cottage in the village of Friezland in Saddleworth.

When Danny had opted to move to Oldham, he'd decided quite quickly that he wanted to live in the slightly upmarket area of Saddleworth, although Danny's run-down terrace was probably the least upmarket property in the area. He didn't care. He rather liked the mix of wild countryside and the nearby frou-frou shops and restaurants, but he told people it was for purely practical reasons: *it's easy to get around Oldham rather than fighting your way out of the town centre all the time, plus the phone signal's pretty good.*

He liked the village's name: Friezland. *Sounds like some Nordic crime series on BBC4.*

He was about to close the front door when he remembered that he'd forgotten the two most important pieces of equipment in his job, his mobile phone plus a portable charger. A mobile was all he needed these days. Not only was Danny the editor of *Oldham Now*, but he was also the owner, chief reporter, photographer, videographer and researcher - a journalistic one-man band. 'Hyper Local News' they called it. *Cheap as fuck and the only job I could get, more like.*

The novelty of driving himself around Oldham hadn't quite worn off yet. He'd finished the driving ban and community service order he'd received in 2016. He'd refused a breath test at the scene and because of the seriousness of the incident… *driving into a tree while pissed, don't dress it up as anything else…* the community service order had been a welcome alternative to the custodial sentence that had been talked about in court.

He loved driving through the hills around Oldham. The villages peeled away as the countryside opened up to its full, stark beauty. This was not a place for tree-lovers; when the rounded, brown hills met the slate grey sky, there was little or nothing to break up the stark, straight border between them. Sky at the top. Land at the bottom. *That's the way it is out here. And it's beautiful.*

Google Maps told him that the quickest route to Hanging Lees was to park at the Bull's Head pub and then walk. *Your destination is on the left.* But Google didn't take into the account the fact that the pub car park was cordoned off with police tape, as was the path behind it. As Danny slowed down to get a better look, he was waved on by an angry-looking police officer in a high vis jacket who was muttering to himself and shaking his head. Danny was no lip reader, but he was sure two of the words the officer had used were 'daft' and 'twat'.

Danny gave the officer a cheery wave, carried on up the road and pulled into the first layby he came across. He checked social media again for any mentions of the incident; he did a geo-located search via Tweetdeck, looking for tweets sent within a 10-kilometre radius of the scene that contained photos or video. It was a good way of shutting down the noise of Twitter and zeroing in on exactly what he was looking for. Still nothing.

Danny had been forced to become a reluctant expert in the art of social media since setting up on his own, but there was one thing he refused to let go of from the previous century: maps. Proper actual physical, dog-eared, tea-stained maps. He preferred them because they were very useful when it came to public rights of way - those little dotted lines that showed you the way to get around police tape while still claiming you were just out for a leisurely stroll. He didn't care for Ordnance Survey maps - too much information that he didn't need and way too pricey. He preferred Philip's *Street Atlas* and there was no finer copy than their Greater Manchester edition. Full colour, large scale sections for town centres and all the footpaths you could wish for, especially out here in the sticks. *Bloody lovely.*

A quick flick through his atlas to pages 32-33 showed him that there was a footpath 100 yards up the road that veered off to the left, following a stream through Cold Greave Clough; and what's more it delivered him directly to the other side of Hanging Lees Reservoir. Danny put on a fleece and the walking boots he kept in the boot of his Honda - *just out rambling officer, honestly* - and trotted down the path.

There were three figures on the other side of the clough as Danny got closer. Two Scenes of Crime Officers stood out against the browney greens of the landscape around the reservoir with their bright, ultra-white 'scene' suits. They were standing next to a pop-up crime scene preservation tent, and one was taking photographs. Close to them was a man whose personal colour scheme also clashed dramatically with the environment. He was dressed in well-worn but expensive-looking neon outdoor gear and his curly red hair was rippling in the moorland breeze. Danny was faintly disgusted as to how young he looked. *A teenage detective. Fucking Nora.* Then Danny reminded himself that the red-haired man was probably well into his 30s. *It's not that he's young, Danny boy, it's that you're fucking OLD.*

With his arms tucked firmly to his sides to minimise camera wobble, Danny started taking video of the scene on his phone. He did two wide, left to right panning shots; on the second pass he noticed another figure had joined the scene. To the right of the police activity, someone was doing exactly what Danny was doing - filming the scene. That included filming Danny himself. The difference was that the other videographer was wearing sunglasses and a baseball cap, plus their face was covered with a bandana that had a grinning skull pattern on it.

While still filming with one hand, Mr. Skull Face waved to Danny. Instinctively, Danny waved back. Then Skull Face gave him the finger and disappeared over the lip of the clough.

That's nice.

Danny found a vaguely comfortable looking rock, sat on it, and then trimmed the video clip he preferred and posted it to the *Oldham Now* Twitter page:

Breaking: reports of a body on the #Oldham #Rochdale border close to #HangingLees Reservoir. Here's the scene right now as @gmpolice search the scene. More details as we get them, rt and follow @oldhamnow for updates.

He posted slightly altered versions on both Facebook and Instagram; his aim was to push people to his website rather than have them linger on any of the social media platforms: *I'd like to see a bit of traffic on this come my way, rather than just Mark Zuckerberg benefitting from my hard work.*

When the story had been posted Danny headed down his side of the clough, stepped over the stream at the bottom and headed up towards the site where the body was. The young-looking detective stepped forward to meet him. 'No closer please, sir,' he said. He didn't sound like he was from Oldham. His accent was flatter, maybe Derbyshire.

'Hi there,' Danny said. 'You the Detective Constable here?'

'Detective Inspector,' he replied.

Fucking Nora. You really are old, Danny.

He went into his patter: 'Sorry, Detective Inspector. I know you're busy. I'm Danny from *Oldham Now*. Just wondering if I could get a few words from you about what's going on?'

'Nothing to say at this time,' the Detective Inspector said. 'Please contact the Press Office. Thanks very much.'

Danny persevered, nodding towards the white-suited Scenes of Crimes Officers: 'You've got SOCOs out, so you must be treating this as suspicious.'

'They're going home,' the detective replied. 'Police Coroner's Officers will be taking over. It's not suspicious… there's nothing for you here. But I'm sure the Press Office will help you, sir. Please. Contact them.'

Danny tried a different tack. 'The top road is getting pretty busy,' he pointed out. 'It might help keep it clear if you can tell people to stay away from the scene. I can get that message out.'

The detective checked that Danny wasn't filming him: 'More likely it'll bring a load of dickheads with packed lunches out here, just to have a nosey at what's going on,' he said. 'The Press Office is your best bet.'

'You know as well as I do that the GMP Press Office is a glorified email account these days,' Danny countered. 'I'll be lucky to get a reply by the end of the week.'

'Move along sir or I'll do you for obstruction,' the detective said.

'Obstruction?' Danny shouted, indignantly. He stretched out both arms, drawing attention to the wide open space of the moors. 'Out here?'

'It was a joke sir,' the detective said with a smile that suggested he felt a bit sorry for Danny. 'Press Office. Please.'

Young, ginger and a comedian. Wow.

The detective turned away. *I'm not having this,* Danny thought. 'Will the Press Office be able to help me with the note that was found with her body?' he asked in a deliberately loud voice. The two Scenes of Crime Officers standing next to Hanging Lees reservoir heard what he said and stopped what they were doing. They looked at the detective and then at Danny.

'Her?' the detective asked.

'Yes,' Danny replied. 'Her.' *Might as well take a swing at this and see what happens. I've got a 50/50 chance at being right.* 'There's a woman under that tent with a note pinned to her jumper.'

'Mr. Johnston,' the detective said, pointing towards a pair of large flat stones by the side of the path. 'Please, take a seat.'

Danny did as he was asked. 'How did this information come your way?' the Detective Inspector asked.

'A direct message on Twitter,' Danny replied. 'I get them a lot. Not many like this one, though.'

'Can I see it?'

'No, you can't. Sorry. Not yet anyway. But the DM also said that the note mentioned a cop. A *paedo* cop.'

'I see. Was there a name attached to that?'

Danny was again going to decline to answer - *make him think I know the name* - when his phone pinged with a WhatsApp message. It was from Kate Smithdown:

> *<Danny. There are police at the house. They've come for my dad and they're doing a search. Please come ASAP. There are people here and it's all over social media.>*

THREE

Danny drove past the end of the driveway to former Detective Inspector John Smithdown's detached home on the Huddersfield Road. It always took him slightly by surprise how close it was to Black Moss Reservoir. He pulled into a small layby just beyond the house. He'd always liked Smithdown's home, a double-fronted stone cottage with views across the small towns and villages that peppered the valleys and hills down towards Oldham town centre. Flower tubs and hanging baskets added to its moorland charm. But today, the outside of the retired detective's home looked very different.

Outside the house, a crowd of about 40 people had gathered. Many were holding up their phones to record what was going on. Most of them were men in their 30s or early 40s. There were several women too and a couple of school age children. The atmosphere was like a slightly raucous party. A man in a skull bandana mask was shouting into the narrow end of an orange and white traffic cone. *Is that the same guy I saw out on the moor?* Danny thought as he got out of his car. Then he noticed that nearly all the people in the crowd were wearing similar skull face bandanas to prevent them from being identified.

'WHO ARE YA?' the man shouted into his makeshift loudhailer.

'JOHN SMITHDOWN,' the crowd shrieked back at him.

'WHAT ARE YA?' he asked.

'BEAST!' the crowd replied.

'WHERE ARE YA?'

'RIGHT! FOOKIN! THERE!' The crowd pointed at the house with each word. 'BEAST! BEAST! BEAST, BEAST, BEAST' they added.

Then the chant began again: 'WHO ARE YA?...'

This is some proper organised shit, Danny thought as he approached the front of the short drive. Several police officers were leaving the house with plastic bags containing DVDs, several cameras, a laptop and dozens of VHS cassettes. Through the milky plastic of one of the bags

Danny could see that one was marked in faded red marker pen.

'WEDDING SUPER 8 FOOTAGE DO NOT
RECORD OVER THIS PLEASE!!'

'Don't you need a warrant to do this?' Danny asked to any of the officers willing to listen, realising as he spoke that he didn't really know what he was talking about. *You sound like some character in a shit TV cop show.*

'Under the Police and Criminal Evidence Act we can search at the point of arrest to look for supporting evidence, sir,' said a male detective at the doorway. He was dressed in a black suit and white shirt - both contrasted sharply with the shock of bright red curly hair that was piled on top of his head.

'Arrest?' asked Danny. 'John Smithdown is in his 80s; he's had a stroke. Is this all entirely necessary? More importantly... the man's a fucking hero - a decorated *police* hero - worth more than you lads all rolled into one.'

'It's Mr. Johnston, isn't it?' the officer said. 'I believe you were waving your iPhone about up on the moors earlier. We'll be checking your Twitter feed at some point.'

'Check it all you want, mate,' Danny said. 'That's what it's there for.'

'Yes, I'm afraid we have arrested Mr. Smithdown...' the officer continued, noticing that Danny was staring at his hair. 'And no sir, Oldham Police do not have a policy of only employing gingers. Just me and my brother. I assume you met him out on the moors?'

'We did meet. He's a comic too.' Danny looked around the detective and through the open door of the cottage. 'Can I see him? Can I talk to John?'

Before the detective could speak, Danny heard Kate Smithdown's voice from inside the house. 'Danny! Get in here, now. Fuck what ginger bollocks says.'

The detective formed his lips into an *ooooh* of mock offence as Danny stepped into John Smithdown's cottage. Smithdown was sitting in his favourite armchair in the lounge with Kate kneeling next to him. She'd clearly been crying but that had now passed. Now she just looked angry. Very angry.

The stroke John Smithdown had suffered several years earlier had dampened the movement in his face a little, but Danny was still able to clearly see the hurt on his old friend's features. Smithdown didn't acknowledge Danny's arrival. He was staring at a set of photographs on a bookcase next to the open fireplace. The photos were mainly of Jean Smithdown, the retired detective's wife and Kate's mum. Jean had died in 2016. Cancer.

'Dad, Danny's here,' Kate said, rubbing her father's arm reassuringly and forcing a smile. 'Look. It's Danny. Here to help. Like always. Oh, Danny thanks for coming.'

'Of course, Kate. No problem. John, how are you, mate?'

Smithdown carried on staring at the photos of his late wife. 'What a woman, she was,' he said, quietly. 'By Christ. Oldham's answer to Audrey Hepburn. Thank God she's not around to see this.'

'John, we need to speak,' said Danny. He looked around and saw the detective was talking to a uniformed officer in the front doorway. 'I had a message this morning, about a woman found dead over at Hanging Lees Reservoir.'

'Oh aye?' was all that Smithdown said in reply; he was still looking at the photographs of his wife.

'She had a note pinned to her,' Danny continued. 'A suicide note. It named you, John.'

'So, I believe,' Smithdown said, still seemingly distracted by the photos.

'That's all Ron Weasley out there would tell us,' Kate added, nodding towards the red-haired detective.

'John, I'm really sorry,' Danny said. 'We're short of time here and you need to know. It said you abused her as a kid.'

'Danny, what the fuck are you talking about?' interrupted Kate.

'Kate, please,' Danny urged. 'John, do you understand me?'

Smithdown looked at Danny, then at his daughter. Before he could reply, the detective stepped into the living room: 'Right, Mr. Smithdown. You've had your usual cautions and explanations. I believe your solicitor is on their way to Oldham police station. It's time you came with us, I reckon.'

Smithdown looked out of the window of his cottage and saw the crowd outside. 'Kate, Danny… what about those people?'

'It's not safe for him,' Kate said. 'Please. Can't you clear them away first?'

'Don't worry, we'll make sure he's alright,' the detective said to Kate. 'He's in good hands.' He turned his attention to Smithdown, making a point of speaking much louder: 'WE'VE GOT TO GO NOW, MR SMITHDOWN. LET'S GET YOU TO OLDHAM STATION. BET

IT'S BEEN A WHILE SINCE YOU'VE BEEN THERE, ISN'T IT?'

'TURN THE VOLUME DOWN, LAD… I'M NOT DEAF,' Smithdown shouted back. 'I'M NOT A CHILD MOLESTOR, NEITHER. Help me up, Kate. Let's get this sorted.'

She grabbed a coat for her father as they headed for the door. Danny helped him on with the light brown windcheater. Smithdown looked at Danny, then he did something that he'd never done in the four decades that Danny had known him - the retired detective gave him a hug. 'I'm *scared*, Danny lad,' he whispered.

Then former Detective Inspector John Smithdown was led away by officers from Greater Manchester Police. Danny watched as two uniformed officers cleared a path so Smithdown could get in their unmarked car. As he walked along the gravel path, the crowd ramped up their shouts as he passed: 'WHO ARE YA?'

'JOHN SMITHDOWN!'

'WHAT ARE YA?'

'BEAST!'

Everyone in the crowd seemed to be pointing a camera phone in Smithdown's direction. Danny held Kate's hand as her father bent his head to get into the back seat of the police car. Danny watched the face of the young officer who was helping keep the crowd back. He was sure he saw him smile and give a wink to one of the ringleaders. Just before the door closed, a young woman holding a child of about three in her arms, got close enough to spit in Smithdown's face.

'BEAST! BEAST! BEAST, BEAST, BEAST!' the crowd sang.

FOUR

BODY FOUND AT HANGING LEES RESERVOIR

Danny Johnston - Oldham Now

Police in Oldham are investigating after the death of a woman at a local beauty spot.

The body was discovered at Hanging Lees Reservoir in Piethorne Valley by a couple out walking early this morning. The woman hasn't been named by police, but it's believed she was in her 50s and lived locally.

Detectives are examining a note that had been left at the scene - it had been pinned to the woman's body.

The moors around the reservoir close to the A627 Ripponden Road have been sealed off and a search of the area is taking place.

Police initially thought that the circumstances surrounding were not suspicious but in a new development, a man in his 80s has been arrested following the discovery.

It's believed he is helping police with their inquiries into what's been described as a 'non-recent abuse' case.

It's expected that the woman will be named later today.

FIVE

When Danny's phone thrummed and 'Kate Smithdown' appeared on the display, he knew he was in for a pretty harsh conversation inspired by his *Oldham Now* story.

He'd written it while sitting in his car outside John Smithdown's house, but he'd done what he always did when covering 'death' stories; he'd left out the code that told WordPress to insert adverts into the story. Despite the fact that doing this cost him money, it had always been Danny's policy. It was one thing to get 15 pence a click thanks to a story about school dinner ladies going on strike or a missing dog being reunited with its owner, but it was quite another to profit from someone's death. This was financially unfortunate for Danny, as the site always experienced a noticeable analytic spike with death stories. *If you weren't so self-righteous, Danny Johnston, you wouldn't be so skint.*

'What the fuck is that piece all about?' Kate shouted. 'Why would you post that? I mean, seriously. Dad's your fucking friend, for Christ's sake. My fucking son will have seen it too, Danny. Did you think about Jonathan's feelings before you wrote it, or do you just not care?'

Danny took a breath before he answered: 'It's exactly what I would have written if I didn't know your dad. Word for word. I can't ignore what's happened just because it involves John Smithdown. Plus, I didn't name him.'

'You don't need to name him, Danny,' Kate said, her anger seemed to have gone up a notch. 'Have you looked on social media? There are videos of him being arrested everywhere. They're chanting his name, for God's sake. Hashtag fucking BEAST is trending locally.'

'Well, there you go,' Danny pointed out. 'It looks like I'm the responsible one, then, doesn't it? That's the difference between a journalist and someone with access to the internet. We adhere to the rules. Look, I did what I had to do - bare minimum, no more. Where are you now?'

'I'm at Oldham Police Station,' Kate said. 'And it would be quite nice if my friend Danny Something would get himself down here and offer a bit of fucking support.'

Danny always knew he was in trouble with Kate when she called him Danny Something - the name she'd used when they'd first met nearly thirty years earlier. He'd been a reporter for Manchester Radio; she was a journalist on the *Oldham Messenger.* 'Jimmy Something, isn't it?' she'd asked in 1990, struggling to remember the person she'd heard on the radio. 'Danny Something,' he'd corrected her, as a joke. And it had struck.

'You want support?' he said. 'Not a problem. Whatever you want. I mean it. What do you want me to do?'

'Get your arse down here, sharpish. Dad's just gone in for questioning. I'm freaking out and I want you here.'

'Of course. I'm literally on my way. I'll be there in 20 minutes.'

There was a pause. A few beats. 'We first met at a police station, didn't we Danny?' she said.

'Yes, we did, Kate.'

'It was a press conference after the kid's body was found at Black Moss. There was only you and me there, do you remember?'

'I do, indeed.'

'God, it was so long ago. Hard to believe I'm in my late 40s now.'

'It's been several years since you were in your 40s, Kate Smithdown. Let's do the maths, shall we…?' '

'Just shut it, will you?' Another moment of quiet. 'I'm scared, Danny,' Kate said. '*Really* scared. I need to ring the school - speak to Jonathan. He needs to find out what's going on with his grandad from me, not from social fucking media.'

'How do you think he'll take it?' Danny asked; he regretted it immediately.

'He's fifteen, he's in a special school for kids with extreme emotional difficulties and his grandad is all over the internet as Oldham's answer to Jimmy Savile. How do you think he's going to take it?'

'It'll be alright,' Danny said, summoning up his best reassuring voice. 'I'm sure it will. I'll be there as soon as I can.'

'Good. Be as quick as you can. And no stopping off to write any more stories. Understood?'

'Understood.'

SIX

'Which one are you again?' Smithdown asked as he neatly hung his jacket on the back of a chair in the interview room. 'You two ginger lads look the same to me. No offence, obviously.'

'None taken, Mr. Smithdown,' the DI said, pulling up a chair. 'I'm Detective Inspector Patrick McIntyre. This is Detective Constable Karl McIntyre. Yes, we are related. You might have guessed that already.'

'Where's the tape machine?' Smithdown said. He looked at his solicitor as she took out a notepad and pen from her shoulder bag. 'Paulina, this should be being taped.'

'It's Digital Interview Recording now, Mr Smithdown,' the DC replied. 'DIR. All recorded evidence goes to a central server. No more sticking pencils into C90 cassettes. Easier for all concerned.'

'It's fine John,' Paulina said. 'Don't worry. We'll soon sort this out.'

'Right then,' DI McIntyre said. 'I'll be asking the questions; DC McIntyre will be observing. Shall we make a start?'

RECORD OF INTERVIEW
Person interviewed: SMITHDOWN, John (11/1/39)
Place of interview: Oldham Police Station
Time commenced: 1340 hours
Interviewer(s): DI3716 McIntyre, Patrick DC2184 McIntyre, Karl.
Other person(s) present: Paulina Scorer - Solicitor from Blanco & Harkness Solicitors.
Usual introductions, cautions and advice.
This is the first interview with JOHN SMITHDOWN - SMITHDOWN confirms that no questions have been asked before the recording begins.

DI MCINTYRE: Mr Smithdown, the person I want to talk to you this afternoon is Margaret Jane Ormrod, known as Maggie Ormrod. Does that name mean anything to you?

SMITHDOWN: I suppose that's the name of the poor woman found out at Hanging Lees this morning?
DI MCINTYRE: That's correct. Did you know that name before today?
SMITHDOWN: I did not, no.
DI MCINTYRE: Are you absolutely sure about that?
SMITHDOWN: Yes, I am. That's why I said it.
DI MCINTYRE: You formerly worked for Greater Manchester Police - when did you become a police officer, Mr Smithdown?
SMITHDOWN: I'd retired by the time you'd worked out where your dick was, lad, put it like that.
DI MCINTYRE: For the benefit of the recording, Mr Smithdown's solicitor Ms Scorer just very quietly advised him to answer the question, though she does seem to find what he said quite amusing. What year, Mr Smithdown?
SMITHDOWN: 1965.
DI MCINTYRE: What dealings did you have with children during the 60s and 70s? In particular, I'm meaning children that were in the care of the local authorities.
SMITHDOWN: Well, in those days you'd basically round them up, take them home, then repeat. There were no child protection units in those days. It wasn't very touchy feely… if you'll excuse the expression. You'd just scoop them up and put them back where they were supposed to be. If they'd done something that they shouldn't have done while they were out and about, then we'd deal with it accordingly.
DC MCINTYRE: You had quite the career, didn't you Mr Smithdown? Commendations left, right and centre. Mentioned in dispatches in 1973 for pulling two kids out of an abusive household. Mum and Dad were proper wrong uns, weren't they? Commended again for saving a teenage lad and a young girl in '88 over at Kinder Scout. You were involved in the Black Moss murder case in 1990 as well, I see. All those kids killed by the two women. Sisters, weren't they? Those poor children. Terrible. But there's a pattern here, isn't there? A common thread. Children, Mr Smithdown. Time and again. Have you noticed? I have. There always seems to be children involved in your heroics. Every time. For the benefit of the recording, Mr Smithdown has just mouthed the words 'Fucking Nora' in response. Have you ever had any sexual interest in children, Mr Smithdown?
MS SCORER: Oh, come on.

SMITHDOWN: DI McIntyre, really? What do you lads call it these days? ABE? Achieving Best Evidence? And this is your idea of Achieving Best Evidence, is it? No, lad. I have zero sexual interest in children.
DI MCINTYRE: You were suspended in 1988 for harming a child though, weren't you? A child in your custody. You split her lip open, I believe?
SMITHDOWN: I was cleared of any wrongdoing.
DI MCINTYRE: Don't see any record of you denying that you did it, though? In fact, it looks like you admitted it at the time.
SMITHDOWN: I was cleared.
DI MCINTYRE: Okay, Mr Smithdown. Can we talk about events up on the moors today, please? At Hanging Lees.
SMITHDOWN: If you want to. Fine. Not sure if I can be of any use though.
DI MCINTYRE: As a result of a note we found at the scene, we removed a variety of items from your house today, Mr Smithdown.
SMITHDOWN: I'm old, but I'm not stupid. Yes, I did happen to notice your lads stomping about the place this morning. I want everything back exactly as it was, some of that stuff is irreplaceable.
DI MCINTYRE: Well, we're examining those items at the moment. They're in safe hands. Are we likely to finding anything that would incriminate you in any way?
SMITHDOWN: Yes… crimes against fashion from my wedding videos. Guilty as charged, but it was the 70s after all. Other than that, no. Nothing incriminating.
DI MCINTYRE: Are we likely to find any material of a sexual nature, Mr Smithdown?
SMITHDOWN: Just me in my Speedos in Benidorm in 1973, if that's the kind of thing that gets you going.
MS SCORER: John, let's keep the answers to the point, shall we, then we can get you home.
DI MCINTYRE: Thank you, Ms Scorer. I agree. I don't think we're finding this quite as funny as you are, Mr Smithdown. A woman has taken her own life. She opened both her arms up from top to bottom. I've spent the morning looking at her body.
SMITHDOWN: You're right. It isn't funny. It's horrible. I'm sorry. But I don't know this poor woman. I never heard about her until Danny… until now.
DI MCINTYRE: That's Danny Johnston, the gentleman who was at

your house earlier. Is he your daughter's boyfriend?
SMITHDOWN: No. Everyone thinks that, but they're just friends.
DI MCINTYRE: Mr Johnston is a journalist, isn't he?
SMITHDOWN: He is.
DI MCINTYRE: And he runs the *Oldham Now* website, is that correct?
SMITHDOWN: Yes, he does.
DI MCINTYRE: Mr Johnston was spotted out on the moors at Hanging Lees this morning, filming the scene where the body was found. He was also asking questions at the scene. He seemed to have a surprising amount of knowledge about what had gone on. Amazing really, how much he seemed to know. How did he come by that information?
SMITHDOWN: I don't know. He's a journalist. A very good one as it happens. He's been ahead of you lads more than once. And me, for that matter.
DI MCINTYRE: You have a very long connection with Mr Johnston, don't you? He was one of the kids you pulled out of that abusive household in '73, wasn't he? I read his book, the one he wrote about the Black Moss case. They called it the house of horrors in the press, didn't they? You probably saved his life, is that fair to say?
SMITHDOWN: Now then, which of the many questions that you've just fired at me do you want me to answer, Detective Inspector? Remember - ABE.
DI MCINTYRE: How does your friend Danny Johnston, who you've known since the 1970s, know so much about the body found at Hanging Lees?
SMITHDOWN: I don't know. Why don't you ask him? Like I say, he's very good at his job.
DI MCINTYRE: For the benefit of the recording, I'm now showing Mr Smithdown a cutting from the *Manchester Evening News* dated the third of February 1973. The article is headlined 'CHILDREN RESCUED FROM HORROR HOUSE'. The article is accompanied by a photograph of a police officer with two young children. I believe the photo is of Danny Johnston and his sister being rescued from the aforementioned house. Is that you in the photograph with them, Mr Smithdown?
SMITHDOWN: Yes, it is.
DI MCINTYRE: I'm now showing Mr Smithdown another photograph. This is a colour photograph, looks like it was taken on a domestic type of camera. It's a bit creased but the people in the picture

are clearly discernible. It's of a man with his arm around a young girl, aged about 11 or 12 years. Is that also you in the colour photograph?
SMITHDOWN: Okay... Let's have a look. Right. Well it certainly looks like me, yes.
DI MCINTYRE: It does, doesn't it? Do you know the girl in the photograph, Mr Smithdown?
SMITHDOWN: I'm afraid I don't. Look, where is this is going?
DI MCINTYRE: This photo was found at Maggie Ormrod's house this morning. I believe that's you in the picture and I believe the young girl with you is Maggie.
SMITHDOWN: Right, so that's why you were bagging up my photo albums this morning, was it? Looking for more pictures? You've got one photo as a piece of evidence and that gives you the okay to take every picture of mine that you can lay your hands on. Right you are. I don't know this girl. And that's that.
DI MCINTYRE: I believe that despite what you have told us you did know Maggie Ormrod, Mr Smithdown. I believe you had a sexual interest in her and that you acted on that sexual interest. I believe that what happened to Maggie has played on her mind for 40 odd years. It tortured her, in fact. And I believe that's why she took her own life this morning. Anything to say, Mr Smithdown? You're very quiet all of a sudden.
MS SCORER: I think we should stop, Mr McIntyre. I think Mr Smithdown is unwell.
DI MCINTYRE: For the recording, here's the letter that Maggie had pinned to herself before taking her own life. In the letter she states: 'He should have helped us but he never. His name is John Smithdown, and he were a detective with Oldham Police. He abused me/raped me. Said he would kill me if I said owt.'
MS SCORER: Please, we need to stop. John, are you okay?
DI MCINTYRE: 'His name is John Smithdown... He abused me/raped me.' That's what it says. Did you, Mr Smithdown? Did you abuse that little girl? What do you have to say? Mr Smithdown? Can you hear me? Right. Okay. We should stop. Mr Smithdown doesn't look right. Okay, let's stop.

End of recording: 13.58

SEVEN

After Smithdown had been taken away from his house, Danny had talked to a few of the more reasonable-looking members of the mob outside and discovered where Maggie Ormrod had lived. He felt bad that he'd lied to Kate about going straight to the police station but justified it in his own mind: *I'm of more use here trying to find out what the fuck has happened. Sitting about like a spare part in the waiting area of Oldham nick isn't going to help John.*

Maggie's terraced house on the outskirts of Denshaw stood out from the others. Not just because there was a policeman stood outside it - though that certainly helped - but because, compared to its slightly upmarket neighbours, it looked ramshackle and uncared for. Denshaw had changed in recent years with incomers and newbuilds taking the area into a higher price bracket. Maggie Ormrod's house had stayed defiantly ungentrified.

The tiny front garden was almost filled with a single, battered sofa that had a large scorch mark on one of the cushions. Several old paint tins and a toy pram accompanied it. The path from the battered gate to Maggie's door was barely ten feet long. There was a hand-written sign taped onto Maggie's door:

BELL NAKKERED, KNOCK REELY HARD!

Danny stood at the gate and looked at the policeman. The policeman looked at Danny and shook his head. 'Good day, officer,' Danny said with a smile. 'You're doing a cracking job.'

Danny changed direction, swung open an altogether less battered-looking gate and knocked on the house to the right of Maggie's. He winked at the police officer as he waited. A man in his 60s opened the door; Danny got as far as… 'Hi, I'm from *Oldham Now…*' when the door was quickly closed again.

'That's a shame,' the officer said, quietly, as Danny walked past

Maggie's house and went to the house to the left. 'Not your day, is it?'

'Least I don't spend all my time standing around like Piffy on a rock bun doing nowt,' Danny replied with a smile. "Piffy on a rock bun" was an old Mancunian expression he'd picked up from John Smithdown. It meant hanging around, doing nothing. *My God, I'm actually turning into the old bastard.*

At the second house, the door was opened by a woman of Danny's age holding a cat. Danny smiled and introduced himself; he was braced for the same treatment, but the door stayed opened and the woman listened to what he had to say. 'I was wondering if I could ask you about the woman who lived next door… Maggie Ormrod, I believe that was her name. Did you know her?'

'Yes, I knew Maggie,' the neighbour said. Her accent was only lightly Mancunian, almost non-existent. *Not from round here. Trendy incomer? Bit like yourself, Danny boy.* 'Hard NOT to know people when you live next door to them in little terraced houses like these.'

'That's a fair point,' Danny admitted. With as little fuss as possible, Danny took out his phone. 'I assume you've heard about what happened up at Hanging Lees… Sorry, do you mind if I record you? Is that okay?'

'I suppose so,' she said. Her eyes darted for the slightest moment towards the policeman who was just a few feet away from them. 'What do you want to know?'

'What was Maggie like?' Danny said, instinctively going for an open question - who, what, when, where, why, which, how - that invited the other person to speak.

The woman thought for a moment. There was a slightly awkward silence. Danny's experience told him to wait… *never interrupt silence, let them think. Wait. The less the journalist speaks the more the interviewee might say.*

'She was alright...' the woman began, hesitantly. 'She had a good heart did Maggie. Yes. A good heart. She was a bit of a… character, you might say. Always cheery and happy. But very much her own person. I'd help her out sometimes. She'd do the odd job for me. Yeah. She was a good un. So sad to hear about what's happened.'

Danny nodded and pulled a gently sympathetic face. He created another few beats of silence and waited to see if she was going to say something else. He was about to ask when the woman had last seen Maggie, when she unexpectedly spoke again: 'Never had any trouble with her. Good as gold. Until recently that is.'

'How do you mean?' asked Danny. Another open question - Danny left some silence. Again, she gave the slightest of looks towards the police officer.

'She always… God, people always say this in these kinds of situations, don't they? She kept herself to herself. That was Maggie. She was very self-contained. But lately, there were more people about next door. Pretty noisy people, to be honest. Making a din late at night. Partying. You know the kind of thing. I had to have words. We didn't fall out, but I did ask her to keep it down a bit.'

'How would you describe these people?' Danny asked.

'Sorry, I just thought you wanted a few nice words about Maggie,' the woman said, sounding slightly annoyed. She motioned towards the officer outside Maggie's door. 'You seem more like a policeman than he does.'

'Sorry. Last thing I'd want to do is sound like that. Can I ask your name?'

'I'd rather not give my name thanks,' she said. 'Look, I've got things to do. That's enough, isn't it?'

'Sure. I really appreciate it, thanks.'

She closed the door. The police officer was staring directly at him now; he seemed to want Danny to know that he'd been taking in everything that had been said. Danny paused and saved the recording on his phone. He marked it as MAGGIE NEIGHBOUR. He noticed a text had come in while he'd been interviewing the woman. It was from Kate Smithdown:

<Danny I know you're probably on the knocker asking questions, you predictable bastard, but you really need to come now. Dad's in a bad Way. He's in the Royal Oldham Hospital. I mean it, come now.>

EIGHT

'It must be handy if there's trouble at the football stadium,' Danny said as he looked at the grainy remains of his tea that was stuck to the bottom of the paper vending machine cup.

'What are you on about?' Kate asked as she prodded at her phone.

'This hospital. It's right next door to Oldham Athletic's ground. If it all kicks off, as it were, then it's not far to come. For the wounded and that. No need for ambulances. The walking wounded can literally just walk around the corner.'

'When was the last time you went to a football match?' Kate asked.

'Do you know what?' Danny replied. 'I don't think I've ever actually been to a football match.'

'Exactly,' Kate said. 'It's not the 1970s, Danny. Nobody does hooliganism anymore. The football fans all work at PC World and have mortgages. The world's changed. It's not all Angel Delight and The Magic Roundabout out there anymore, you know. We have Thai food and Amazon Prime nowadays. You live in the past, that's your problem.'

'I wouldn't say I *live* in the past,' he huffed.

'Well, you've certainly got a holiday cottage there, put it like that.'

'It was a genuine loss to comedy when you decided to become a... whatever it is you are now,' Danny said.

'I'm a lady of leisure...' she pointed out. Kate took great delight in reminding Danny of her 'retired' status. The media businesses she'd built up over the years had all been bought out, meaning she never had to work again. 'But what I really am right now is pissed off about waiting here for news about Dad,' Kate added. 'It's been over an hour.'

A woman of about 60 wearing a volunteer's badge approached them with a trolley; she put a hand gently on Kate's shoulder and smiled. 'How are you two doing? It's awful just waiting isn't?'

'Was I moaning?' Kate said and smiled back. 'Nobody likes a moaner, do they? Not in a hospital anyway. We're just waiting for someone to tell us how my dad is. Sorry.'

'Don't be - they'll be back to you as soon as they can,' she said. 'Promise.'

Her voice was quiet and calming. Danny liked to listen out for accents; hers wasn't from around Oldham. *Derbyshire maybe. Not sure. Either way she must be from a factory where they make really nice volunteers. Why can't everyone be like that?*

'I've got some biscuits and a spot of cordial spare if you want it,' the woman said. 'Teas and coffees have all gone. Would you like a bit to keep you going?'

'Oh, yes please,' Kate said, as if she'd been offered the finest champagne. 'Got any Vimto?'

'I have indeed. Two Vimtos, coming right up.'

The woman handed them two plastic cups of juice and two mini packs of digestive biscuits. 'Thank you so much,' Danny said.

'I'll be back round later on,' the volunteer said, pushing her trolley. 'Hopefully, I won't see you… if you know what I mean. Everything will be fine, you'll see. By the time I'm back you'll be on your way home. Best of luck with your dad.'

'Thank you,' Kate said as the woman left. 'She was so nice. God, I fucking love Vimto.'

Danny spotted a doctor walking towards them in the waiting area. 'Is that the guy who admitted your dad?' he asked.

'Yes, that's him,' Kate confirmed. 'He's Spanish. Christ, it must have been a shock for him ending up in Oldham...'

'He's very young-looking,' Danny pointed out. 'Fuck. That's exactly the kind of thing your dad would say.'

'Oh shit, Danny, look at him. His face is so stern.' Kate wiped her eyes then took hold of Danny's hand and squeezed until it hurt. Danny could feel that she was shaking.

They both stood up. The doctor smiled: 'Hello. Hi. Please. Don't be worried. Please. He's doing okay. He's doing good.' His accent was an eccentric mix of Spain and Oldham. 'Please, won't you sit down?'

'Do you know happened?' Kate asked. She had slightly loosened her grip on Danny's hand, but it still hurt.

'He had a stroke in the past, correct?' the doctor checked.

'Correct,' Danny and Kate said at the same time. *He's not your dad you know, he's Kate's,* Danny reminded himself.

'Well, your dad has had a Transient Ischaemic Attack - a TIA. That's a kind of mini stroke. The symptoms are the same, but the difference is that they pass. No lasting harm. His arm and face were numb when he arrived, but that's fading now. His speech hasn't degenerated. He's doing okay. He's upset. A bit confused. But all in all, not too bad.'

'Oh, thank you,' Kate said, freeing her hand from Danny's and touching the doctor's arm. 'Thank you so much. Can I see him?'

'I would like you to see him very much,' the doctor said. 'Because I think it would be a very good idea if he were to stay here tonight. Your father, on the other hand… he disagrees.'

'Stubborn old bugger,' Kate whispered and rolled her eyes at Danny.

'Maybe you could help convince him for me?' the doctor added.

'Bloody right I will,' Kate confirmed. 'Lead the way.'

'Of course,' the doctor said. He took Danny and Kate through a set of double doors, down a corridor and into the Stroke Unit. Lying in bed, John Smithdown mouthed the words 'fucking' and 'Nora' when he saw his daughter approach and pulled himself slightly upright.

'Mr Smithdown,' the doctor said introducing Kate as if she was entering a stage. 'I'm afraid you are in very serious trouble now…'

'Don't you fellahs take an oath or something, promising not to cause harm to your patients?' Smithdown said. He nodded at his daughter: 'You've put me right in harm's way here.'

The doctor held up his hands as if to indicate there was nothing he could do.

'Dad,' Kate began. 'This lovely doctor is too polite to say it, but I'm not. Stop being a silly twat and do as you're told. I mean it. If he says you need to stop here, you need to stop here. There's no reason for you to go home, we need you at your best to fight this Hanging Lees bollocks. Am I making myself clear? You're staying put and that's final. DO YOU UNDERSTAND?'

'Yes,' Smithdown said quietly.

'Good. Any more of this crap and I'll smack your legs, understand?'

'Fully,' her father confirmed. Danny smiled. He knew that Kate's mum used to use that expression when she was being troublesome as a child. She never actually smacked her legs - that's why it became a family joke. *God, imagine growing up like that.*

'I'd say that was very much settled then,' the doctor said. He looked at Kate. 'Go home, you and your husband need rest too.'

'Oh, he's not my husband,' Kate said, winking at Danny. The doctor flashed what Danny had to admit was a very winning smile at Kate. *She's practically old enough to be your mum, mate,* Danny thought. *Pack it in. These lads can't help themselves when Kate's around, can they?*

'Danny,' Kate said. 'We need to go and see Jonathan. Tell him what's happened. Will you come with me?'

'Yes, of course I will,' Danny confirmed.

'It's my son,' Kate explained to the doctor, unnecessarily, in Danny's opinion. 'He's at a residential school. We have to treat news like this very carefully.'

The doctor nodded sympathetically. 'You do what you need to do. We'll take good care of your father.' Inside his head, Danny repeated the doctor's words back, only in a whiny voice. *You do what you need to do. Meeeh, meeh, meeh I'm so caring.* The moment he'd done it he felt bad. He looked around just in case he'd accidentally said it out loud.

'Hey… Danny,' John Smithdown said, indicating that Danny should come closer with a weak wave of his hand. 'Here a minute.'

Danny squatted next to Smithdown's bed and looked at the retired detective. Close up, the jokiness wasn't as apparent. His eyes were grey and watery, and he looked afraid. 'What is it, John?'

'Too good looking for my taste, that doctor,' Smithdown said in a whisper.

'Dead right, mate,' Danny winked. 'Fucking Antonio Banderas with a stethoscope. Coming over here, being all professional and handsome. Bollocks to him.'

Smithdown smiled for a brief moment. Then it slipped away: 'Listen to me,' he said quietly. 'I'm being serious, now. I'm no angel. Never said I was. I've done some things that wouldn't be tolerated in this day and age. I accept that. But I'm telling you now, I don't know that woman up at Hanging Lees. And I certainly didn't know her as a kid. You must believe me. You do believe me, don't you, lad?'

'Of course I do, John,' Danny said. 'Totally. Don't worry. We'll put this right.'

NINE

30 March 1975

Maggie Ormrod slipped a finger into the coin return holder of the pinball machine and scooped out a ten pence piece. *Ace!*

She paused a moment and looked at the machine's flashing lights; a cartoon drawing of a confident-looking man with light brown way hair was on the main upright panel alongside a flashing red, white and blue NUMBER 1. The boys at the care home had been talking about the man the other day after there'd been a piece about him on *John Craven's Newsround.* The boys said he was mad - *not John Craven, he's not mad, he's nice* - and that he'd broken every bone in his body. They'd been arguing about how to pronounce his name and John Craven had settled it when he said: *Evel Knievel.*

Maggie looked at the man's image on the pinball machine: *fancy being called Evel! It must cause all sorts of mither… No one would believe a word you said! If you got stopped by the police and they said, 'right, what's all this then? You were going right fast on that bike, sir… what's your name, then?' And then you said, 'Evel', they'd be like, 'right then, smart arse, you'd better come with us.' You'd never get NOWT done being called Evel.*

Maggie slipped the coin into the flapped pocket on the front of her dungarees and fastened the button to secure it. She gave it a little pat and the coins inside made a satisfying tik tak sound. She watched the flashing lights of the pinball machine for a few moments more. Pinball machines didn't interest Maggie. *Just a load of noise and lights and what do you get at the end? Nowt. Another go if you're lucky. Waste of money.*

No. What Maggie liked was Penny Falls. Now THAT was a game worth playing. *I'll have to go next door for that. Just daft pinball in here.* Maggie sorted out her 'shiny coins' from her 'not shiny coins'; the 'not shiny' ones went back into her special pocket. Then she crossed the arcade tent, stood on her tiptoes and pushed her 'shiny coins' across the counter of the change booth. The man behind the counter barely looked at her as he swapped them for two pence pieces, the accepted currency of the experienced Penny Falls player.

Maggie left the pinball 'arcade' - in reality a canvas rectangle supported by scaffolding poles - and stepped outside into the warm, Spring air. The pinball area smelled of boys: cigarettes, sweat and cider. *Yuk! Have a bath now and again yer mucky buggers.*

But outside was different. Outside had all the best smells ever all rolled into one: doughnuts, candy floss, popcorn, hot dogs, onions and that difficult-to-pin-down oily odour that seemed to hang over every travelling fair. Maggie wasn't sure what was better: the smell of the fair or the fact that no one knew that she was here smelling it. For a moment she thought about spending a few of her precious coins on a burger - she'd barely eaten all day - but decided to be cautious. *I'll have a double burger with my winnings. With chips n'all!*

The rides added a wonderful soundtrack to the smells. The Cyclone, the Mad Mouse and the Walzters; each had its own special set of clanks and rattles, sending out a message that expressed the possibility of real danger and genuine mishap. Maggie heard the cries of the fairground workers too: 'Readyboyzangirlz?' a man shouted over the Waltzer's fuzzy PA system, dipping the pounding music slightly to make sure his slurry words of warning could be heard. 'I SAID... AREYOOREADYBOYZANGIRLZ?'

'YEAH!' came the replies from the excited teenagers who were bracing themselves for the ride to start.

'OKAYTHEN... HEREWEGOHOLDTIGHT!'

Then the ride lurched into life and there were screams. Lots of screams.

Maggie looked beyond the rides and out towards the huge expanse of dark water next to the fairground site. She watched as the cascading, spinning funfair lights danced across the surface of the Alexandra Park boating lake; the skittering reflections made the fair seem twice the size that it really was. Maggie didn't like the lake. It's featureless sheen uneased her. She didn't like water full stop - lakes, ponds, pools and reservoirs all gave her chills. But she also felt weirdly excited by them too; the same fear that she imagined people experienced when they went on fairground rides. Maggie didn't like fairground rides much either; she liked Penny Falls.

As she headed for the slot machine arcade, Maggie made a point of staying as close to the tents as possible, brushing the canvas with her hand as she walked past. The touch of the heavy-duty material made her feel safe. Safe from the water. Safe from anyone who might spot her and wonder why such a young girl was on her own. Just... safe.

As she entered the tent there was a new smell to add to the already heady list - the coppery smell of coins. Lots of coins. *There must be millions… no, BILLIONS of them,* she thought.

Inside were at least twenty variations of her beloved penny machines. Each one had a slightly different theme and design to entice the player: some were six-sided, some had four, others two. One had a surfer theme, another had cartoon lumberjacks riding logs over waterfalls. They all shared the same simple idea: put your coins in and - if you timed it right - the electric pushers and paddles would slide your money into the teetering pile of coins left by other, less skillful players and force it towards the edge. Then gravity would do its work and a great chunk of cash would tumble into the chutes below. *And then it's all mine. All for little Maggie.*

With an expert eye, Maggie walked around the machines, looking for especially vulnerable piles of coins that were ripe and ready to be released. After a lap of the tent, she decided on one machine, a multi-sided unit designed to look like a spaceship. *Penny Planet! That's so ace…*

Maggie unbuttoned her special pocket and dug out a handful of two pence pieces. She watched intently as the pushers moved backwards and forwards and waited until experience told her the time was just right time, then she pushed three coins very quickly into the same slot. They tumbled down, and then fell into line, guided by the paddle; then they snuggled up against the existing money. Maggie's coins then helped push the coins already inside the machine forward towards the edge. They were close, but not quite close enough to tip them over. She repeated the action in exactly the same way; three coins, one after the other, pushed into the same slot. Nothing. She did it again. And again. By now the money at the edge - much of it prized, shiny ten and five pence pieces - seemed to be defying all logic by clinging on and refusing to budge.

Maggie looked at the wobbling mass of money and checked what she had left… *three coins. Bloody Nora.*

As she debated whether to change her strategy there was a bang on one corner of the machine and a large pile of money fell into the chute nearest to Maggie. She looked up. A man in a beige raincoat had bumped the machine with his hip. He smiled and made a 'oops' face as if it had been a terrible accident and he hadn't actually meant to send all those coins down the chute and into the collection point right near where Maggie was standing.

'Mister!' she said, her eyes wide with shock and pleasure. 'Yer can't do that, the fairground lads will call the police!'

The man smiled again. 'I wouldn't worry about that,' he said. He looked around then bent down to Maggie's eye level. *He smells of beer and mints.* His voice dropped to a friendly whisper. 'I *am* the police.'

TEN

It wasn't hard to tell that Hunter's Hollow Residential School on the outskirts of Diggle had, in a previous life, been a hotel. As a child, Danny - along with his older sister - had spent six months in a care home while they waited to be fostered. That home had been nothing like this.

Set back from the road by a 200-yard driveway, Hunter's Hollow and its various add-ons and extensions through the decades fanned back from an impressive former coaching inn that now served as its main entrance. Behind the main doors were former conference areas that now served as classrooms, an ex-health club that was now the school gymnasium and hotel rooms that could accommodate up to 70 pupils aged eight to eighteen. Behind the site were extensive grounds, including tennis courts and climbing walls, that stretched into the distance before a craggy ridge known as Hunter's Edge took over.

Danny had looked at the school's website on the way there. The care home he'd been sent to had been little more than a holding pen for kids that people either didn't want or couldn't handle. Hunter's Hollow had carers, teachers, therapists and clinical psychologists to help pupils overcome their problems and learn at the same time. One of the school's specialties was helping young people who'd suffered 'adverse childhood experiences'; Kate's son Jonathan had certainly had more than his fair share of those.

At the front entrance a woman dressed in slightly muddy softshell trousers and a hoodie was waiting for them: 'Kate! Hi. I'm so sorry to hear about your dad. How's he doing?'

'They're keeping him in overnight,' Kate replied as she and Danny stepped from her Mercedes and climbed the steps to the main entrance. 'He's comfortable I suppose. That's the word they use, isn't it? Comfortable? Sorry, Susan, this is my friend Danny Johnston. Danny, this is Susan Matlock. She's the manager here.'

Susan smiled at Danny. 'Hi, Danny. Nice to meet you. I've read your book.'

'Oh dear,' Danny said. 'I don't like the sound of that…'

'No, it's all good,' Susan said, reassuringly. 'It's great, in fact. Fascinating. Terrible title though. *Twister Sisters*? Bet the publishers forced that on you, didn't they?'

'They did,' Danny admitted. 'I wanted to call it *Black Moss*, but I got overruled. That's showbiz.'

'We should get you into the school sometime,' Susan said. 'You could talk to the pupils about journalism and writing. You up for that?'

'Sure,' he said. 'Why not?'

Susan made Danny shake on it: He looked at her: *Late forties but looks younger. Sporty. Super confident. No messing about. Not what I imagined… I was expecting someone in dungarees.*

'Done!' Susan exclaimed. 'You heard him, Kate? That's a binding contract, right there.'

'I did indeed,' Kate confirmed, pointing a finger at Danny then at Susan as if to indicate… do as you're told. 'Best to sort it on email,' Susan said. 'The phone signal is shit out here.'

'How's Jonathan?' Kate asked as they went through the reception and into the main body of the school. Susan used her electronic identity card to open up multiple, secure doors as they went.

'Do you know what?' Susan said. 'Considering what's been flying about on the internet today, he's not too bad at all.'

'It's all crap,' Danny said. 'I've known John Smithdown since I was seven. Trust me. He's innocent.'

'Yes, I read about that in your book. He saved you and your sister, didn't he? Very brave of you to write about it. You've had quite the journey Danny, haven't you?'

'You make me sound like I'm on my way out,' Danny replied.

'Not at all,' Susan replied, again she was smiling at Danny. 'You never know what excitement could be waiting for you just around the corner, do you?'

'You really don't,' Danny agreed. *Did I just blush a bit then? Fucking Nora.* He looked at the artwork on the corridor walls as they walked and tried to avoid eye contact with Kate.

Susan led them into a medium-sized room with soft furnishings and low-key lighting; there were posters on the wall with uplifting messages on them about achievement, potential and determination. 'Jonathan has said that he'd prefer to meet in one of these quiet areas rather than in his room,' she said. 'His choice. Really important we respect that. If you'll both just wait here, I'll go and get him.'

Danny walked around the room, looking at the positivity posters; he was still trying to avoid Kate's look. *Don't you dare, Kate Smithdown. Don't. You. Fucking. Dare.*

Kate waited for Susan to leave the room. 'Danny Something,' she sighed. 'Was that your attempt at flirting back there? God, I think I'm going to be sick.'

Danny ignored her and leant in to examine one of the posters more closely: 'Do you know what it says on this poster, Kate?'

'What does it say, Danny?'

'It says… shut your cakehole,' he replied, tapping the poster that was actually about life goals with the knuckle of his forefinger. 'Right here. Shut your cakehole. That's what it says. Those are very wise words and I think you should take them to heart.'

'Danny Johnston, flirting,' she said quietly. 'Christ Almighty, I've seen it all now.'

Susan came back into the room with Jonathan, relieving Danny of the need to say something clever in return. Kate's son had been 10 years old when Danny first met him - a tiny ball of energy, all curly hair and smiles, charging about on his bike. Now it looked like he'd been on some kind of teenage stretching machine; his arms and legs seemed 20 percent too long for his torso, and his face had lost every trace of its youthful roundness. He wore ultra-skinny black jeans that had been strategically ripped in key places and a red t-shirt with a Soviet Coca Cola logo on it. He raised a hand, smiled at Danny and sat down. The seat he chose was nearer to Danny than to his mum.

'Right, I'll leave you guys to it,' Susan said.

'Actually,' Jonathan said, his voice took Danny by surprise. It was deep, calm and insistent. 'Can you stay, Susan? Is that okay?'

Susan looked at Kate before she answered: 'Of course, not a problem.' She perched herself on the windowsill facing them, crossing her arms and looking at her feet.

'Right… okay… Jonathan,' Kate began. 'It's about your grandad. He's in hospital. He's had a very minor sort of stroke. Just a mini one, honestly. He's okay, but he's been told to stay at the Royal tonight so he can rest and get his strength back.'

Jonathan said nothing. He looked at the ends of his fingers as if they were the most fascinating thing imaginable.

Kate sighed and carried on: 'You may have seen some stuff about him on social media. Or in the local press.' There was a darting look towards Danny when she said that. 'It's not true. I'm telling you now, it's all fake. You know that I'm sure you do. But until we can clear things up, your grandad is better off in hospital where he can rest and stay out of the way. Okay?'

Jonathan played with the skin on the edge of his fingernails. There was silence. 'Jonathan,' Kate said, her voice was wobbly with tiredness and emotion. 'If you're still angry at me for placing you here at the school… I get it. I understand.'

'You don't get it though, do you?' the teenager said, looking at his mother for the first time since he'd entered the room. 'I'm not angry at you. Not for that, anyway. I actually like it here. I feel safe. Protected. That's a nice feeling, that is. The feeling of being… protected.'

'Jonathan, please…' Kate said; she was struggling now to keep from sounding upset.

'Danny gets it,' Jonathan said. 'You know what it's like to be uncared for as a kid, don't you, Danny?

'Mate, come on,' Danny pleaded quietly. 'There's no need for this.'

Jonathan then turned his attention towards Susan: 'When I was 10, my mum let me be kidnapped, Susan. You know that don't you? Of course you do. It's all there in my records. We've talked about it in group sessions. I was drugged and kidnapped. By two fucking weirdos. The twisted fucking sisters. They were going to kill me, Susan. Just like they'd killed all those other kids. If it hadn't been for Danny, I'd be at the bottom of Black Moss Reservoir instead of being here. So, you're wrong, Mum. I like it at Hunter's Hollow. I feel safe. I AM safe.'

'Jonathan,' Danny said, speaking despite the strong feeling that it wasn't really his place to talk. 'It was your mum that saved you, don't you remember? I was no use. One of them, Jan Cave, had banged a knife in me. Your mum took care of Beth Hall with a bat - took her jaw clean out of its hinges - then she just about drowned Jan in Black Moss. It was her, Jonathan. Your mum. My friend Gary Keenan helped too. He died trying to help you. But it was her,' he jabbed his forefinger in Kate's direction. 'She was the one that saved you. She protected you like no one has ever protected a kid before. She's the reason you're alive. Her. Right there.'

'She's the reason I was taken in the first place,' Jonathan muttered. 'Her. *Right there.*' His voice was harsh and sarcastic now. He looked at Susan. 'Are we done?'

'You're free to go to your room at any time, Jonathan,' Susan confirmed. 'You know that.'

Jonathan jumped up from his seat, nodded to Danny and left. A few moments after the door closed behind him, Kate began to cry.

ELEVEN

That night, for the first time in several years, Danny dreamt about The Shirtless Boy.

He'd become aware of The Shirtless Boy after he'd stopped drinking. The Boy had been one of many unpleasant side effects. Danny often wondered if The Boy had always been there, and that alcohol had just taken away his ability to remember his presence.

The boy he saw face down in the sand at Black Moss in 1990 had no shirt on. He had weights strapped to his chest, admittedly, but no shirt. When he'd crashed his car in 2016, he was sure he'd seen a boy with no shirt on just before he'd hit the tree that had stopped his car, his career and his drinking all in one instant.

He even thought he'd seen such a boy out on the moors; it was while he was doing his community service after his drink driving conviction. Danny had always convinced himself that the boy with no shirt that he'd seen that day, the boy at Black Moss, the boy at the crash scene and The Shirtless Boy in his dreams were all very separate things. *Different boys with no shirts on. Coincidence. Not connected. No way*

Danny's dreams were always harsh and unpleasant when The Boy made an appearance; the waking was inevitably sweaty, cold and jarring. Even within a dream, Danny was able to think… *oh fuck…* when The Boy showed up. He wasn't the kind of person who would attempt to trying to 'interpret' a dream, but even Danny had to admit - to himself, never to anyone else - that things were usually about to take a bad turn when he dreamt about The Shirtless Boy.

In his dream that night, his car had broken down in a layby out on the moors. *Have I run out of petrol? Not sure. You never are in a dream, are you? Anyway, the car definitely won't start. Hazard lights on? Yes.*

It was late at night but the moon and the tangerine glow of lights from a distant town provided just enough illumination for him to see down the curving moorland road. It stretched away from him and seemed to get longer and longer the more he looked. The inside of the car was cold - *really* cold - and Danny could see his own breath wisping upwards in front of his face.

As Danny's hazard lights clicked on and off, he saw The Shirtless Boy through his windscreen; no shirt as ever but wearing grey shorts and holding something in his hand. Each time the lights flashed, The Boy got a little closer to the car, though his legs never seemed to move.

Danny looked at his face. He couldn't see his features. The Boy definitely had features, it's just that Danny could never quite see them, no matter how hard he tried to make them out.

He could definitely see what was in The Boy's hand though: a candyfloss on a stick. There was no doubt in Danny's dream-mind that this was the biggest, brightest and best candyfloss he'd ever seen in his life. It was fluffy, pink and beautiful. He felt jealous that The Shirtless Boy had it. *Lucky little bastard. Why can't I have one? Wonder if he'll give me a bit?*

Although Danny couldn't see his mouth, The Boy was clearly eating the candyfloss and really enjoying it. *That must be the best candyfloss in the world and that tight little twat is hogging it all for himself.*

With every flash of the hazard lights, The Boy got closer and closer, and the candyfloss got smaller and smaller.

Flash. Closer. Flash. Closer. Flash. Closer.

Then the lights flashed again but The Boy wasn't there. Danny leant forward and stared though his windscreen. It was misty from his breath and he wiped the inside of the glass with the sleeve of his jumper. The Shirtless Boy was gone.

Then Danny heard a tac tac sound. The Boy was by the driver's window. He stood there for a moment; then he tapped the glass with his empty stick and motioned for Danny to lower the window. Danny shook his head. The Boy tapped again.

Absolutely no fucking way, you little bastard.

They looked at each other through the car window. The Shirtless Boy then pulled his arm back and pushed the stick through the glass as if it wasn't there and straight down Danny's throat.

Danny woke up. His mobile was ringing. *Unknown caller. Maybe it's the hospital. Oh God.*

'Hello?'

'Lad's Grave.' The voice was male. There were other voices in the background. They sounded like they were running.

'What?' queried Danny, still fuzzy from being woken from his dream. 'What are you on about?'

'LAD'S GRAVE MOOR,' the voice shouted. Look it up. That's where you need to be, right now.'

TWELVE

Danny passed Hanging Lees Reservoir and the Bull's Head pub, eased up the moorland Ripponden Road and saw the huge, skeletal frame of the Windy Hill transmitter up ahead. It stood guard next to the M62 motorway at the border between Greater Manchester and Yorkshire. Lad's Grave lay ahead, just as the road cut across one of the bleakest sections of the moors. *Lad's Grave? Seriously? Why the fuck do they give places names like that around here?*

The pre-dawn light showed the elegant silhouette of the Pennine Way footbridge on Danny's left as he drove under the M62 and out onto the other side. He pulled into a layby; behind him, lorries clattered up and down the motorway between Manchester and Leeds. *The highest bit of motorway in England, this is. There's a fun fact to distract you from being scared out of your fucking mind, Danny boy.*

In front of him were the moors. Layer after layer of peaty bogland with only patchy sheets of heather, crowberry and cottongrass to break it up. The land dipped, swooped and disappeared into the darkness; there were no trees to interrupt the bleak dominance of the land. Not one. In any direction. There was only one vertical that broke up the endless lines of moorland horizontals - a lone wind turbine whooshing a circular beat on the crest of the second or third rolling hill of Lad's Grave Moor.

Shit. I suppose I've got to go up there, haven't I? Brilliant.

Having learned some hard lessons in relation to inappropriate footwear and the moors around Manchester many years earlier, Danny was prepared. He pulled a pair of walking boots from the box in the boot of his car and took a torch too. He closed the boot and took a look around; all he could see was that very special brand of nothing that was the only true defining feature of the moors. Once he was booted up, he headed off across the open land towards the turbine.

As a young man, the hills and moors that curved around Greater

Manchester had baffled Danny. It was an alien landscape that didn't welcome the likes of him. Now, in his mid-50s, he understood the landscape a little better. He knew the hags that could trip him, the gullies and hidden streams that might take hold of his ankle and the cloughs that could distract him and lead him astray. He liked the reliable nothingness that the moors provided, and he was wise to the dangers that lay hidden underneath its mossy folds.

He moved quickly and efficiently across the terrain, zig zagging his way up the moor towards the turbine. The lone unit up ahead was only about 40 feet high, no match for the 200-foot monsters to the west at the Scout Moor Wind Farm. There were no actual farms on this section of the moors - the landscape was far too harsh for that; the wind farms had taken over that responsibility now.

Danny guessed that the turbine was probably to provide emergency power for the motorway or the nearby Green Withens Reservoir; perhaps it was a test unit to feed energy into the National Grid with an eye on a fully-fledged wind farm in the future. Either way, it looked strangely alone, quietly fulfilling its purpose on there on the moors without any company.

As he got closer, Danny shone his torch and noticed what looked like a sack or a bin bag at the turbine's base. The light shak shak shak sound of the blades as they cut through the chill air got louder as he approached. The dawn light was just starting to creep across the top edge of the moors that surrounded him.

Shak shak shak.

The sack at the bottom of the turbine was bent at the middle as if it had been tied to the base of the unit.

Don't be a person, don't be a person, don't be a person.

Danny was about 20 feet from the turbine now and he could see that it was indeed a person. Or at least, what was left of one. Danny could tell it was a man because he had no shirt on; his hairy arms, chest and shoulders were all matted with blood. His jaw hung loose, and his cheekbones were now dents in the remains of his face; there were holes and parallel gouges in his balding head. Underneath the blood and around the holes, the numbers '1812' were just about visible on the man's forehead. What looked like a mobile phone was strapped to his chest; the grey tape holding it there was also streaked in blood.

There was an A4 sign between his legs, printed out in a strangely jaunty, knockabout typeface and pinned down by rocks at each corner.

HERE LIES BARRY 'THE BEAST' MORTIMER
CHECK HIS PHONE.
LET THIS BE A WARNING TO ALL PAEDOS.
NONCE AND YOU WILL DIE.

Danny stood and stared. He looked around the moors. 'Just you and me then, Barry,' he whispered. 'Christ Almighty, what the fuck did you do?'

He looked at the phone strapped to the man's chest and the four-digit number on his forehead. He thought for a moment about activating the screen and putting the number into it. *Don't be a tit, Danny. For once in your life, don't be a tit.*

Taking out his own phone, Danny rang 999, told the operator what he knew and then rang off. He then sat on a large rock nearby and stared at the man's body. Then he searched Facebook for the name Barry Mortimer. It didn't take him long to find what he suspected was the man's account. *Local guy. Family man. Wife and three kids. Holidays in Spain and Florida. Happy, happy, happy. Fucking Nora.*

The latest post on the man's page - put there two hours ago - was certainly eye-catching:

STAND BY FOR A MAJOR ANNOUNCEMENT…
I, BARRY MORTIMER, AM A MASSIVE NONCE.
DETAILS TO COME LATER TODAY!

So that was what was 'on your mind' when you were on Facebook at 2.10 am this morning was it, Barry? I suspect you didn't actually post that yourself, did you?

Underneath the post, some of the man's friends had already added likes, laughing emojis and comments: 'Think someone's been at your phone, Baz!' one said. 'Don't tell me, you've been hacked. Ha! Ha! Ha!' said another. 'Always suspected it Bazza!'

Danny took screen grabs of the page and saved copies of Barry's photos, then he scrolled through his 'about' information to find his place of work. He also took note of a Strava post showing that the man had managed a 5K run earlier in the year. There was a photo of a tired and sweaty-looking Barry wearing running gear; he had his hands in the air in triumph. *Looking to drop a few pounds there, Barry?* The looped Strava route highlighted where the run had started and ended. *That's probably his home address, right there in Delph. People give so much information out; in the old days I would have had to ring every B. Mortimer in the phone book.*

Not anymore. You need to think more about your privacy settings, Barry. Bit late now, I suppose.

Danny took several photos of the scene, including the sign, but was careful to keep anything gruesome out of the frame. Then he started writing. He didn't care for doing stories on his phone; he couldn't do that double-thumb thing that everyone under 35 seemed able to do with ease. After ten minutes and a few tweaks, he was ready to post the story; then he hesitated. *If you weren't so self-righteous, Danny Johnston, you wouldn't be so skint.*

Danny looked at the body and the sign. The wind pushed across the moor and rattled the paper. He added the code that inserted adverts into the story and pressed 'publish'.

THIRTEEN

'VIGILANTE' FEARS AFTER MUTILATED BODY FOUND NEAR MOTORWAY
Danny Johnston - Oldham Now

Murder squad detectives, investigating the discovery of a man's body on moorland near the M62, fear he may have been subjected to a vigilante-style attack.

The grim discovery was made in the early hours of this morning at an area known as Lad's Grave. It's close to the motorway underpass on the A672 Denshaw to Ripponden road. Police were alerted after an anonymous tip off to *Oldham Now*.

The badly mutilated body had been strapped to a wind turbine and a note found at the scene suggested that the man had been targeted as an alleged paedophile. The note said:

'LET THIS BE A WARNING TO ALL PAEDOS,
NONCE AND YOU WILL DIE.'

The note named the man, but *Oldham Now* is withholding his identity until relatives can be informed.

A post-mortem examination is expected to be carried out later today to establish the exact cause of death. Police will also spend the day examining a phone found at the scene. A four-digit passcode had been written on the victim's head, indicating that those responsible were keen for police to look at the dead man's online activity.

It's the second body to be found in the area in the last 24 hours. On Monday morning, the body of a woman was found at Hanging Lees Reservoir, which is also just off the A672 road. The woman has since been identified as Maggie Ormrod, aged 57, of Ripponden Road, Denshaw.

It's not yet known if police are linking the two finds, but Detective

Inspector Patrick McIntyre and his brother Detective Constable Karl McIntyre are believed to be leading both investigations.

Danny checked how the story looked via Facebook. Nearly all the traffic to his website came via Facebook, so it was always his priority. *Twitter is just noise. FB is where the engagement comes from. Hook them there, then get them onto the website sharpish. That's how to make money in this game.*

He watched as the comments, shares and angry emojis began to grow, even though it was barely six o'clock in the morning. The first comment was from Jill from Coldhurst (Love my hubby, my two beautiful boys and nites out with my Girl Squad): 'Good fookin riddance. Scum,' it said.

Jill's comment began racking up likes and laughing emojis straight away. 'Spot on, Jill'... 'You go, Jill'... 'No arguments from me, one less nonce to lock up. Whoever did this... good on them I say!'

Danny flicked through some more of the comments and reactions that his story was provoking:

Royton Ray: 'About time someone started tackling this head on. Cops have got their hands tied. A dead nonce can't nonce again. Fact.'

Juliepops: 'Made my day this. Get in!!! If they need a hand getting rid of anymore give me a shout!!!'

Jake and Janet's Mum: 'Someone should set up a fund to buy these vigilantes a pint. Good work lads!'

Like after like. Laughing emoji after laughing emoji. Heart after heart.

The sun began to rise behind Manchester city centre. Danny could see the sharp silhouette of the Beetham Tower at the end of Deansgate from his vantage point next to the wind turbine. It was cold and he wanted to go back to his car, but it seemed wrong to leave Barry Mortimer out there alone strapped to the wind turbine. Danny wasn't sure why it felt wrong - no one had less sympathy for the likes of Barry than he did - but it just didn't feel right. He managed to justify staying for entirely practical reasons: *I'll get some video of the cops when they arrive. That's good content, that is.*

Plus, Danny reasoned, he felt obligated to be on standby to shout a warning to any early morning walkers or joggers who might go by... *What should I say? I wouldn't go this way if I were you, mate. There's a nonce with his head caved in. You're welcome!*

So, Danny sat down, pulled his jacket tight around his neck and waited. Down the M62 motorway he saw flashing lights bouncing off the slopes that hemmed in the carriageway on the westbound carriageway. The sound of the sirens came seconds later. *By God, that was quick. Maybe I wasn't the first person to call.*

Across the other side of the motorway, close to the Windy Hill transmitter, he saw two figures in the morning light. One was holding out an arm as if holding up a phone. Both seemed to have their faces covered. Danny stood up to get a better look. There was a growling, mechanical sound and then they were gone. *I can hear motorbikes; is that from the moors or the motorway?*

Down the moor he saw the police pull up into the layby next to his car; he waved to them and pointed at the turbine.

Five minutes later the McIntyre brothers arrived at the scene: 'Mr Johnston,' Detective Constable McIntyre said. 'Always a pleasure.'

The two detectives looked at Barry Mortimer's battered body and the sign in front of him. 'Well, I don't like to jump to conclusions,' his older brother said,' But I suppose you're going to say it was like this when you found him?'

'That's exactly what I'm going to say, because that's what happened,' Danny confirmed.

'...And that you absolutely haven't touched anything,' DC McIntyre added. 'Especially the phone that's strapped to his chest.' The two brothers were like a double act, almost finishing each other's sentences.

'Again, correct,' Danny said.

'Are you familiar with the expression "helping police with their inquiries" Mr Johnston?' DI McIntyre asked.

'I am indeed,' Danny replied, blowing into his cupped hands to keep warm.

'Good,' the DI said. 'Well, how about me and my brother here get you out of the cold, get a nice mug of Oldham police station hot chocolate down you and then you can do just that.'

FOURTEEN

RECORD OF INTERVIEW
Person interviewed: JOHNSTON, Daniel (12/7/66)
Place of interview: Oldham Police Station
Time commenced: 0810 hours
Interviewer(s): DI3716 McIntyre, Patrick DC2184 McIntyre, Karl.
Other persons present: Paulina Scorer - Solicitor from Blanco & Harkness Solicitors.
Usual introductions, cautions and advice. JOHNSTON has been informed that he is not under arrest and that he is free to leave at any time. JOHNSTON has opted to have a legal representative with him (Ms P Scorer).
This is the first interview with DANIEL JOHNSTON - JOHNSTON confirms that no questions have been asked before the recording begins.

DI MCINTYRE: Mr Johnston, I want to talk to you about two matters today. One is the discovery of a woman's body - a Maggie Ormrod - at Hanging Lees Reservoir. But I'd like to start with some questions about the discovery of another body, that of Barry Mortimer, which was found at Lad's Grave Moor in the early hours of this morning. Did you know Mr Mortimer at all?
JOHNSTON: I didn't. I spent a bit of time with him out on the moor in the early hours of this morning. He didn't say much. So…no, it's fair to say that I didn't know him.
DI MCINTYRE: Can you tell me how you came to be out on the moors at that time?
JOHNSTON: I got a call telling me to get myself out to Lad's Grave. They do love spooky names for places around these parts, don't they? So, the call said go there… and that's what I did.
DI MCINTYRE: Do you know the identity of the caller?
JOHNSTON: No. I don't. It was anonymous. You don't kill someone then call a reporter and leave your name and number, do you?
DI MCINTYRE: What can you tell me about the person who called

you?
JOHNSTON: Male. Not young, not old. Northern accent, not strong. Might have been from round here, maybe not. He just told me to get myself out to Lad's Grave, sharpish. When I tried to get more out of him, he told me to Google it and hung up. That's it.
DI MCINTYRE: Did you recognise the voice?
JOHNSTON: No.
DI MCINTYRE: And where were you when you got the call?
JOHNSTON: At home. On my own.
DI MCINTYRE: And prior to that?
JOHNSTON: I'd been to Hunter's Hollow School to see John Smithdown's grandson…To tell him what's been happening with his grandad. Left there about nine. Called in for a takeaway at Valentino's on the main road near my house. Took it home. Ate it. Watched the news. Updated my website. Went to bed. That's it. I've got a receipt. For the pizza, I mean. I had a thin crust with anchovies by the way. In case you need to know. For the record and that. It was nice. Not everyone cares for anchovies on pizza, but I do.
DI MCINTYRE: Let's stick to the matter in hand, shall we? What happened then?
JOHNSTON: I went up onto the moor and… well, there was Barry. He was in a bit of a state, to say the least. Yeah. Quite a sight.
DI MCINTYRE: There was a note left at the scene, wasn't there?
JOHNSTON: There was indeed.
DI MCINTYRE: The note read: HERE LIES BARRY 'THE BEAST' MORTIMER. CHECK HIS PHONE. LET THIS BE A WARNING TO ALL PAEDOS. NONCE AND YOU WILL DIE. You know that because you rather unhelpfully put a picture of it on your news site. What did you take that note to mean?
JOHNSTON: Well, I'm not a detective like you and your brother are, but I took it as a warning. Someone's out to get paedophiles. And whoever did this had clearly fingered Barry. If you'll excuse the expression.
DI MCINTYRE: So, you took this to be a threat to paedophiles?
JOHNSTON: They'd caved his head in. So, yes… a little bit of a threat.
DI MCINTYRE: Did you notice anything else about the body?
JOHNSTON: A phone was taped to his chest… I assumed it was his. A four-digit code had been written on his forehead. Very thoughtful of them, I thought. Clearly a better class of vigilante - a cut above.
DI MCINTYRE: Did you touch the phone?

JOHNSTON: Absolutely not. I looked at his Facebook page from my own phone. They'd obviously posted something on there on his behalf, too.
DI MCINTYRE: I'm a massive nonce.
JOHNSTON: I think we should stick to talking about Barry, don't you?
DI MCINTYRE: Hilarious, Mr Johnston. You know exactly what I mean. That was the message they posted. Why do you think they wrote the number on his head?
JOHNSTON: I'd be guessing.
DI MCINTYRE: What would be your guess?
JOHNSTON: My guess would be that the code was for Barry's phone. Then you lot could unlock it and scroll through all Bazza's slickest chat up lines aimed at the younger end of the market. Then you could see that he was, as the note so eloquently stated, a nonce. One less for you to worry about, I suppose. The youngsters of Oldham are safe. Facebook is loving it. Everyone's happy. Apart from Barry, of course.
DI MCINTYRE: That's a rather cynical way of looking at it, Mr Johnston. A man's been murdered. We will be putting every resource we have at our disposal to see that those responsible for this are caught and prosecuted.
JOHNSTON: Of course. Every resource. Right you are. Anything else?
DI MCINTYRE: Well, you were also at the scene of the body found at Hanging Lees Reservoir on Monday morning. Could you tell me how that came about?
JOHNSTON: Similar scenario. Got a message via an anonymous Twitter account that disappeared immediately afterwards. Advised me I should get myself to Hanging Lees. So, I did. I saw you out there. That was nice. Took a few photos and a bit of video. That's it.
DI MCINTYRE: Was there any mention of anyone else in the message?
JOHNSTON: No.
DI MCINTYRE: No name?
JOHNSTON: No.
DI MCINTYRE: Any mention of anyone you might know?
JOHNSTON: No names, like I said.
DI MCINTYRE: Did you screenshot the message?
JOHNSTON: No.
DI MCINTYRE: You're normally a very chatty sort of man, Mr

Johnston. Now it's all one-word answers.
JOHNSON: That's not a question. Try a question.
DI MCINTYRE: Did you know Maggie Ormrod, the woman found at Hanging Lees?
JOHNSTON: See, that's a closed question. Did you, were you, are you - all closed questions. It just invites me to offer a one-word answer. So here it is. No.
DI MCINTYRE: Did Mr Smithdown ever mention the name Maggie Ormrod to you?
JOHNSTON: Closed question again. Come on. No.
DI MCINTYRE: What's the nature of your relationship with John Smithdown?
JOHNSTON: Open question. That's better. Well done. We're making real progress. John Smithdown saved me and my sister's lives when we were kids. Got us out of our parent's house and into a care home. The house of horrors the newspapers called it at the time. I met up with him again during the Black Moss murder investigation in 1990, then again when I moved up here from London in 2016.
DI MCINTYRE: After your arrest for drink driving?
JOHNSTON: That's correct, as you well know. These days, I help his daughter look after him. I see him several times a week. He's like a father, uncle and best mate to me, all rolled into one. Look at your police records. He's a hero, too. The real deal.
DI MCINTYRE: You mentioned your sister - did she continue her friendship with John Smithdown?
JOHNSTON: You're back on the closed questions again, but I'll let you off. No, she didn't. She didn't feel the need, plus she died of cancer recently and that tends to limit your social life. And if you're mentioning my sister to have a little dig around about whether John Smithdown liked young girls or not, then fucking shame on you.
DI MCINTYRE: I wasn't, but I have to ask. Have you ever known John Smithdown show an interest in young girls?
JOHNSTON: Absolutely not.
DI MCINTYRE: Okay, let's leave it there.

End of recording: 0831 hours.

Danny put on his jacket and smiled at his solicitor. 'That okay, Paulina? I told you I'd be on my best behaviour.'

'I was pleasantly surprised,' she said cheerfully, packing her notebook into a briefcase. 'Well done.'

'Did you get everything you want?' Danny asked the Detective Inspector.

'That's a closed question, Mr Johnston,' the DI replied. 'As a special treat I'll give you the benefit of a two-word answer. For now.'

'Can I ask you a question?' Danny said. Paulina gave him a warning glance and shook her head.

'You can ask,' the detective said. 'Whether I can give you a reply, that's a different matter.'

'It's a closed question,' Danny said. 'Based on what you've presumably seen on his phone… private messages and so on… do you think Barry Mortimer was a paedophile?'

DC McIntyre got up from his chair and stood alongside his brother: 'We can't answer that, as you well know.'

'I rather think that you just have. Here's another one. Do you think he was trapped and killed by vigilantes?'

'You definitely know we can't answer that,' the DI said.

'Again, you kind of just did…'

'Mr Johnston, we're all on the same side here, as far as I know,' DC McIntyre said.

'That depends whether you seriously think John Smithdown harmed that poor woman up at Hanging Lees when she was a kid,' Danny said. 'If you do, then we are definitely not on the same side.'

'We have to investigate it,' the DI said. 'Non-recent abuse cases are a big deal right now, and rightly so. You know that better than anyone. As soon as we can get this sorted out, the better it'll be for all concerned.'

'Can I go now?' Danny asked.

'You were free to go at any time,' the DI responded. 'We appreciate your help. Here's my number. If you think of anything else - or get any similar messages - please get in touch.'

Danny took the detective's card and made an 'after you' gesture to Paulina Scorer.

'Mr Johnston,' DI McIntyre said. 'One other thing. Please stay away from Barry Mortimer's family, okay?'

'Absolutely,' Danny replied. He smiled at his solicitor.

'We mean it,' the DC added, firmly. 'Don't go near them.'

'Absolutely,' Danny said.

FIFTEEN

From the woods that peppered the streets on the outskirts of Delph, Danny spotted the back garden of Barry Mortimer's new-build house. *Trampoline in the garden. Built-in barbeque. Living the suburban dream. You had it pretty good, Barry. Until you fucked it all up.*

He saw a woman in her 40s leaning on the sliding patio doors smoking a cigarette. Danny had spotted the police standing outside the front of the house - along with a removal van - and decided to take the more scenic route around the back. He'd noticed another thing about the front of the house too: it had the word NONCE written across the front window in white paint.

Danny knew the woman was likely to be alarmed by his presence as he approached the low back fence behind the house, so he had to work quickly. She spotted him straight away: 'What the fuck are you doing?' she said, shielding her eyes from the thin morning sunshine with her hand.

'Mrs Mortimer, I'm so sorry to disturb you. My name's Danny from *Oldham Now*. Can we talk please?'

'Why exactly should I talk to you?' she said, stubbing out her cigarette and heading indoors.

Her accent was strong, typical of people from areas of Oldham close to the Yorkshire border. Using a technique he'd been taught many years before Danny tweaked his nondescript accent so it more closely reflected hers. 'Because it was me who found him out on the moors,' Danny replied. 'I was there. I saw him. And I want to know why someone would do that to him.'

The woman stopped. She looked through the house to the silhouette of the police officer at her front window. Then she closed the patio doors and walked over to the fence. 'I'll bet you do,' she whispered.

'As I said, my name's Danny… what's your first name, Mrs Mortimer?'

'It's Christine,' she replied and lit another cigarette. Danny had given up the previous year. *God, I could murder a ciggie.*

'How are you doing, Christine?' he asked.

'I'm muddling through,' she said with a tinge of sarcasm in her voice.

Danny thought about the photos he'd seen on Barry Mortimer's Facebook page. 'What about your kids, how are they doing? Two girls, yes?'

'How d'you know that?'

'It's all on your Barry's Facebook page. No secrets anymore, Christine. A 20 second glance at someone's social media tells you everything you want to know about them these days.'

'Yeah,' she agreed, sending a jet of exhaled smoke in Danny's direction. He really wanted a cigarette. 'Well, he did like a bit of Facebook did our Barry. My daughters aren't doing too well, as you can imagine. They're at my sister's. We're leaving. Have you seen the front of our house? Our neighbours seem to have gone off us a bit. They were here drinking our wine on Saturday night, now they're redecorating our front windows. People can be funny like that, can't they? Anyway, what do you want then Mr Danny Johnston from *Oldham Now*?

'The police know more than they're letting on, Christine,' Danny said. His voice was soft and reassuring. 'Two bodies have turned up in 24 hours. Your Barry and a woman up at Hanging Lees. A friend of mine has a saying, Mrs Mortimer. TFC. When more than one strange thing happens at about the same time, he says…TFC. It stands for That's a Fucking Coincidence. When the woman died up at the reservoir, I got a message telling me that it had happened. I got there just after the police did. Then I get a similar call about your husband. This time I get there *before* the cops. Two bodies and I get a tip off about them both? TFC if ever I heard it.'

'You reckon?'

'I do, Christine.'

'You saw my Barry up at the moor, did you?'

'I did,' Danny replied.

'Bit of a state, was he?'

'I'm afraid so.'

'Do you reckon he suffered?' the woman asked.

Danny paused, not sure how to answer. 'I think it's fair to say he did, Christine.'

She looked across at the woods, flicked her ash and scratched at some invisible mark on the fencing. *Looks freshly creosoted, that fence,* Danny thought. *Say what you will about Barry, he kept on top of the jobs around the house.*

'There was a sign there I hear,' she said. 'Telling everyone my Barry was a nonce.'

'There was. I don't know where all that came from. That's why I wanted to talk to you. Do you know why someone would leave a note like that?'

'Well, I've got a theory,' the woman said. 'Would you like to hear it?'

'I would, Christine,'

'Well, this might sound a bit harsh Mr Danny Johnston from *Oldham Now*...But there's no way to sugar-coat this. I reckon he WAS a fucking nonce.'

SIXTEEN

ONLINE OBSESSION OF 'VIGILANTE' VICTIM

Danny Johnston - Oldham Now

The wife of a man found battered to death close to the M62 motorway says she had fears over what her husband was doing online in the months leading up to his murder.

A post-mortem examination on Barry Mortimer, 44, from the Delph area of Oldham has revealed he'd been repeatedly hit with a blunt instrument, possibly a hammer. His body was found strapped to a wind turbine on Lad's Grave Moor. He'd been missing for several days and it's thought he'd been tortured for some time before he died.

The discovery of Mr Mortimer's body was made after a tip off to *Oldham Now*. His mobile phone had been left at the scene and the code to unlock the device had been written on his forehead. A sign had been placed nearby stating:

'LET THIS BE A WARNING TO ALL PAEDOS.
NONCE AND YOU WILL DIE.'

Mr Mortimer's wife, Christine, says she thinks her husband was targeted by online vigilantes who set up fake profiles online to ensnare paedophiles. 'I had my concerns about what he was up to online,' she told *Oldham Now* in an exclusive interview. 'He seemed to be obsessed with it. He'd spend hours chatting to people late into the night. He said he was contacting old mates from school, but I knew that wasn't true. I thought he was contacting women, then a friend's daughter told one of my kids that Barry had been messaging her. She's only 15. It's not right. He promised he'd stop, then he started going out at night. Said he was looking at new business premises, but he was meeting girls. Young girls. Looks like he arranged to meet someone, and that it wasn't a young girl at all. It was these vigilantes.'

Mrs Mortimer has now moved out of the area, fearing for her safety and that of her children.

Detective Inspector Patrick McIntyre, who's leading the hunt for Mr Mortimer's killers, has refused to comment. But he confirmed that police are now looking at Facebook groups dedicated to exposing people they believe to be paedophiles. There's been a huge rise in such groups in recent years. Some have resulted in prosecutions but there's mounting concern over people going one step further and taking the law into their own hands.

Meanwhile, police are appealing for anyone who knows Barry Mortimer's whereabouts in the days leading up to his death to come forward.

SEVENTEEN

Danny was at home, listening to music and calculating how much money he had made in the last 36 hours. Engagement on his social media was up and so was the number of hits on his website. He was being offered block bookings for adverts on the *Oldham Now* site stretching into next year. The money that was coming his way was at a far higher rate than he was used to. *Two grand from a chain of nurseries, three from a double-glazing company, five grand from a betting firm. Fuck.*

When he'd established *Oldham Now,* Danny had gone on a seminar to find out how to make money from local news. He remembered what he'd been told: *good content makes people stay longer on the website. That means more eyeballs on the adverts. That makes for better analytics for the advertisers. Then you can charge them more for the adverts.*

He also had a growing pile of messages from TV companies and news outlets wanting to interview him about the vigilante murder. He had ignored them all. *Why should I help them put eyeballs on their adverts? Fuck 'em. This is my story.*

He carried on adding up the money - he kept messing it up and having to start again - when his phone rang; it was Jonathan.

'Hi mate,' Danny said. 'Where are you?'

'I'm up in the hills near the school. It's about the only place you can get a signal around here. I'm sure they built the school here on purpose. What's that music you're listening to?'

'It's an album called *Adventure*, by a band called Television.' Danny held his phone up so Jonathan could hear it better.

'Nice,' the teenager said. 'Is it new?'

'It came out when I was your age. Younger than you, in fact. Steal it off the internet and have a listen. Now then, something makes me think that you didn't ring me just to talk about music.'

'Yeah. Okay. You're right. I want to go and see Grandad in hospital. Will you come with me?'

'Of course,' Danny said. 'When are you and your mum free?'

'Thing is,' the teenager said. 'I don't want Mum to go.'

'Bloody hell, Jonathan,' Danny said. 'You're putting me in a tricky situation here. I don't get why you've got it in for your mum at the moment. She's amazing and she only wants to protect you. That's all she's ever wanted. Honestly.'

'I just want to do this without any drama,' Jonathan said. 'There's always drama with Mum. I just want to see Grandad… that's reasonable, isn't it?

'I suppose it is,' Danny admitted. 'But I don't think I'd be allowed to take you out of the school, even if I wanted to. I'm not family, am I? Not actual family, anyway.'

'Susan from the school can come along too, then it's all fine.'

'Oh right. Susan? Yeah. Course.'

'Thought that might change your mind.'

Danny scratched on his phone with his fingertips and whistled into the microphone: 'Sorry, Jonathan. The signal's really bad. I can't make out what you're saying…'

'Yeah, right. I'll get Susan to email you. Thanks, Danny. Got to go. Time to do healthy, outdoor stuff. See ya.'

'See you, Jonathan.'

God, Kate's going to kill me when she finds out.

Danny sat back down and looked at the Adventure album sleeve. He had very few possessions when he moved to Friezland and Kate had harassed him into buying some 'stuff'. One of his few purchases had been a proper record player and he'd been buying up old vinyl, mainly stuff from the 70s and 80s. Music was one of the few things from the past that didn't make him feel unhappy. Television singer Tom Verlaine was shouting 'Foxhole, Foxhole' from the song of the same name when there was a knock at Danny's front door.

When people go to someone's house they tend to knock and take a step back; DC Karl McIntyre was right in Danny's face when he unlocked the cottage's battered front door. 'You fucking dickhead, Johnston,' he said.

Danny took a step back. 'And a very good evening to you too, officer,' Danny replied. 'I'd invite you in, but I don't want to, so I won't. Does your big brother know you're out this late on your own?'

'What did I tell you? It was literally the last thing I said to you; stay away from Barry Mortimer's family. What's the first thing you do? Go and interview his missus, for fuck's sake.'

'Well, with the greatest respect, DC McIntyre… and you can

probably tell that I'm going to say something rude now, because I've prefaced it by saying with the greatest respect… but I don't need your fucking permission to do an interview with someone. As it happens, Mrs Mortimer was happy to talk. More than happy, in fact. So, with the greatest respect, fuck off.'

Danny went to close the door, but the DC had his foot in the way. 'Then you go and splash it all over your shitty little website,' the detective added. 'You honestly don't know what you're messing with here. Not a fucking clue.'

'I think you should go,' Danny said. The DC was 20 years younger and fitter than he was; if he wanted to push his way in, he could do it very easily. Danny reached into his pocket. 'I like your feisty policing techniques, though. Very energetic. Let me get them on video for posterity.'

With his weight still on the door, Danny pulled out his phone and unlocked the screen. The DC stepped away. His tone immediately changed. 'Good night, Mr Johnston. Thank you for your assistance.'

Danny watched as the young DC marched off down the street. 'Well, you're very welcome,' he replied. 'I suppose.'

Without turning around, DC McIntyre waved a hand: 'We'll be in touch, Mr Johnston. You can rely on it.'

EIGHTEEN

Danny arrived at the Hunter's Hollow reception to find Susan Matlock and Jonathan already waiting for him. With them was a tall, well-built man in outdoor gear who looked too old to be a student. Susan clasped Danny's hand with both of hers: 'Danny, lovely to see you again. Sorry I've got to act as chaperone. But as Jonathan didn't want his mum to come and you're not actually a relative... Rules are rules and all that.'

'Of course,' Danny said. 'Kate's not going to be happy, I reckon.'

'The child takes priority here at Hunter's Hollow,' Susan said. 'Always.'

Danny realised that Susan was still holding his hand; she let it go. 'Oh, sorry, Danny, this is my son, Ben. He works here too. He does the rufty tufty out and about stuff... climbing, quad bikes, orienteering and all that. But his main job is to be everyone's big brother. Isn't it love?'

'Hi, Danny,' Ben said, putting out a hand. 'Great to meet you. I wondered why Mum was all dressed up.'

'Not wearing a tracksuit doesn't qualify as getting dressed up, Ben!' she laughed. 'Be aware that I'm not just your mum, I'm also your boss. I'm quite happy to sack you, right now.'

Danny laughed and shook Ben's hand. He had always adhered to John Smithdown's theory about handshakes: they had to be the correct kind. Not too firm - *a bullshitter's handshake, no thanks.* Not too weak - *like a wet lettuce, a vicar's handshake, no thanks either.* Ben Matlock's handshake was just right.

'Did you hear that, Danny?' Ben said. 'Workplace bullying! I'm going to have to take that up with our HR department.'

'I am the HR department, Ben,' Susan said. 'So, shut it. I'll see you later.'

Ben held up his hands in mock surrender: 'Nice to see you, Danny. Hope your grandad's on the mend, Jonathan.'

'Thanks, Ben,' Jonathan said. Danny put an arm around the

teenager's shoulder.

'Don't be home late, Mum,' Ben added as they walked away. 'You know how I worry!'

'I swear I will kill him,' Susan muttered.

When they got to the six-bed ward at the Royal Oldham Hospital, Danny peaked around the corner to double-check if Kate was there. She wasn't.

Smithdown was dozing in his bed, so Danny quietly pulled up three chairs for him, Johnathan and Susan and they just sat quietly by the retired detective's bedside. A few photo frames had been placed on the cabinet next to the bed; one was of Smithdown with Kate and Jonathan at what looked like a fair; another was of Jean Smithdown, looking glamorous at a party from the 1980s.

Danny felt a hand on his shoulder. The volunteer who had given him and Kate cups of Vimto last time was there. She put a finger to her lips and handed Danny a cup of tea in a proper cup and saucer. She smiled and Danny took the tea. He noticed the name on her volunteer badge: 'Thanks Jennifer,' he whispered. Susan whispered, 'coffee, please' and Jonathan pointed to the bottle of Vimto. When all three had a drink she once again put a finger to her lips, gave Danny the thumbs up and left.

'You'll never be accepted into the SAS, Danny,' Smithdown said a few moments later with his eyes still closed. 'I could hear you coming from halfway down the Manchester Road. Have you brought me anything or are you just here for the free tea?'

'Largely for the tea if I'm honest,' Danny replied. He put a box of Maynard's Wine Gums on the cabinet. 'There, you old sod. Hope they choke you.'

'Lovely to see you too, Danny,' Smithdown said. 'Oh, Jonathan. Come here, lad. If ever your grandad needed a bloody big hug, it's right now.'

The teenager bent over and held Smithdown tightly. Danny thought for a moment that Jonathan was about to start crying, but the young man buried his face in his grandad's shoulder to hide it. By the time he let go, the tears had largely gone.

'And who's this, then?' Smithdown said, nodding in Susan's direction. 'Is this your new lady friend, Danny?'

'Jesus Christ, don't you start,' Danny sighed.

'Hello, Mr Smithdown I'm Susan Matlock from Hunter's Hollow

School. I'm just here to accompany Jonathan. Hope that's okay?'

'It's more than okay, love. It's a pleasure. Lovely lady like this and you brought her to a hospital, Danny? Not my idea of a romantic location...'

'Shut it,' Danny said. 'Or I'll euthanise you, right now.'

Danny sat back and let Jonathan and his grandad talk. He smiled as they chatted about school, football, and why Jonathan had deliberately torn holes in the knees of his trousers. Susan leant over and whispered in Danny's ear: 'It's such a shame that Kate's not here.'

'I know,' Danny whispered back. 'But I'm sure he'll come around.'

'Maybe it's Kate that needs to come around, Danny. Not Jonathan.'

'Right,' Smithdown announced. 'Sorry to interrupt you two lovebirds, but it would be nice to get an update about what the fuck is going on out there, Danny lad. Excuse my language love.'

'I hear a lot worse on a daily basis, Mr Smithdown. Trust me.'

Smithdown started to pull himself further up in his bed; Danny helped him. He could feel the retired detective's bones through his hospital issue bed shirt.

'It's all happening,' Danny said. 'Paedo vigilantes… torture… murder. You'll be pleased to hear that you're yesterday's news, mate.'

'I wish I was,' the old man said. 'I had one of the flying ginger brothers in here earlier on. My case is pending further inquiries. They'll be looking for other victims, I suppose. But there aren't any victims in the first place, so that'll go nowhere. Plus, there's all this other caper going on.'

'The damage is already done though, isn't it?' Danny said, picking up the Wine Gums and helping himself to a few. 'Your name is already shitted up, whatever happens. That's the power of the internet, John.'

'Do you want us to go?' Susan asked.

'No, it's fine, love,' Smithdown said. 'I've nothing to hide. Give me a Wine Gum, Danny, you tight get. They're supposed to be mine, you know.'

Danny offered the sweets to Susan and Jonathan first, then gave the box to Smithdown. There was quiet for a few moments. 'I don't like those two detectives,' Smithdown finally said. 'There's something off about them.'

'I don't like them either,' Danny agreed. 'The DI is alright, I suppose, but his little brother is a headbanger.'

'You don't like any cops, Danny,' Smithdown pointed out.

'Apart from you, John. You're just about bearable.'

'Thanks for those kind words, lad. Proper moving, that is.' Smithdown shook the box of Wine Gums. 'Don't take the black ones. They're my favourites.'

There was silence again. 'I don't want to die with this hanging over me, Danny,' Smithdown said. Jonathan reached out and held his grandad's hand.

'You're not going to die, John,' Danny said. 'It was a mini stroke, that's all.'

'I am going to die, Danny. In case no one's told you, we all are. It doesn't matter if I die when I'm 103 or a week on Tuesday, I don't want this on my name. Understood?'

'Understood,' Danny confirmed. 'It's not going to be easy. There's the note. The photo too. It all points to you. What should I do?'

'Go back to the start,' Smithdown said. 'Look at it afresh with your…'

'I know,' Danny said, remembering what the detective had once told him. 'With my eyes open and my gob shut.'

NINETEEN

'Oh... It's you again,' Maggie Ormrod's neighbour said as she opened her front door to Danny. The weather had taken a turn for the worse after he had dropped Jonathan and Susan back at Hunter's Hollow. It was raining heavily now and the woman's tiny, terraced cottage opened directly onto the street, offering him no shelter. 'I suppose you think I'm going to ask you in because it's raining, don't you?' she said.

'It would be nice,' Danny said, pulling the collar of his jacket tightly up.

'Well, I'm not going to,' she said. 'What do you want? I've been reading your website. You're a proper trouble magnet, you are, aren't you?'

'I'm not here to cause trouble,' Danny said. 'I'm not after an interview or anything. Just information. No phones, no recording. Just help. Something's not right and I want to make it better. For Maggie if nothing else.'

The neighbour looked at Danny, then glanced up and down the street. 'Go on then,' she said. 'I must be mad. Take your shoes off.'

Danny did as he was told and followed the woman into the kitchen. It was deliciously warm from an AGA cooker. Art prints covered the walls and an old, contented-looking cat was curled up on a cushion-covered seat at the wooden table. 'Your house is really nice,' Danny said. 'Mine's an old cottage like this but it's a tip compared to yours.'

'Hmm. Flattery now. You're trying all the tricks, aren't you? Take a seat, but mind the cat. Do you want tea?'

'I'd love a tea. Thank you.'

'I'm Joy, by the way. Joy Pritchard. It's Danny Johnston, isn't it?'

'It is.'

'Well, allow me to throw a little flattery your way,' Joy said. 'I read your book about those child murders. Amazing story. Hard to believe that Smithdown guy is a wrong un, to be honest.'

'He isn't. That's why I'm here. He's in hospital; he's had a mini-stroke but he's still cracking on and the least I can do is put this right while he's getting better.'

'Okay,' she said, cautiously. 'He's lucky to have a friend like you, I suppose. But… what if he actually is a wrong un? What would you do then?'

'I'd wheel his hospital bed into Oldham cop shop myself,' Danny stated. 'And that's a promise.'

The cat next to Danny made a light snoring sound. 'What do you want to know?' Joy asked.

'You said that Maggie was a character. How did you mean?'

'It's a polite way of saying she was piss artist, I suppose,' Joy replied with a smile. 'What little money she had, she spent in the pub. The Bull's Head up the road, mainly. She'd been barred from most of the other local places.'

'Why?' asked Danny, sipping his tea from a rustic-looking mug that looked hand made.

'The pubs around here have gone a bit upmarket, and they like it quiet. Maggie was loud and could be a bit of a handful. She upset the diners having their sea bass and crushed potatoes, that kind of thing. Have you spoken to anyone at The Bull's Head?'

'I've just come from there. They didn't want to know. I'm a so-called journalist, apparently and they don't want my sort in their pub. Did she drink at home?'

'Not really. She craved company. She'd sit here with me sometimes and have a few glasses of wine. Well, I had wine, she preferred Carlsberg Special Brew. But she knew I wouldn't put up with any nonsense, so she was always on her best behaviour.'

'You also said before that things had changed at her house. Noisy parties, that kind of thing.'

'Yeah, maybe she was short of money. She hadn't been working very much and supermarket tins of beer are cheaper than pub pints, aren't they?

'They are indeed, Joy. I can vouch for that. What did she do for money?'

'Cleaning, mainly. Wherever would have her. She went here and there. Offices, schools, that kind of thing. She cleaned at the police station for a while last year.'

'She was a cleaner at the police station?' Danny asked. 'The main Oldham station in town? The cops never mentioned that.'

'Yes, she did. Used to cycle there and back first thing in the morning. Had to push her bike up halfway up the hill to get home.'

'A cleaner at the cop shop… Fucking Nora. Sorry Joy. No need for that, is there?'

'I've heard worse, Danny.'

'Fucking cops. Why is it always the bastard fucking cops?'

'Okay, I think you've used up all your swearing tokens now.'

'You're right. Sorry. Did Maggie ever talk about her childhood?'

'She'd been in children's homes, I knew that. You could tell she was damaged. No question about it. It was clear she'd really been through it. A few times when she was really drunk, she'd take out a photo of her and a guy from the 70s. Rant and rave about it. I rescued the picture from the bin a few times after she'd screwed it up and thrown it away in a rage.'

'Do you still have it?'

'No. She'd taken it back for the umpteenth time. The police have got it now. But I took a photo of it just in case she destroyed it. Thought it might come in useful one day. I suppose it has, in a way.'

Joy pulled out her phone and flicked the screen until she found what she wanted. She showed it to Danny. Little Maggie Ormrod with a young, smiling John Smithdown. Danny looked at the detective's arm around her slim shoulders. It gave him a cold feeling. 'Could you send that to me?' he asked. 'I'll show you how to Airdrop it if you like?'

Danny's phone pinged with an Airdrop notification. 'I know how to Airdrop,' Joy said. 'I'm not that past it. I've got a recent picture of Maggie too, if you want it?'

Before he had time to say yes, a second alert hit Danny's phone. This time it was of a much older Maggie. Her eyes were closed in pleasure as she nuzzled Joy's cat. 'You're very much on the ball, Joy,' Danny said, saving the pictures. 'Why do I get the impression you know what you're doing?'

'Kind of,' she confirmed. 'I used to work in telly, like you. Down the road at Granada TV. I worked in the gallery on the news, so I know the importance of a good picture.'

'One last thing,' Danny said. 'Do you know why she stopped cleaning at the police station?'

'I don't. Sorry.'

'Don't be. You've been really helpful, Joy.'

'I have?'

'Yes. You really have. It'd be interesting to know why she stopped cleaning at the nick, wouldn't it?'

‘I suppose it would,’ she agreed. ‘How do you propose to find out?’

‘Well, it just so happens that I’m going to Oldham Police Station tomorrow.’

TWENTY

DEATH AT HANGING LEES - DID YOU KNOW MAGGIE ORMROD?

Danny Johnston - Oldham Now

Oldham Now is trying to trace anyone who knew local woman Maggie Ormrod, whose body was found on Monday morning at Hanging Lees Reservoir.

Police say there are no suspicious circumstances surround her death and are not looking for anyone else in connection with the find. That is the usual statement police put out when there has been a suicide, pending an inquest.

In a separate development, a man in his 80s, who was being interviewed by detectives about allegations made in a note left at the scene, has been told he won't have to answer further questions about the matter for the time being. He fell ill while helping police with their inquiries at Oldham police station.

Do you know Maggie? A recent picture shows her cuddling a neighbour's cat. She was a familiar figure in the area near her home on Ripponden Road, Denshaw.

She worked locally as a cleaner and was known to frequent several local pubs, including The Bull's Head, which is close to Hanging Lees Reservoir. Staff at the pub declined to comment when asked about Maggie earlier today.

It's believed that she spent time in children's homes in the 1970s. Were you in care at that time? Do you remember Maggie? If so, please contact danny@oldhamnow.net

TWENTY-ONE

Danny set up a tripod with his iPhone clamped to the top, focussed it on the top table and set it to record. He attached a note to one of the legs with the word TV people use for tripod.

MIND MY STICKS

He then placed another iPhone on the top table next to the nameplate that said:

DETECTIVE INSPECTOR PATRICK MCINTYRE.

He set that one to record audio via the Voice Memo app; he'd synch the two up later. Then he took a seat on his own; he wanted to sit away from the other journalists who were waiting for the police press conference to start.

He looked around the large conference room at Oldham Police Station. *Decent turn out.* The usual faces were here from the regional news operations: *Manchester Evening News,* BBC North West, ITV Granada, Press Association, local news agency Cavendish Press and Kate's old paper the *Oldham Messenger.* But there were network TV reporters here too, and Sky News were also in attendance. *This story is definitely taking off.*

An onscreen TV reporter he knew from when she was a researcher on his ITV show mouthed, 'Hello Danny' from across the room. She then pointed to herself and then at Danny and made the internationally recognised sign for 'talking' with her thumb and second finger. Danny mouthed back, 'Later' and gave her the thumbs up. He had absolutely no intention of talking to her afterwards and had already worked out how he could slip out of the room at the end of the press conference without answering any questions from the other journalists. *Fuck 'em. This is my story.*

DI Patrick McIntyre then entered the room, accompanied by a

Greater Manchester Police Press Officer. Danny noticed DI McIntyre's brother Karl standing to one side of the room. He was looking right at Danny. The 'look' went on for what Danny felt was a rather strange amount of time. *Is he trying to intimidate me? Really? What a massive weirdo.*

After a little thought, Danny came up with a way to diffuse the situation - he stood up, waved to the DI and shouted: 'Karl! Hey, Karl! How are you mate? Nice to see you last night. Drinkies later, yeah?'

Everyone in the room stopped and looked; first at Danny, then at Karl McIntyre. *I do believe he went a bit red there.* The DC walked over, crouched down and leant in to talk quietly into Danny's ear. 'You're a witness in this case, Mr Johnston. Not sure it's appropriate for you to be here.'

'Well, you know what I'm not sure about?' Danny replied, not bothering to speak quietly at all. 'I'm not sure GMP is telling the whole story here. Not about this and not about the suicide at Hanging Lees either. And I'll bet you a tenner that what we are about to witness here is your brother talking a load of copperspeak bullshit that will add fuck all to what you've released already. So don't come the big bollocks with me. I've had coppers ten times more frightening than you have a pop at me in the past. Trust me.'

The detective stared at Danny; his face was close, and his breath was deep and slow. 'You shouldn't be here,' the DC repeated. As he walked away, he gave Danny's sticks a kick, tipping it over. Danny caught it just before it hit his chair.

'Bye Karl,' Danny shouted. 'I am single, actually. Thanks for asking.'

Standing next to the top table, the Press Officer spoke: 'Right then. Morning all. Thanks for coming today. This is Detective Inspector Patrick McIntyre. He has an appeal that we hope you can help with - it's in connection with the discovery of a man's body close to the M62 motorway. Before we start, as you may know there has been a certain amount of information about this case that's already appeared online.' Several of those present turned to look in Danny's direction. *Oh, okay, it's going to be like this is it?*

The Press Officer continued: 'We are going to give you the correct version this morning. We would ask you to ignore what you may have seen and heard and stick to the details you are about to get from DI McIntyre. The purpose of the exercise here is to find the person or persons responsible. I think we can all get behind that, yes? Okay. Great. DI McIntyre, over to you.'

'Thank you very much,' the detective said. 'Yes, good morning, everyone. The reason we've called this press conference is to make some specific appeals in relation to the death of Barry Mortimer. Mr Mortimer was 44 years of age and he was from the Delph area of Oldham. His body was found at a wind turbine at an area known as Lad's Grave Moor. He'd been subjected to a sustained and brutal attack that we believe had lasted for many hours before he was found dead. Mr Mortimer ran a printing business in the centre of Oldham and security footage shows him leaving work early at 4pm on Saturday afternoon. We believe he then headed east towards the Greenacres area. His wife reported him missing at 9pm that evening. We are keen to trace anyone who saw Mr Mortimer in the Greenacres area after 4.30pm on Saturday.

'Secondly, we also want to speak to anyone who saw anything suspicious close to the Junction 22 turn off of the M62 on the night Mr Mortimer's body was found. So that's Monday night or the early hours of Tuesday morning, some two days after he was last seen. This is a very remote section of the motorway, surrounded by open moorland. Despite this, it's a hugely busy section of the motorway, with thousands of cars and lorries passing, even in the middle of the night. We'd ask any motorists or lorry drivers who were in that area on Monday night or the early hours of Tuesday to think hard. Did you see anything out of the ordinary that night on the motorway?

'Thirdly… I'm appealing to anyone involved in the so-called online vigilante community, particularly those based on Facebook, to examine their consciences and come forward with any information they might have. They can do so anonymously if they like via Crimestoppers. The number, as ever, is 0800 555 111. I know there's been a lot of speculation about why Mr Mortimer was murdered and what kind of person he was. I know there's a lot of anger out there, which can sometimes boil over. But the legal system is the best way to deal with criminals, whatever type of crime they may or may not have committed. So, I'm appealing for calm. Let us do our job. Please.

'And finally… I know there has been some reporting on this case so far that can, at best, be described as unhelpful to this investigation. Mr Mortimer's background will obviously form part of this inquiry. Mr Mortimer was a family man and his family want to know what happened to him; we are committed to finding that out. The key thing here is that he was the victim of an horrific attack. The worst I've ever seen. Whoever did this needs to be caught quickly before they do it again. That's our focus. That's why we need your help. I'm very happy to take any questions; please be aware though that there will be certain aspects of the case I can't talk about.'

'Thank you, DI McIntyre,' the Press Officer said. 'Right then. Please tell us who you are and what organisation you represent before asking your question, thank you.'

Danny leant back in his chair and folded his arms. He watched as the other journalists asked their questions. It was all perfectly orderly. *Not like in the TV dramas where the journalists attending the press conference all stand up and shout questions at the same time. Absolute bollocks.*

The BBC asked about the sign found next to Barry Mortimer's body. DI McIntyre politely declined to comment, repeating his key appeals and asking for people not to speculate. ITV Granada wanted to know more about what kind of person Barry Mortimer was. The DI talked about the murdered man's wife, his children and his business. Sky News went straight to the point and asked: 'Was Barry Mortimer a paedophile?' DI McIntyre said largely the same words he'd already spoken but delivered them in a slightly different order. Again, he mentioned irresponsible reporting and repeated his appeals.

The Press Officer held up his hand: 'Okay. Any other questions?'

One by one, all the journalists in the room turned and looked at Danny. He did nothing. Eventually he stood up, walked over to where DI McIntyre was sitting and stood right in front of him. They looked at each other. 'You need to keep a tight leash on your brother, Detective Inspector,' he said. 'He's a bit excitable.'

Then Danny picked up his iPhone from the top table, collected his other phone on the sticks and walked out.

He got as far as the reception doors when he heard a shout behind him: 'Danny, Danny, Danny! Wait, please!'

Danny kept walking but the TV reporter who he used to work with - try as he might, he couldn't summon up her name - quickly caught up with him. 'Come on Danny, wait a sec,' she said. 'I'm in heels here, they're not made for running.'

'I'm in a rush, sorry,' he said. 'Can't stop.'

'Come on. I just need a few minutes with you for our package. You know me… help me out here.'

'I do kind of know you,' he said. 'But to be honest I can't remember your name. Sorry, but it was during my pissed years, so don't take it personally.'

'It's Carrie!' she cried indignantly. 'Carrie O'Connor. Oh my God.

You don't even remember my name? I groped you at a Christmas party once!'

'I definitely don't remember that,' Danny muttered, quickening his pace across the car park. 'Look, I'm not doing any interviews, Carrie and that's that. Journalists interviewing other journalists… it's a load of crap. Plus, there's nothing in it for me. Thanks, but no thanks.'

'Course there is,' she said. 'It'll be great exposure for your website.'

Danny stopped walking and looked straight at her: 'Exposure? Fucking Nora! Oh, well that's different. Print me off a bit of that lovely exposure so I can spend it on rent for my house. My landlord much prefers exposure to cash. For fuck's sake… *exposure.* That old chestnut. The answer's no, Carrie. Lovely to see you again. Thanks for the grope, although I genuinely don't remember it. But the answer is most definitely… no.'

TWENTY-TWO

THE FIVE KEY THINGS WE DIDN'T FIND OUT FROM TODAY'S 'VIGILANTE' MURDER PRESS CONFERENCE

Danny Johnston - Oldham Now

Greater Manchester Police held a press conference today to appeal for information about the murder of Oldham man Barry Mortimer - but refused to talk about why the 44-year-old was targeted.

And that isn't the only thing the police aren't talking about.

Mr Mortimer's body was found strapped to a wind turbine close to the M62 motorway. He'd been tortured for some time before he was discovered on a stretch of moor known as Lad's Grave.

The person who found him was me. I went to the moor after getting an anonymous tip-off. I got a similar alert about the death of Maggie Ormrod at Hanging Lees Reservoir.

Let me tell you something: these press conferences are pantomimes. The detective in charge, Detective Inspector Patrick McIntyre said nothing of any note and declined to answer anything about what is really going on. His brother, Detective Constable Karl McIntyre was openly hostile towards me, almost threatening in his manner.

So much that goes on between journalists and the police in this country is done behind closed doors. I should know, I've been a journalist for 35 years. So, I've decided to be completely transparent and publish the questions I have for Greater Manchester Police right here to see what *Oldham Now* readers think of them. If officers from Greater Manchester Police want to respond, they know where to find me.

1.Why was Barry Mortimer targeted?

Mortimer's wife confirmed to me that she had real concerns about what he was doing online. *Oldham Now* reported this earlier in the week. Yet, police seem to be pretending that this information isn't out there.

It definitely is out there, so they need to take their fingers out of their ears and start listening. Mrs Mortimer seems convinced that her husband was a danger to young people online. Why don't GMP?

2.Why won't the police discuss the sign found at the scene?

As reported earlier this week a sign was found at the scene close to Barry Mortimer's body. As our exclusive pictures show, it features a chilling warning:

HERE LIES BARRY 'THE BEAST' MORTIMER. CHECK HIS PHONE. LET THIS BE A WARNING TO ALL PAEDOS. NONCE AND YOU WILL DIE.

The whole of Oldham has seen this sign via *Oldham Now;* yet the police seem to be pretending it doesn't exist. It does.

3.Why have Oldham detectives kept their connection with the Ormrod case a secret?

Maggie Ormrod's body was found in the early hours of Monday morning at Hanging Lees Reservoir. She was a cleaner at Oldham Police station, yet detectives have kept this vital fact a secret. Why did they do that?

4.Who is contacting *Oldham Now* with details of these incidents?

Twice now, I have received tip-offs about serious incidents in the area from anonymous but extremely well-informed sources. Where is this information coming from?

5.Why do masked 'vigilantes' keep appearing at the crime scenes?

I was the first person at the spot where Maggie Ormrod's body was found. I was also the first person on the scene of the Barry Mortimer murder. At both places I saw one or more masked people filming the scene. What do the police know about these people and why were they in attendance at both of these apparently unconnected incidents? These masked people also turned up at the house of a man in his 80s who was being taken in for questioning about historic abuse allegations. Who is feeding these people such detailed information?

The Oldham Division of Greater Manchester Police has a grim record of being involved in the most serious of crimes. Officers from Oldham were involved with murders and incitement to cause a race riot in the town in the late 1980s after the so-called 'Mermaid's Pool murder'. An Oldham detective was also responsible for the horrific 'Twisted Sisters' killing spree that started with the discovery of a child's body at Black Moss reservoir in 1990.

Promises of change have always followed these terrible crimes. Assurances of inquiries, recommendations and new practices, followed by root and branch removals of so-called 'rogue' officers.

The problem isn't an institutional one, we are told, it's just a few 'bad apples'. We've heard the excuses and explanations before. But did anything really change after Black Moss and the Mermaid's Pool? Or are we witnessing a new breed of bad apple in the famously rotten barrel known as Oldham Police?

It's starting to look like the bad old days are back. With a vengeance.

TWENTY-THREE

31 March 1975

'Flippin eck Maggie, you proper frightened me then,' Alma Richards said from under the covers of her bed in the Greenacres Children's Home. 'Where've you been? It's really late.'

'To the fair,' Maggie whispered, taking off her clothes as quickly as possible and getting into bed in just her pants and vest. 'Shurrup and go back to sleep.'

'How can I go back to sleep with you banging about like a baby elephant?' Alma moaned.

Maggie closed her eyes for all of ten seconds then threw back the covers and leant out of bed so far that she was almost upside down.

'What you after now?' Alma pleaded in a hushed voice.

Maggie was digging around in the pockets of her dungarees that were on the floor by her bed. She found what she was looking for, pulled herself back upright and tucked the precious item under her pillow. She closed her eyes for another ten seconds, then opened them again and lay on her back, staring at the ceiling.

'What's up with you?' Alma whispered. 'You're driving me mad.'

Maggie rolled over, propped herself up on her elbow and looked at Alma: 'If you could have any treat, I mean anything, what would you have?'

'Oh God, stop mithering me!' Alma said, covering her face with her blanket.

'Go on,' Maggie said. 'What would you have?'

Alma turned to face Maggie; their beds were just feet apart. 'Anything at all?' she asked.

'Anything,' Maggie confirmed.

'A Wimpy Special Grill…' the girl began.

'Oh!' Maggie interrupted. 'The one with the sausage that bends around the tomato!'

'A Wimpy Special Grill, a Knickerbocker Glory and a banana milkshake.'

'Not strawberry?' Maggie queried.

'No, definitely banana,' Alma confirmed.

There was silence. Maggie smiled: 'I'll get it for you. On Saturday in town. My treat.'

'Don't be daft,' Alma sighed. 'A Special Grill is 49p on its own. With the other stuff as well, it'd be nearly a pound!'

The two girls lay quietly in their beds. 'Can you keep a secret?' Maggie asked.

'I'm no grass, Maggie Ormrod,' Alma pointed out, slightly indignantly.

Maggie reached under her pillow and took out a blue piece of paper. She unfolded carefully then held it up so Alma could see it. 'Bloody Nora!' the younger girl cried, then slapped a hand across her mouth to keep herself silent. 'A fiver! Where did you get that? Did you nick it?'

'No, I did not!' Maggie said. It was her turn to sound indignant now. 'It's mine. My new friend gave it to me. Not nicked. All mine. And I was going to treat you to a Wimpy, but if you're going to be rude…'

'I'm sorry!' Alma squealed. 'Oh God. Are you serious? I've looked at the menu of the Wimpy that many times, I could tell you everything on it by heart.'

'You and me, Saturday dinner time,' Maggie said. 'The Special Grills are on me.'

TWENTY-FOUR

For the next few days, Danny kept a low profile and watched as the police tried to rattle as many cages as possible in the online vigilante community, largely centred on Facebook.

He saw how carefully invited journalists accompanied police officers on early morning raids to arrest 'people of interest' in the Barry Mortimer case. Doors were kicked in for the benefit of the cameras and sallow-faced men in shell suits were taken away for questioning. The raids made the lead story on both *Granada Reports* and *North West Tonight* and some of the clips got big numbers on social media *Nice PR for the police, good ratings for the news. Everyone's happy.*

Danny wasn't surprised that there was an underground digital hub dedicated to baiting, catching and exposing men with fake profiles and promises of underage sex. But he was stunned by the sheer size of it. He was also very disappointed by the lack of creativity that had gone into naming the various Facebook groups dedicated to it.

He'd lost count of the sheer numbers of 'Noncebusters' there were, though 'Paedohunters' ran a close second. A few bucked the trend: he quite liked 'Pae-DON'T' for its brutal simplicity; he'd slowly developed a soft spot for 'Molester Testers'; but his firm favourite was 'Nonce Upon a Time in the West (of Oldham)'. It had a winning mix of fairy tale and western film references, along with a pun no one else had so far thought of. The sheer levels of interaction that each page generated was also staggering - thousands of angry emojis, positive comments and likes for every video. *With engagement like this no wonder I've been skint for so long. These guys are hoovering up all the online traffic. Looks like they're in it for the likes as much as the noncebusting.*

The contents of the Facebook pages were depressingly repetitive. A middle-aged man - usually white, but not always - would be confronted in a car park, bus station or occasionally at his own home. This was normally done by some slightly younger white men. The confrontation would be filmed as the target discovered that the liaison they'd set up online wasn't quite what they had expected. Some denied all knowledge, even as the proof was shown to them. Others were struck mute by a strange mix of shame and bafflement. Some ran away, only to be chased and caught by the younger, fitter hunters with their cameras still rolling. As an ex-television reporter, Danny was impressed with some of the production values; many had a reasonably professional air, using graphics, music and even animation to 'sell' the sting. Most were shot on single iPhones but some were multi-camera affairs that had been well edited and even sound mixed.

He watched one video that showed a man identified as Paul being approached in his car at a McDonalds in Chadderton. The video team approach him and ask who he was waiting for. 'My brother-in-law,' Paul said. 'What's with the cameras?'

'Is your brother-in-law called Briony, mate?' the lead vigilante sneered, off-camera. "Cos that's who you're actually waiting for, isn't it?'

'No idea what you mean, sorry.' Paul's face clearly showed that he knew he'd been found out, despite his denials.

The vigilante affected a sarcastic, singsong tone of voice: 'Briony, I will treat you right. You're first time is precious... once in a lifetime... and should be with someone who will respect you and make sure you feel like a princess and a lady…'

The camera zoomed in on Paul's face: 'Ring any bells, mate?' the vigilante continued. 'Remember messaging those words to Briony? Little 14-year-old Briony? Do ya, Paul? Beautiful words, mate. Genuinely. Shame you were actually messaging us, Paul, ya fookin paedo.'

Paul tried to move his car, but he was now pinned in from all sides by the video team. 'Now, if anyone else wants Paul to write them some beautiful words like these, here are his contact details, starting with his home address...'

Paul had started to cry now. 'Please. Oh God, please, I'm sorry. So, so sorry. I've never done this before. Swear to God. It was stupid. Absolutely fucking stupid. It'll never happen again. I swear. Please can you delete this? Please?'

'Too late for that mate. So here we go. Paul's a local lad, from right here in sunny Chadderton and can be found at 23a Montague Close. That's near the chippy, yeah? Thought so. So yeah, that's the place to meet up with Paul to discuss anything you've seen or heard here tonight. It's a good chippy too, so you can get some grub after you've put his windows in. If you want to pre-book a visit to Paul, no problem. Just call him on 07913...'

Danny watched as Paul started up his car and tried to nudge it past his tormentors. They cheered and jeered as his pulled out of the car park, throwing stones and takeaway milkshake cups at the back of his car. As he pulled away the camera zoomed in and then focussed on his number plate.

Danny looked hard at each video to see if he could find anyone claiming responsibility or knowledge of either the murder of Barry Mortimer or the death of Maggie Ormrod. Nothing.

These are exactly the kind of people who were outside John's house. Definitely. But are they the same kind of people who'd kidnap and torture Barry Mortimer? That's a stretch. The cops are looking in the wrong place, I reckon. These guys want likes. They want comments. They want people to follow what they're up to. The other lot… they don't give a shit about Facebook and all the online clout. They're probably not even on Facebook. They don't need to be. They're a straight up execution squad.

TWENTY-FIVE

Danny didn't really have the time to do a talk for pupils at Hunter's Hollow School. The Barry Mortimer murder and the Hanging Lees suicide were two of the biggest stories he'd ever had on *Oldham Now.*

His Twitter following had gone up by 25 per cent; the *Oldham Now* Facebook group page had been liked by an extra thousand people and he was getting a lot of 'Hi Danny, can you follow me back so I can DM you?' messages from other news organisations wanting to use his pictures and videos. He had bypassed the usual 'sure, if you give me credit' response; he'd written up a rate card and had started charging for them.

Plus, requests to advertise on *Oldham Now* were still coming in. Another six local firms had offered him four thousand pounds each to run ads for the next twelve months. Revenue from banner ads, filler ads, job ads and the financial kick back from the analytic spike on all his stories was really starting to add up, especially now that he'd added the code to accept adverts on all the 'death stories' in his archive.

So, Danny was far too busy to give a talk to a bunch of teenagers at the Hunter's Hollow School. But Susan Matlock had emailed him, saying how much it would mean to the students if he came. So, instead of politely declining he'd said... *yes, absolutely, love to, when do you want me to be there?*

Danny had worked in TV for years so expressing himself to an audience was in his bones. But as he buzzed the main entrance door to the school, he felt a tug of nerves. *That's weird. I can talk to anyone. Maybe it's because of Susan. It's almost as if I really want to please her. Which is weird because I don't normally give a shit about pleasing anyone.*

He had even invested in a new, white tee-shirt at his local supermarket while he'd been doing his weekly shop. And he'd ironed it too.

Danny buzzed through the main door and Susan Matlock met him in the reception. *Jeans, white shirt, fancy pumps. Definitely no outdoor gear today… Why am I even noticing this stuff?*

'Danny, thanks so much for doing this,' she said with a smile. 'The pupils are really looking forward to listening to you.'

'No problem at all,' Danny said, trying not to smile too hard in return. 'It's going to be good.'

'How long can you give us?' she asked.

'Do I need to keep it clean?'

'If possible, yes,' Susan replied.

'I'll do you two minutes then.'

Susan laughed and very lightly touched Danny's forearm; it was like he'd experienced a tiny static shock on the spot where her fingers had connected with his skin.

Ben Matlock joined them and shook Danny's hand. 'Aright, Danny?' he said with a grin. 'Nervous?'

'It's fine, I've done loads of talks in my time,' Danny replied.

'No, I meant nervous about seeing Mum again… it's technically a date this, isn't it?'

'Ben!' Susan cried. 'For Christ's sake, shut it! Sorry, Danny. Let's get you signed in and badged up, then we can get cracking before I punch Ben in the throat…'

With the paperwork done, Danny was taken down a long corridor lined with certificates and awards and into a conference room that was clearly a leftover from the school's time as a hotel. There were forty teenagers waiting for him; three-quarters were boys. The room had that blunt, musky smell that comes with large groups of lads: *Hair gel, body spray and laddishness. Oh, to be young.*

Danny spotted Johnathan sitting at the back of the room. He nodded towards the teenager, and he got the smallest of nods in return. *Can't be seen to be too friendly when you're with your mates. Not cool.*

'Right then!' cried Susan, putting both hands in the air and waving them to get the group's attention. 'Bums on seats, please. Let's be having you.'

Susan pointed to a pale-faced teenage boy who had two hoods over his head. 'Josh… are you staying?' she asked. 'You are? Then take your coat off then, you're making me nervous. At least take one of your hoods down. You look like a bank robber. Thank you. So! As promised, this is Danny Johnston. He's a journalist and an author and he runs the *Oldham Now* news website. So as there's no news at all currently happening in the Oldham area, he had nothing better to do… so he's come here to talk to you lot.'

Susan winked at Danny and motioned for him to step forward. He stood at the front of the meeting room and took out a small bottle of sparkling water, opened it and then had to shake his hand dry when it bubbled over and splashed onto the floor. 'That was a good start,' he muttered, wiping his hand on the back of his trousers. 'Okay. Right. My name is indeed Danny Johnston and Susan has asked me to come and talk to you about being a journalist.'

He paused and looked around the room. Forty pairs of young, slightly puzzled eyes were trained on him. He noticed at least twenty pairs of folded arms too. 'So… I think being a journalist is a calling: like being a doctor. Or a teacher. Or a nun.'

He'd done talks before and that line usually got a small laugh. Not today. He took another sip of water. 'Being a journalist has totally changed. When I started you were sent out with a pad, a pen and a bag of two pence pieces.'

Danny noticed some puzzled faces: '…So you could phone your story into the news desk from a phone box. That's what the coins were for. Now all you need is a mobile phone. You can write on it, film on it, edit on it and publish on it. What's more, everyone's got a phone. Everyone. Doesn't make everyone a journalist, though. So, what's the difference? Well, accountability for one thing. A journalist doesn't just stick something online anonymously. A journalist puts their name to their story and stands by it. They take responsibility for it. They understand the law and how to stay on the right side of it while still holding people to account. They appreciate the importance of consent and how vital it is to respect it when people agree to talk to you. They get the fact that to be given a platform to tell stories to other people is a privilege. It's the best job in the world but it's also a massive responsibility. You've got to get the balance right; make sure you talk to plenty of people who don't have much of a voice… and at the same time, challenge as many people as possible who maybe have too much of a voice. That's what being a journalist is.'

Danny looked at the pupils. The same number of arms were still folded. *I'm dying on my arse here.*

He decided to try a different approach: 'Look. To be honest, I'm not sure what being a journalist actually is any more. It's become very confusing in recent years, for me anyway. I do know this, though. I got really lucky. I didn't have the nicest start in life when I was a kid. Me and my sister were taken away from our parents because they were shit at looking after us. We were in care - not for long, but long enough to know it was better than where we'd come from. We got lucky that we were adopted by two amazing people who did their best to give us a better life. I didn't like school and school didn't like me, but I did better at college and fluked a job on a local paper. Then I fluked another job at what used to be called Manchester Radio. I think it's called All The Fucking Hits now, or something shit like that.'

There was a small ripple of laughter in the room. 'Sorry, Susan,' Danny said. 'I promised to keep it clean. Anyway, when I was working at Manchester Radio, I found a story - literally stumbled across it - that changed my life. A kid's body had been dumped on the edge of Black Moss Reservoir. It's only a few miles from here. No one cared about the kid because there was a much bigger story down the road that was sexier and more high profile. The Strangeways Riot. Look it up. Not now, obviously. Later. Anyway, no one gave a shit about this kid apart from me and a policeman called John Smithdown. A really good man… don't let anyone tell you otherwise. I didn't know it at the time, but John Smithdown was a hero. Still is. He stopped Oldham going up in a race war in the 1980s. Seriously. He did. Then I got lucky again and got a job in London with the national TV news and then my own current affairs series. I was in showbiz! Then I fucked it all up because I was pissed all the time and crashed my car into a tree. I got sacked because everyone saw what I did. Do you know why? Because someone filmed me with their phone and put it on the internet. Oh, the irony. So, I came back up here a few years ago. Me and John Smithdown managed to find out who killed that kid, you've probably heard about that. But we never found out who the kid actually was. One day I will though. That's a promise. So maybe that's what being a journalist is all about. Wanting to put things right and never giving up until you do. I don't know. Does that make sense? Sorry. I went off on one there, didn't I? I probably shouldn't have sworn as much either. Sorry. Any questions?'

There was a silence - quite a long one - then Josh, the boy in the coat and hoodie, put up his hand and asked: 'How much do you earn?'

'Fuck all,' Danny replied. That got a laugh too, and the room relaxed a little bit more. He felt the need to mouth 'sorry' again to Susan. 'Seriously, not very much at all, I'm afraid. It's Josh, isn't it? Well, Josh… I turned over about 15 grand last year. You can earn more at McDonald's. I won't starve and I've got a few quid stashed away from the old days, but if you want to go into journalism for the money, you're in for a big surprise. And not a nice one either, I'm afraid. Yes, you?'

Danny pointed at a girl of about 15 in a shell suit: 'Hi. What's your name?' he asked.

'It's Carly. Hi. How many people work for you?'

'Ha! None, Carly. Zero. I'm it. A one-man band. I do everything myself. Everything. But, on the plus side, no one tells me what to do. And not many people can say that.'

Josh put up his hand again: 'What was it like seeing that dead paedo guy out on the moors?'

There were a few sniggers. Susan was about to say something, but Danny answered: 'It was horrible, Josh. One of the worst things I've ever seen. No one deserves to die like that.'

'Not even paedos?' Carly asked.

'Not even *alleged* paedos,' Danny confirmed. 'The law is there to decide things like that, not vigilantes. Anyone else?'

Josh put his hand up again. *Josh is in an inquisitive mood tonight,* Danny thought.

'You said you only made about 15 grand, yeah? But how do you actually make that money?'

'Advertising,' Danny replied. 'I get paid to include adverts on the website.'

'So, the more people go on your site, the more money you make?'

'Correct.'

Josh looked at his phone: 'I'm on your site now. There's a sidebar showing this week's top stories. The top three are about the paedo murder, the fourth and fifth are about the woman who did herself in at Hanging Lees.'

'I haven't looked since this morning,' Danny said. 'I'll take your word for it.'

'So, the more people die - preferably in really nasty ways - the more money you make?'

'Technically, yes. I'd love to be funded by the public like the BBC or by some rich benefactor… but I'm not. The reality is that without me there'd be little or no local accountability around here. Local newspapers have all but fizzled out. Local radio stations are essentially national franchises with shared news content. No one goes to council meetings or covers the courts like they used to. That world is gone. Someone needs to tell local stories that hold local organisations to account, otherwise it's all just clickbait bollocks about celebrities. I wish that my top five stories weren't the ones you mentioned. But that's not under my control. The public decides that, not me. The popular stories pay for the unpopular ones. What I do and the way I do it isn't perfect, but it's probably the least worst way of doing it, put it like that.'

There was quiet. 'Right then,' Susan said. 'Any more questions? Preferably ones that don't contain the word paedo.'

Danny fielded a few more questions. They asked about reading an autocue on TV (*I never used one, I only ever did short pieces to camera when I was out and about filming stories and I memorised the words I had to say. I had a go once and I was rubbish at it*); they asked about the most famous person he'd ever met (*Probably Margaret Thatcher, but she probably isn't that famous to you, I'd imagine. Fame is generational, isn't it?)* and they asked about the most embarrassing thing that had ever happened to him (*went out on a tip off that there was a riot in Rusholme, South Manchester. Lot of South Asian people. Turned out to be Eid. Still, I thought it was a great story, so I interviewed loads of lads, the police, shopkeepers, everything. Turned out the whole time I thought I was recording I was on pause. When I thought I was on pause I was actually recording. So, I got nowt but the sound of my own footsteps. When I got back to the radio station, I was so embarrassed I lied and said that when I got there, there was no one about so I'd just left. I still cringe myself to sleep about it*).

After half an hour Susan smiled and looked around the room: 'Right, if there's no more questions, let's thank Danny, please.' A medium strength ripple of applause came from the audience. He tried to catch Jonathan's eye but he was already on his way out of the room, talking to Josh, who's hoodie and coat were now back in their original positions.

'Was that alright?' Danny asked, finishing his water. 'I'm not sure that was any use to anyone.'

'It was great,' Susan said. 'What was that you said? *Trying to put things right and never giving up until you do.* Those are golden words, right there.'

'Well, that's very kind. Josh is a character, isn't he?'

'Clever lad,' Susan smiled. 'He wants to be a journalist.'

'He's got the charm, that's for sure,' Danny said.

'You need charm to be a journalist?' she asked with mock incredulity. 'How did you get under the wire then?'

'Oh, that's nice...'

'I'm only messing. I really appreciate you coming. And by way of a thank you, I'd like to buy you lunch sometime. Somewhere local. Saddleworth, maybe? Could you pick me up from here? Ben needs the school Land Rover most days. What do you think?'

Danny felt slightly flustered and didn't do a very good job of hiding it: 'Well… I…I think that's the least you can do after hurting my feelings like that,' he said.

'Ha! Great. Thursday alright?

'Thursday is very alright,' he said with a smile.

'That's settled then. I'll show you out.'

Danny and Susan walked across the room and through the reception and he returned a wave and a thumbs up from Ben. As they walked, Danny turned his phone back on. There was a text message from a number he didn't recognise.

<MIDNIGHT ON THE M62 FOOTBRIDGE.>

'Everything okay?' Susan asked.

'Cracking, yes,' he replied. 'Just a potential new story. See you Thursday.'

TWENTY-SIX

Danny looked at Kate's outfit as they headed up the foggy path past the Windy Hill transmitter. She was sporting hiking boots and a slightly shabby looking faux leopard skin coat. 'You look like Richey Edwards on a Duke of Edinburgh expedition,' he said.

'What are you on about?' Kate said, sounding annoyed and out of breath.

'The coat. The boots. You look like the guy from the Manic Street Preachers. But on an outward-bound course. Absolutely bizarre choice of gear.'

'The boots are Jonathan's from years ago,' Kate pointed out. 'The coat is the warmest thing I could find at short notice. It's fucking freezing out here. No wonder they call it Windy Mountain.'

'Hill,' Danny corrected. 'It's Windy Hill. You're telling me the warmest jacket you could find was that thing? Who left it at your house, Bet Lynch off Coronation Street?'

'Sorry, Danny,' she said, looking at Danny's outdoor clothing. 'I didn't have time to get properly kitted out in all the weekend warrior gear like you're wearing. Next time you get another weird tip off from Paedo Killers R Us, I'll make sure I'm better prepared. Where the fuck are we going, anyway?'

'The Pennine Way bridge. It goes over the M62. You'll have driven under it a thousand times. It's very distinctive. It's called a parabolic arch.'

'This whole thing is parabollocks if you ask me,' Kate added. 'Why am I here, exactly?'

'I need a witness,' Danny said. 'Plus, you're my only friend. Apart from your dad. And he's a bit old to be knocking about on the moors at this time of night.'

'I'm genuinely touched,' she said. 'How far is it?'

'Just over this ridge. Can you hear the motorway? It can't be far now.'

As the path crested the hill, the noise suddenly increased and the rolling landscape was crudely interrupted by the M62. Cars and lorries thundered past in both directions below them, fog lights pushing through the late-night haze.

Connecting the gap across the east and westbound lanes was a strangely elegant footbridge, curving more than 60 feet above the carriageways.

'Such a weird bridge to be plonked out here in the middle of nowhere,' Kate muttered, pulling her coat around her for warmth. 'It's wasted on ramblers and Boy Scouts. It's too fancy, isn't it?'

'Apparently the transport minister at the time was a keen walker and insisted on something a bit special,' Danny offered. 'Quite European, isn't it?'

'Très chic, Danny, I'm sure.' Kate looked across at the empty bridge. The far end of the structure over the eastbound carriageway almost faded away into the fog. 'There's no bugger here anyway,' she pointed out. 'Another fun night out, Danny. Nice one. You should ask Susan Matlock out, see if she fancies coming up here. Very romantic.'

'She's already asked ME out,' Danny said. 'Get with the times, Grandma, this is the modern world and Susan is a very modern woman.'

'She's a very strange woman if she's asked you out,' Kate replied.

As they got closer to the eastern entrance to the narrow bridge, two groups of figures scurried onto it from either end. They gathered into two separate huddles and then stopped. There were four people in each group, and they were all looking directly at Danny and Kate. One person from each of the groups then waved to them. 'Okay, that's a bit freaky,' she said. Danny took out his phone and started filming. *It's like they really want me to record it.*

Danny and Kate walked slowly toward the edge of the footbridge. It was surprisingly narrow; two people coming in opposite directions would struggle to pass each other. The traffic below the bridge seemed to push and pull at the fog, making the figures clear one minute and indistinct the next.

'Oh good,' Kate added as they got closer still and the lights from the traffic below revealed more about the people on the bridge. 'They're all wearing masks too. Nice touch.'

'Not quite,' said Danny. 'Look.'

The two gangs all sported variations on the skull bandanas Danny had seen before, but there were two people without masks. Instead, they each had a strip of gaffer tape across their mouths. Danny couldn't see the gagged man at the far side of the bridge too well because of the fog, but the one closer to him clearly had dried blood caked onto his bare chest and his hands were tied behind his back.

One of the masked figures held out a hand, motioning to Danny and Kate that they shouldn't come any further.

'Are we stopping?' Kate asked.

'I reckon we are,' Danny replied.

Danny and Kate stood still. The masked figures stared at them. After 20 seconds they seemed satisfied that their instruction was being followed. Then, with very deliberate, exaggerated movements, two of the group produced mobile phones, held them high and then taped them to the upright spokes of the bridge railings close to where the two shivering, shirtless figures were standing.

'What the actual fuck are we watching here, Danny?' Kate asked. 'This is beyond weird.'

'You know the guy I found over at the wind turbine? It can't have been more than a mile from here. Barry Mortimer was his name. They'd taped Barry's phone to his body to make sure it was found. Not sure why they're taping these phones to the railings.'

Then Danny got his answer. Two people from both of the groups grabbed an ankle each and tipped both men head-first off the bridge.

'Shit, Danny!' Kate cried. 'What the fuck!'

One of the men hit the roof of a passing lorry with a terrible clattering sound before bouncing off the top and crashing onto the carriageway. He was then hit by a series of cars and vans as his body was flipped and battered this way and that before landing in some bushes by the westbound carriageway. The other man somehow managed to find a gap between the traffic as he fell; he went straight down onto the motorway before a gravel truck flattened the top half of his body. The downward force of the truck made his crushed and bloodied figure stick to the road surface; then it was hit by a series of vans, lorries and cars. Over and over and over again.

'Fucking Nora,' Kate whispered. Then she shouted: 'I mean, Fucking Nora, Danny! Jesus Christ Almighty, what the fuck just happened?'

The masked gang raised their fists in triumph and ran towards the far end of the bridge. The foggy night took them and they disappeared from view. But Danny could hear the sound of revving engines - *motorbikes? God, they came on motorbikes* - which roared away as the sound was swallowed up by the moors.

Danny and Kate opened their mouths at the same moment; both were about to scream a warning to the drivers below. No sound came out. Danny realised there was no point; there was no question that both the men were dead.

They stood and watched as the Manchester bound side of the motorway started to slow down. Not before two lorries and a car had skidded through the side crash barrier and onto the steep grass verge to avoid the vehicles up ahead. Then a motorcyclist rear-ended a car and somersaulted the rider onto its roof. It took at least two minutes for the traffic to come to a complete halt on the westbound carriageway. On the eastbound side, where the dead man's body was still stuck to the motorway, the vehicles kept hitting what was left of his body for another three minutes.

Traffic on both sides finally came to a stop; drivers were getting out of their cars to see what had happened. When they saw the bodies, several of them took out their phones to call the police. Others took out their phones and began filming the scene.

On the bridge above the chaos, all that was left were the two mobiles strapped to the railings.

'On second thoughts, Danny,' Kate said. 'Don't bring Susan here. Ever.'

TWENTY-SEVEN

THE VIGILANTES ARE IN CHARGE NOW AND OLDHAM POLICE KNOW IT

Danny Johnston - Oldham Now

It's usual when covering stories like last night's double motorway murder to use expressions like 'execution-style' or 'so-called vigilantes'. It protects the journalist from any comeback as they are essentially guessing at what actually happened.

Not this time.

What happened on the M62 footbridge was a double execution, pure and simple. I know. I saw it with my own eyes.

The two men murdered last night, were put to death because the vigilantes decided that they deserved to die. Simple as that.

They were thrown onto the M62 because a new breed of vigilante has declared themselves to be judge, jury and executioner in their fight against online sexual predators.

They made it very easy for the police to see what they wanted them to see. The victim's phones had been left at the scene attached to the footbridge railings close to the Windy Hill transmitter. The passcodes had been written on the mobiles in fluorescent white marker pen.

The deliberate placing of the victims' phones at the scene - so police can see what the two men had been doing online - is identical to the method used in the murder of Barry Mortimer less than a mile away. His body was found close to the motorway at Lad's Grave Moor last week. He'd been beaten to death and strapped to a wind turbine alongside a sign threatening more murders:

'NONCE AND YOU WILL DIE'

It looks like at least two people in Oldham didn't listen to that warning. Now they're dead.

It's the third time in less than a week that a message sent to this website has led to the discovery of a dead body or bodies. Last Monday a Twitter message alerted *Oldham Now* to the apparent suicide of local woman Maggie Ormrod. This was followed by another tip off concerning the murder of Barry Mortimer.

Last night I was told to be at the M62 footbridge at midnight. The vigilantes waited for me to arrive before putting on their vile show. I believe they want as many people as possible to know what they're doing and why they are doing it. That's why the tip-offs are being sent to me and that's why they are giving police access to their victims' phones.

Their message is clear: online groomers are fair game. But it's no longer about being named and shamed on a video that gets sent to the police or posted on social media. The rules have changed: online paedophiles are in their sights and if they get caught by the vigilantes, they'll be killed.

A quick look online shows that there's a huge amount of support for the vigilantes. Social media is awash with praise for the killers and there are reports that the usual 'paedophile hunters' - using fake profiles to trap and film suspects - may soon be out of business. Oldham's sexual predators are now in hiding, too scared to ply their sick trade.

I wonder if Oldham Police are secretly delighted by the actions of this new breed of vigilante.

TWENTY-EIGHT

RECORD OF INTERVIEW
Person interviewed: JOHNSTON, Daniel (12/7/66)
Place of interview: Oldham Police Station
Time commenced: 0940 hours
Interviewer(s): DI3716 McIntyre, Patrick DC2184 McIntyre, Karl.
Other persons present: Paulina Scorer - Solicitor from Blanco & Harkness Solicitors.
Usual introductions, cautions and advice. JOHNSTON has been informed that he is not under arrest and that he is free to leave at any time. JOHNSTON has opted to have legal representative with him.
This is the second interview with DANIEL JOHNSTON - JOHNSTON confirms that no questions have been asked before the recording begins.

DI MCINTYRE: Mr Johnston, can you tell me how you and Ms Smithdown came to be out on the moors last night?
JOHNSTON: I'd been out at Hunter's Hollow giving a talk to the pupils. I got a text telling me to go to the bridge. I didn't recognise the number. I guess it was from a chuckaway phone. We parked up near the transmitter and the rest is on the video… which I have very helpfully provided for you so as not to be accused of getting in the way of justice and all that. I don't really have anything else to say. For now.
DI MCINTYRE: And why was Ms Smithdown there?
JOHNSTON: As an extra pair of eyes. And back up. And a bit of company. Its scary out on the moors and she's tough as fuck.
DI MCINTYRE: What did you see on the bridge when you got there?
JOHNSTON: It's on the video.
DI MCINTYRE: Just run though it for me.
JOHNSTON: Well, as you can see on the video… some well-organised, masked men executed two people that they probably thought were paedophiles. They made a proper show of it too, real pantomime stuff.
DI MCINTYRE: Did you hear any voices? Any accents?

JOHNSTON: No one actually spoke. Like I said… a pantomime. It was all acted out for the benefit of my camera phone. Like… Ooh, look at this… it's some very bad men. What's that, children? Should I throw them off the bridge? All of that. But no one spoke. Not a word. Then over they went…splat, splat. Then they took off on motorbikes. Then you lot miraculously turned up.
DI MCINTYRE: Did you see the motorbikes?
JOHNSTON: No, I didn't. I just heard them.
DI MCINTYRE: Could you identify what type of bike you heard?
JOHNSTON: Not really. I don't know much about motorbikes. What kind of bikes do the police use? Maybe ones with Greater Manchester Police Paedo Death Squad written on them.
DI MCINTYRE: I don't know what that means.
JOHNSTON: Of course you don't. You and your brother are a pair of choirboys, aren't you? Little angels, the pair of you.
DI MCINTYRE: Are you saying that the police are somehow involved in these killings?
JOHNSTON: Are you saying that they aren't?
DI MCINTYRE: Okay, I think we'll leave it at that for the time being.

End of recording: 0949 hours

'Was that alright, Paulina?' Danny said to his solicitor as he put on his jacket. 'I didn't want to come across as rude or sarcastic or anything.' He winked at Detective Constable Karl McIntyre who'd been observing while his brother took Danny's statement.

'Let's just go, Danny,' Paulina said, gathering her things. 'I think you've said quite enough.' She turned to the two detectives. 'I assume you'll be naming the men killed at some point today?'

'After relatives have been informed, yes Ms Scorer,' the DI replied.

'That was quite the piece you posted on your website, Mr Johnston,' DC McIntyre added as they were leaving. 'I particularly liked the bit where you suggested we were dead chuffed about people being chucked off bridges. Made my day, that did. Such insight.'

'Come on, Danny,' Paulina said. 'You've given a statement, let's leave it at that.'

'It's okay,' Danny replied. 'Perhaps the McIntyre lads are just annoyed that they didn't manage to put me in hospital with their line of questioning… like they did with John Smithdown.'

'Danny, please,' Paulina said. 'You have told the DI what you saw.

That's what we came for. Time to go.'

They headed for the door of the interview room, but Danny couldn't stop himself from talking: 'These dirty bastards are up to something, Paulina. If there's a trail of slime stinking the place up in Oldham, there's always a cop at the end of it. Every time.'

'Speaking of which,' DC McIntyre said. 'How is Mr Smithdown doing?'

Danny turned and kicked his chair in the detective's direction. It clattered against the edge of the table separating them. 'Hey, Danny!' Paulina said, grabbing the arm of Danny's jacket and pushing him towards the door. 'Out. Right now!'

'You and your brother are wrong uns,' Danny said, pointing at both of the detectives as Paulina coaxed him in the direction of the door. 'I know it and John Smithdown knows it. This is just as much a panto as that shit out on the bridge. Maggie Ormrod killing herself… That's all part of the show too, I reckon. I'm being played for a prick here. Not anymore. That's it. This is the last time I'll be coming in here. Unless it's to watch you two dickheads being arrested for whatever it is you're up to. Because I'm going to fucking well find out. And that's a promise.'

TWENTY-NINE

Danny had been sitting in the café with Paulina for 20 minutes, eating toast and laboriously tapping his story into his phone, when Kate finally arrived from giving her statement.

'How was it?' Danny asked. 'Did you confess?'

'Yes,' Kate confirmed. 'I'd admit to anything to get out of being in the same room as those tools. Especially the younger one. He's an arse.' Kate pulled up a chair next to Paulina; she nodded at Danny. 'And did this lad behave himself?' she asked.

'He did really well,' Paulina said. 'Until right at the end. Things went downhill, you might say. Kicking a chair at the DC was probably a low point.'

'Oh dear, Danny,' Kate sighed. 'Not like you to antagonise the police.'

'It would break my heart if I thought I'd upset them in any way,' Danny said; he didn't look up from writing his story.

'Speaking of you annoying people,' Kate continued. 'I believe you took Jonathan to see Dad at the hospital the other night.'

Danny slowly looked up from his phone: 'You can't kill me in a public place in front of a solicitor, Kate.'

'I'm sure Paulina would look away for a few moments, wouldn't you, mate?'

'Justifiable homicide…' the solicitor smiled.

'Oh, don't worry… I forgive you,' Kate said. 'Me and Jonathan would probably would have gotten into a massive argument anyway. I'll go and see Dad myself later.'

'How did you find out?' Danny asked, completing his story in draft form; he'd left a gap where the dead men's names could be inserted when they'd been positively identified.

'Susan told me,' Kate said, taking a piece of Danny's toast. 'The future Mrs Johnston.'

'Shit! I'm supposed to be seeing her at lunchtime. I'd better get home and clean myself up.'

THIRTY

As Danny waited in the Hunter's Hollow reception for Susan Matlock, he spotted her son Ben talking to a group of teenagers. Danny decided that he felt slightly uncomfortable with the idea of making small talk with a man just before taking his mother out to lunch, so he pretended to be on his phone to avoid eye contact. It didn't work. Ben saw him and shouted across the reception area: 'Hey, Danny!'

Please, don't.

'I hear you're off on a hot date with my mum?' Ben added, walking towards Danny but still speaking in a very loud voice.

Oh fuck.

'Hope you're going to behave yourself,' Ben said with a grin; he playfully punched Danny on the arm.

Shit, it just gets worst.

'Ben, pack it in,' Susan Matlock shouted as she appeared from a side meeting room. *She looks nice. I should have made more of an effort. Shit.* 'We're just going for bite to eat,' she continued in a slightly louder voice than Danny cared for. 'You don't have to start calling him Dad or anything.' She smiled and winked at Danny. 'Not yet anyway.'

Jesus Christ, take me now.

'Sorry to keep you waiting, Danny,' Susan said and pressed her cheek against his. 'And sorry about that dickhead. Try not to set fire to the place while I'm out, Ben!'

'Can't promise,' Ben said as Danny and Susan walked towards the door.

'It's alright,' Danny said. 'Could be worse, I suppose. It's not like he wants to beat me up or anything. He doesn't want to beat me up, does he?'

'Not as far as I'm aware,' she said. 'Depends if we have a nice time or not, doesn't it?'

As they reached the door, Ben shouted one last time: 'Oh Mum… don't be back late or I'll lock the front door.'

'Fuck right off, Ben,' Susan muttered.

As the main security door closed behind them, Danny heard a

barrage of laughter. 'Well, that wasn't awkward in the slightest,' he said.

'I'm so sorry,' Susan offered as she got in Danny's car. 'Looks like they've practically married us off before we've had so much as a packet of crisps. Ben shows off a bit for the pupils sometimes. He doesn't mean any harm. Like I said before, he's like their big brother in a lot of ways.'

'It's okay,' Danny said, starting the car. 'I'll live. I think. I could do with a laugh at the moment.'

'I'll bet you could,' Susan said. 'That stuff out on the motorway bridge. Just unbelievable. Are you okay? Kate was there too, right?'

'I'm fine. She's fine too. It was some really weird stuff, that's for sure. This town seems to be going mad at the moment.'

'Who do you think is doing all this vigilante stuff?' she asked as Danny headed off down the school's driveway.

'I don't know. I have a few ideas… let's see how they pan out. Can we talk about something else, is that okay? I just want a break from it all for an hour.'

'Of course,' she said. 'Sorry. That was insensitive of me. I should know better, shouldn't I?'

'Not a problem,' Danny said. 'Right, where are we going? You're paying, aren't you? So, hopefully somewhere really expensive.'

Susan had chosen a café that backed onto the Huddersfield Narrow Canal in Uppermill. It was far from expensive, but the bacon rolls and thick slabs of tray bakes that they served were just the kind of thing Danny would have chosen himself. As they watched the canal boats chug past in the light sunshine, Danny felt happy and relaxed; similar to the ease he experienced when talking with Kate, but subtly different. They discussed the canal (nice and clean on this section), whether either of them could see themselves living on a boat (Susan, yes; Danny absolutely no chance), the cake (they swapped when they saw what the other had ordered) and Kate (all the young guys get goo-goo eyes when they see her - how does she do that?).

'It's quite a place, your school,' Danny said when the talk turned to work. 'Imagine if there were places like Hunter's Hollow when I was a kid. Maybe I wouldn't be so screwed up.'

'You seem pretty together to me,' Susan said. 'You're right. It is an amazing place. But no one would be happier than me if it were to be closed down.'

'How do you mean?' Danny asked.

'Wouldn't it be great if we didn't actually need places like Hunter's

Hollow? If there weren't any kids with SEMH needs?'

'You've lost me now,' Danny pointed out.

'Sorry. Social, Emotional and Mental Health… kids who've been abused and damaged. Kids who need protecting from the outside world just to give them a chance, just a *chance*, to claw something back of themselves so they can function. We can't keep up with demand for places. We're overwhelmed. One kid once said to me - he'd been horribly abused - he said… it's like I've got a black hole inside me instead of a heart. He was 11. A kid that age with a *black hole* where his heart should be, Danny. I never get used to hearing things like that. Never. So, yes… it's an amazing place and Ben and the other staff do fantastic work. But I'd love to be thrown out on my ear and told that I was no longer needed. Does that make sense?'

'Yes, it makes total sense,' Danny nodded.

Danny got an alert on his phone. He looked at it. 'Can you excuse me for one minute while I just do this?' he asked.

'Of course.'

'The police have just named the two guys killed on the bridge. I just need to put it into my story and then publish it. Bit of cut and paste… Nearly got it… aaaaaaand there. It's done.'

'Who were they?' Susan asked. 'Sorry. You said you didn't want to talk about it.'

'Bit late now that I've just interrupted our lunch to publish a story about it. Two South Asian guys. That'll go down a storm on Facebook.'

'The whole thing just freaks me out,' Susan said dabbing up the last of her cake crumbs with her finger.

'I know. It's mad. But pretty clever too, in a terrible sort of way.'

'In what way is it clever?'

'It's going to be very hard to trace the victims' movements before they were killed, because they had gone out of their way to hide where they were going before they were snatched,' Danny pointed out. 'Of course they did… they were up to no good.'

'Never thought of that. Good point.'

'Another thing… You can forget about CCTV. Any cameras on the M62 are going to be pointed at the motorway not at the moors. And if the evidence on their phones shows they really were paedos, which it will, then the great British public are going to be right behind the killers. Have you seen the *Oldham Now* Facebook page? It's already 99.9 per cent behind the vigilantes. Same with Barry Mortimer out at Lad's

Grave. No one is going to come forward with information that'll catch the killers… because no one wants them caught. Keep going lads, you're doing a cracking job… that's the feeling in Oldham right now. I hate to say it, but it's almost perfect.'

'They're perfectly insane, more like. They're not the only mad ones… what were you thinking, taking Kate out onto the moors with you like that? God knows what might have happened.'

'She was a proper journalist once, you know. Tougher than me any day of the week. Not the first time she's dealt with horrible shit out on the moors. Plus, she's my friend. When you need help you ask your friends, don't you?'

'I suppose so,' Susan agreed. 'She's so great. I love her. Coolest kid in the class. Everyone thinks you're a couple, you know.'

'Well, we're not,' Danny said with a smile. 'Never have been. Just mates.'

'Is that right?'

'Yep. Mates. Nothing more.'

'I see.'

There was quiet for a moment. Danny looked at the light on the surface of the canal. He was just about to say something when Susan spoke first: 'Look at the time! I should get back. Ben will be reporting me missing!'

THIRTY-ONE

VIGILANTE VICTIMS NAMED AFTER M-WAY DOUBLE KILLING

Danny Johnston - Oldham Now

Police have named the two men thrown from the M62 footbridge by vigilantes in the early hours of yesterday morning.

They were 42-year-old Kabeer Sajid and Adil Aziz aged 35. Both were from the Glodwick area of Oldham and are believed to be brothers-in-law.

Both died after being tied up and thrown from the Pennine Way footbridge by a gang of masked vigilantes. The killings were captured on video by *Oldham Now*, but we are not showing the moment when the two men were actually killed.

After the double execution, the gang are believed to have made off from the scene on motorbikes.

Both the men's mobile phones were left at the bridge, taped to the railings. It's thought that detectives are currently examining the phones to see what online activity the pair had been engaged in before they were killed.

The M62 has now been re-opened after the carriageway was closed in both directions while forensic teams carried out fingertip searches of the area around the scene. The footbridge across the M62 remains closed and the public has been asked to stay away.

Many questions remain about the police's handling of this case so far. *Oldham Now* would like to hear from anyone who knew the two men and has any information about how they got out onto the moors. I'm also interested in any information from serving police officers or support staff who can shed any light on the case that hasn't so far been revealed by Greater Manchester Police.

THIRTY-TWO

Danny got a smile from Kate and a thumbs up from John Smithdown as he entered the ward at the Royal Oldham Hospital. 'How was your hot date, Danny lad?' Smithdown said as he approached the bed.

'Oh, for fuck's sake,' Danny sighed. 'Not you as well. Any more of this and I'll wheel you down to the morgue and leave you there.'

'Come on, Danny,' added Kate. 'We want all the gossip.'

'I'll take you down there with him in a minute, Kate,' warned Danny. 'We had bacon rolls, some cake and a nice chat. That's it.'

'Bacon rolls, eh?' Kate said, raising her eyebrows. 'You dirty bastard…'

'Shut it, the pair of you. I mean it. I don't suppose that nice volunteer lady is about with a cup of tea?'

'He's changed the subject, Kate,' said Smithdown. 'Did you notice that?'

'I did indeed, Dad. Classic technique. The dirty bastard. Honestly.'

'That's enough, you pair. Jesus. First things, first. How are you, John?'

'I'm not too bad actually,' Smithdown replied. 'They reckon I can go home later. Any joy with that appeal story you did about anyone who knew Maggie Ormrod?'

Danny checked his email: 'Nowt so far, sorry. I'll keep plugging away at it, though. The woman next door was very helpful. The picture she gave me of Maggie with her cat should create a bit more interest, too. You never know. Everyone loves cats, don't they?'

'We appreciate it, Danny,' Kate said. 'We know you won't give up. You never do.'

Danny looked to see if there were any Wine Gums left in the box next to Smithdown's bed. It was empty. 'I'll tell you what, John. Those two cops are getting to me. There's something not right about them. It's making my teeth itch, know what I mean?'

'I do, Danny lad.'

'When I'm 60, John, will you stop calling me lad?'

'Probably not,' Smithdown said. 'You'll always be a young pain in the arse to me.'

'So, what's the plan?' Kate said.

'Well, we need some more Wine Gums, that's for sure,' Danny said. He stared into the empty carton. 'The vigilante victims aren't just being lifted off the street at random. They're being targeted. The cops are concentrating on Facebook, but it's got to be cleverer than that. They're laying bait somewhere; I need to find out where they're putting it.'

'Why do I get the feeling something dodgy and dangerous is on its way?' Kate sighed.

'Meet me at my house later if you fancy getting a slice of it,' Danny said with a wiggle of his eyebrows. 'After you've settled John back in at home.'

'Surprised you've got time to do that,' Kate said. 'What with your commitments as Oldham's number one ageing gigolo…'

'Oh, do fuck off,' Danny said, a little louder than he intended to. The other hospital visitors and a few of the staff turned to look in his direction.

'Right, I'm off before I get chucked out,' he said. 'See you later, Kate. I'll get a takeaway; I'll save you some if you like.'

'See, those are the kind of slick lines that make him such a hit with the ladies, Dad.'

Danny showed her his middle finger, then placed a hand on John Smithdown's shoulder. 'Take it easy, mate.'

Smithdown nodded and smiled: 'Danny?' he said. His voice was hoarse and tired sounding. He motioned for Danny to come close. Danny leant in. The retired detective signalled for him to come even nearer. Danny put his ear close to the old man's mouth. He could feel his breath on his neck and his heart went a little faster, fearful of what he might hear: 'You're a dirty bastard,' Smithdown said.

After a few words with the staff, Danny and Kate went their separate ways at the car park. Danny waited until Kate's blue Mercedes with its KTS1 number plate pulled away. He pulled a packet of John Player cigarettes from his jacket pocket and lit one up. He knew she'd be furious with him if she knew he was sneaking the odd smoke behind her back - they'd given up together less than a year ago. *There's something about getting stuck into a story that makes me need a cigarette. God, smoking was compulsory in newsrooms back in the old days.*

He looked around the car park and caught the eyes of a few more guilty smokers. *I know. Smoking outside a hospital. Ludicrous.*

As he finished his cigarette, he spotted Jennifer the volunteer outside the hospital doors. He was about to wave to her, but she spotted someone else and stepped off the pavement as a car pulled up next to her. She got in and gave the driver a peck on the cheek. As the car pulled around the waiting zone and out towards the main road, Danny saw the driver. It was DC Karl McIntyre.

THIRTY-THREE

Several times during the half hour drive, Danny lost sight of the car with DC McIntyre and Jennifer inside. But the ebb and flow of the traffic through Lees, Mossley and then Stalybridge seemed to favour him, and each time he thought they had slipped away, the car came back into view. After Mottram in Longdendale they headed towards the outskirts of Glossop before stopping at a neat, detached house on a new build estate in Simmondley. *That's a fucking long way to come just to volunteer at a hospital.*

Danny watched and waited as the Detective Constable escorted the woman to her door while carrying her bag. They chatted for a moment and the woman touched the detective's face and gripped his hand. Danny took a few photos, making a note of the address. The detective kissed her on the cheek; then she went inside and McIntyre drove off.

Danny sat in his car trying to make sense of what he'd seen. *As a great man once said... TFC. The cops are investigating Smithdown and one of them knows a volunteer who's hanging around his hospital bed? That really is a fucking coincidence.*

He thought about the situation for a moment then sent a text to Kate: 'I'll be a bit late. Get me a sweet and sour chicken. I'm buying. Got some weird stuff to tell you.'

'Okay, just leaving the hospital now with Dad,' Kate replied.

Danny then sent Kate several of the photos he'd taken.

<Know her? She's that nice volunteer at the hospital.
Mrs Vimto. She seems to know the Oldham DC that's
looking at Maggie's suicide.>

Kate replied:

<Hang on a sec>

A minute later a photo came back. It was a clear, closeup picture of Jennifer. She was smiling and wearing her volunteer's badge.

<Yes, that's her…Where did you get that?'>

*<Her pic's on the wall with all the other volunteers.
Clever, aren't I?>*

A few seconds later, another text from Kate:

*<I just showed your pix to Dad and he's freaking out.
Come to his house ASAP.>*

Danny put his phone on the passenger seat and started his car; a second after he'd put it into first gear the driver's side door opened and he was grabbed by the open zip of his jacket. As he was yanked from the car his foot came off the clutch, stalling the vehicle and jerking it forwards. The attacker stumbled as the car jolted and momentarily loosened his grip on Danny's jacket. Twisting his position in his seat, Danny brought his foot up and kicked DC Karl McIntyre square in the chest, sending him stumbling backwards into the road. *Oh shit. I've just assaulted a police officer.*

Danny stepped quickly out of the car and raised both his hands in apology. *Why are you saying sorry? He attacked me.* McIntyre was back on his feet and on him within a moment; his forearm slammed across Danny's throat and his hand gripped his shoulder. 'What the fuck are you doing here?' the young detective shouted. 'Answer me, right now. And it better be fucking good.'

Danny felt the pressure on his throat increase. *He's younger, fitter and better trained than me. Plus, I'm in the top three of the shittest fighters in the world. So, it's probably best to think of another way out of this.*

While Danny tried - and failed - to think of something, a hand reached out from behind the detective; his arm was pulled firmly away, allowing Danny to step away from the car. Danny watched as the detective's arm was expertly pushed up his back and he was firmly shoved to one side. The detective lost his footing and had to put a hand out to stop himself from falling. It was all done in one very quick, efficient move. It was only then that Danny saw that the person responsible for this impressive physical display of man management was Jennifer, the hospital volunteer.

'Leave it, Karl,' she said, using the same calm, pleasant voice Danny had heard in the hospital. 'It's not necessary.'

'He shouldn't be hanging about outside your house, Mum,' the detective said, holding his shoulder in obvious pain. 'He's a fucking dickhead.'

'He may well be a dickhead, son,' Jennifer agreed. 'But this isn't the time or the place. So, let's try and play nice boys, shall we? It's Danny, isn't it? You okay?'

'I'll live,' Danny said, straightening his jacket. 'I was just about to take him down… you saved me the bother. You've got some pretty good moves yourself, Jennifer. I wouldn't want to fight you for the last Wagon Wheel on the hospital tea trolly.'

'I think that's very wise, Danny,' she said. 'Very wise indeed. I think it's probably best if you leave now.'

'It's a bit weird, you being their mum and all that,' Danny said. 'A mate of mine has a saying…'

'Is it… that's a fucking coincidence, by any chance?' Jennifer offered.

'Yeah,' Danny said. 'TFC. The very same. You're not making this any less weird, you know. Quite the reverse, in fact.'

'I can imagine what you're thinking,' she said with a sweet smile that Danny found rather unnerving. 'But, honestly, what's going through your head right now isn't the truth. Really, it isn't. So, I'd suggest you put your energy elsewhere.'

'Oh really?' Danny shouted. 'What am I thinking, exactly? That you're spying on John Smithdown so that your lads can fit him up as a child molester? That? Well, it's fucking tempting to think it, isn't it?'

'Bye Danny,' Jennifer said, beckoning the DC to come into the house. 'Take care.'

THIRTY-FOUR

When Danny arrived at Smithdown's house, he could hear the retired detective shouting from the kitchen. 'Danny! Here! Now!'

Sitting at the kitchen table and surrounded by untouched Chinese takeaway cartons, Smithdown was holding Kate's phone and jabbing at the screen with his finger. 'I never saw her at the hospital, but I know who this is,' Smithdown said, showing Danny the photo on Kate's phone.

'Calm down, Dad,' Kate said. 'Please.'

'Do you know who this is, Danny?' Smithdown shouted, as if he were the only person with any sense in the room.

'It appears to be the ginger cops' mum, John,' Danny said.

'It's Jenny fucking Seddon! That's who it is!'

'Remind me, John,' Danny said. 'Remember, I was pissed for 25 years; my recall isn't as good as yours.

'Jenny Seddon!' Smithdown shouted, as if he couldn't believe how stupid Danny was being. 'Mermaid's Pool Jenny Seddon... Kinder Scout Jenny Seddon... ex-Detective Constable with Derbyshire Con-stab-u-lary Jenny Seddon. THAT Jenny fucking Seddon! She had three kids when I met her back in the 80s. Little ginger sods they were, always charging about the place. Those detectives must be two of her lads. Once a ginger sod, always a ginger sod. DI Patrick and DC Karl McIntyre…. McIntyre was her fellah's name. They weren't married. Very fucking modern for Glossop in the 80s, that was.'

'He's been like this all the way home,' Kate said. 'Effing and jeffing all the way up the Huddersfield Road. Detective Constable Jenny Seddon. Look her up.'

Danny Googled DC Jenny Seddon; when he didn't produce a result straight away, Kate pulled out her phone: 'Come on, Danny,' Kate said. 'It's the internet. How difficult can it be?'

'You've been watching too many films, Kate,' he pointed out. 'Only a tiny percentage of information and press articles from before the internet properly kicked in are actually online. *Manchester Evening News* pieces before the year 2000 are practically non-existent. No one can be bothered archiving them. I'm looking for anniversary pieces, follow ups, stuff like that.'

Then Danny found what he was looking for.

MERMAID'S POOL HEROINE COP RETIRES EARLY
Glossop Chronicle - 9/7/2001

A Glossop police detective who helped foil a terror plot by Far-Right extremists has retired from the Derbyshire Constabulary.

Detective Constable Jenny Seddon received a commendation for her part in the arrest and conviction of neo-Nazi thug Tom Lennon at the Mermaid's Pool near Kinder Scout in 1988. Greater Manchester Police Detective John Smithdown was also honoured at the time for his bravery.

Lennon was the leader of a hate group known as the White Wolves, based in an abandoned shooting lodge in the moors close to Kinder Scout. He plotted to start a race war in the Oldham area as a means of seizing political power on the local council.

The plot was uncovered after Oldham Councillor Sharmeen Chowdhury and sex worker Naomi Wells both went missing in April of 1988. Both later died as a result of events at the Mermaid's Pool.

Lennon was charged with multiple killings, including the machete murder of DC Seddon's partner, Brian McIntyre. Mr McIntyre was a teacher and local mountain rescue volunteer and had three children with Ms Seddon.

Tom Lennon died in prison in 1993, the victim of an apparent revenge attack by South Asian inmates.

His co-conspirator, Bob Donaldson, a former detective with Greater Manchester Police, is still in jail, serving a 'life means life' sentence for his part in the conspiracy.

Ms Seddon was today thanked for her service at a special ceremony at Derbyshire Constabulary headquarters in Ripley. She says she now plans to spend more time with her teenage children, Jordan, Patrick and Karl.

Danny, Kate and Smithdown had formed a huddle to read the article. They broke away and looked at each other. 'That deserves a fucking Nora I think, John.'

'Dead right it does, Danny,' Smithdown agreed. 'Fucking... Nora.'

'So, a woman whose husband was murdered after he'd helped Dad at Kinder Scout in 1988 has been hovering around him at the hospital?' Kate said. 'And two of her sons are trying to fit dad up with historic sex abuse crimes against this poor Maggie Ormrod woman? Allow me to join in... Fucking Nora!'

'I'd save your fucking Noras if I were you,' Danny said, showing them his phone again. 'Look at this.'

CORONER: SON OF MERMAID'S POOL HERO TOOK HIS OWN LIFE

Glossop Chronicle - 5/6/1998

A promising law student - whose father was killed during an incident at the Mermaid's Pool beauty spot in 1988 - died after hanging himself nearby, a coroner has concluded.

The body of Jordan McIntyre was found at the Bowden Bridge car park at the foot of Kinder Scout on the 5th of April this year, ten years to the day after the murder of his father.

Glossop teacher and mountain rescuer Brian McIntyre had been hacked to death by neo-Nazi Tom Lennon during an incident at Kinder Scout. Brian McIntyre's partner, Detective Constable Jenny Seddon, later arrested Lennon at the scene and gave evidence at his trial. Lennon died in prison in 1993 after being stabbed to death by other inmates.

Jordan McIntyre, the eldest of three brothers, had never come to terms with his father's death, the inquest heard. He had often struggled around the anniversary of his father's death. According to family and friends, these feelings had intensified as he got older.

Jordan had gone to Leeds University to study law, but on the night of the 5th of April, he told fellow students he had to return home to Glossop because of a family emergency. It's thought he drove instead to Kinder Scout, stopped at Bowden Bridge and hanged himself from a tree in the car park.

Recording a verdict of suicide, Assistant Coroner Deirdre Castle said: 'Jordan had clearly made the decision to take his own life, hence the remote nature of the spot he chose. There was nothing anyone could have done to stop him or to save him. He was resolute in his decision. My heart goes out to his family, especially his mother and two younger brothers.' Verdict: Suicide.

There was quiet in Smithdown's living room. Kate prodded at her takeaway with a fork, then pushed it away. There was a variety of 'Oh my Gods', 'Jesus Christs' and the inevitable 'Fucking Nora'.

'So, those two cops investigating Dad have quite the axe to grind, don't they?' Kate said. 'I'm not being unreasonable when I say that, am I? Their dad's dead, their brother went and topped himself…. All because of DI John Smithdown. In their minds, anyhow. Christ Almighty. You said they made your teeth itch, didn't you, Danny?'

'All cops make my teeth itch,' Danny said. He nodded at Smithdown: 'Present company excepted.'

'I'm touched,' Smithdown said, quietly.

Kate continued: 'And if they're keeping secrets like these, fuck knows what they're hiding when it comes to these vigilante murders. Danny, you've got to stay away from this, it's gone too far and it's getting too dangerous.'

'You're absolutely right, Kate,' he said sarcastically. 'I'll call the police immediately. I'm sure they'll be a massive help.'

'See, it's that stupid attitude of yours that causes half the problems, Danny,' Kate shouted, banging the table and knocking over a tray of noodles.

She got up to fetch a cloth. As she was away from the table, Danny received an anonymous WhatsApp message. He tried his best to maintain a blank expression as he read it. Kate came back to wipe up the mess; he waited 20 seconds before saying: 'I'm not hungry, to be honest. You finish mine. I can't take all of this in. My mind's like a tub of mushy peas. I think I need to sleep on it. I'll ring you in the morning.'

Danny was aware that Smithdown was staring at him; he avoided the retired detective's suspicious eyes. *Nothing gets past that old bastard.*

'Why don't you stop here with us, Danny?' Kate asked. 'The spare room's already made up, you can stay the night.'

'No, I need to get home,' he said. 'Clear my head. We can't just go charging in with this. We need to be clever. And calm. Let's speak tomorrow and decide what to do then.'

Kate stacked the takeaway cartons and moved them to the draining board. Smithdown looked at Danny and whispered: 'Be… fucking… careful.'

THIRTY-FIVE

I need to move somewhere where every single place isn't called after something weird-sounding, Danny said to himself as he slowed down close to the path leading to Crow Knowl. *It's like the Ordnance Survey people are deliberately trying to freak me out. Hanging Lees, Lad's Grave... now Crow Knowl.*

Danny parked his car in a layby at the point where the Huddersfield and Rochdale roads met and looked at his map. There was a service track that wound a steady path through Crompton Moor and up to Crow Knowl - the highest point on the moor - but it was gated and locked.

Yes, that's another thing for the list. As well as going to places that aren't called something scary, it would at least be nice to be able to drive there. Just once.

He stepped over the stile next to the gate and headed up the track. Behind him was the Windy Hill transmitter and Piethorne Valley. To his left he saw the lights of houses, farms and pubs marking out the small village of Denshaw. On his right were the moving illuminations of the M62, with Rochdale and the Scout Moor wind farm beyond it. Danny could see the lights on top of the giant turbines; some winked and blinked as the rotor blades whizzed past and momentarily blocked them from view.

Ahead of him was the blank moorland canvas of Crompton Moor. There was little to see but as he got higher the view beyond opened out. The sharp rise of Oldham Edge hill and the town centre appeared first, then in the distance, Manchester. He recognised the tall yet bizarrely slim structure of the Beetham Tower at the end of Deansgate. Then he saw the faint outline of the Arndale Centre. To the right was the unmistakable tower and rotunda of Strangeways jail. The sun had nearly set now - silhouetted on the horizon were the towers of the Fiddler's Ferry power station, way out west in Warrington.

Danny realised he was running through the geography of the area in his mind for one reason only: he was very scared. *I can't involve Kate in this one, it's not fair and it's too dangerous. I can't call the cops, don't trust them. For all I know, it's the cops sending me these tip offs… they could be waiting for me right now at the top of Crow Knowl. If only you were 30 years younger John Smithdown, we'd be out here together. Christ we'd be the same age. You'd know what to do, John, wouldn't you? I'm just making it up as I go along.*

The track began to curl in on itself as it snaked around the summit of Crow Knowl. At the top, three transmitter stations, 20 yards apart, came into view. All three had single storey redbrick bases of varying sizes depending on the height of the mast; two had metal chain link fencing around them to protect the buildings and the telecoms masts that stood next to them.

Next to the first and largest of the masts was the remains of an ancient boundary; all that was left was a wall of crossed stones just a few feet high and barely six feet in either direction. Not a huge wall, but just about big enough to prop up the body of a man. Danny stopped and stared at the body. His head had a series of two-pronged jagged holes in it - *claw hammer by the looks of it* - and was covered in blood.

A sign was on the man's lap and his hands were curled around its edges, like he was holding an advert.

PAUL DOCHERTY.
PAEDOPHILE.
GOOGLE HIM.

No threats, no abandon-hope-all-ye-that-nonce style threats. Just a name and job description. That's weird.

Danny took out his phone and did as the sign suggested and carried out an internet search for Paul Docherty. When that provided too many results he added the word paedophile. A series of local news articles came up detailing the man's abuse of children. *Oh dear, Paul. Can't argue with this one. You really were a very nasty piece of work, weren't you?*

Danny took several pictures of the scene, even though he knew he'd probably be unable to publish them. *I suppose I'd better call the police then. Maybe they already know. Wouldn't surprise me in the slightest.*

He was about to publish the details as a breaking news alert on his social media when he heard a noise from the other side of Crow Knowl. Accompanying the low growl of the motorway traffic in the distance and the light wind from the moors he heard a crackling sound. *Like someone's eating a giant bag of crisps.*

He walked around the second transmitter; the building at its base was derelict and open and he could hear birds moving around inside. The crackling noise was further away.

He moved on to the final mast; it was taller and slimmer than the other transmitters and had no protective fencing. It stood on a brick building the size of a domestic garage that had a large and ornate graffiti tag on it. There was something lying next to the mast base, covered in a plastic sheet that crunched and crackled in the wind. *This isn't right. This really is different. It's still fucking horrible, but it's definitely different.*

In the distance he could hear the sound of motorbikes fading then disappearing into the moorland. Then nothing. Just the sound of the M62, and the wind pushing and pulling at the plastic sheeting.

A message had been gaffer taped to the wall next to the sheeting; it looked different to the other sign, and to the one left next to Barry Mortimer's body. There were no shouty, upper case letters making a declaration this time around; the letters were smaller, more low-key.

We are sorry.
This was not supposed to happen.
This is a war and casualties are inevitable.
Do not interfere like he did. Leave us to our work.

Danny looked at the sheeting; the corners had been pinned down by rocks, but it still moved and rippled in the moorland breeze, as if something was moving underneath.

Don't touch it. Leave it be. Do… not… touch… it.

Danny knelt down and pulled the sheet aside. It crackled as it moved. He looked at the bloodstained face staring up at him. The side of the man's head was misshapen and dented inwards, like someone had scooped a section of it away; blood pooled around the upper part of the body and was making its way down the slope of Crow Knowl away from the transmitter. Danny looked at the face - the jaw was open and slack, and the eyes were wide open. Despite the severity of the injuries, there was no doubt in Danny's mind who this was. It was Detective Constable Karl McIntyre.

So much for your theory about the cops being in on it, Danny boy.

THIRTY-SIX

PAEDO KILLERS SAY 'SORRY' OVER COP DEATH
Danny Johnston - Oldham Now

Vigilantes thought to be responsible for the murder of at least four suspected paedophiles have apologised for the death of an Oldham detective investigating the case.

The body of Detective Constable Karl McIntyre was discovered on Crompton Moor last night after another anonymous tip off to *Oldham Now.*

A note was left at the scene, saying that the vigilantes were sorry for his death and that police shouldn't interfere with their murderous campaign. 'Let us get on with our work,' the killers stated.

Another body found at the scene is thought to be that of 46-year-old Paul Docherty. Unlike the previous victims who had no criminal records, Docherty was a convicted sex offender. He was out on licence after serving half of a nine-year sentence for abusing two girls in the Coldhurst area in 2014.

DC McIntyre was the brother of Detective Inspector Patrick McIntyre, who is also working on the vigilante case.

The brothers come from a policing family: their mother, former Detective Constable Jenny Seddon, received a bravery award for her part in foiling a plot to start a race war in Oldham in the late 80s.

It's not the first time the McIntyres have had to deal with tragedy in their family. Their father, Glossop teacher and mountain rescue volunteer Brian McIntyre, was murdered on Kinder Scout near Hayfield in Derbyshire in 1988. Their brother Jordan later took his own life nearby on the 10th anniversary of his father's death.

The McIntyre brothers had also been working on the death of local woman Maggie Ormrod, who committed suicide at Hanging Lees Reservoir ten days ago. It's still not known if the death of Maggie Ormrod is linked to the vigilante killings.

THIRTY-SEVEN

After Danny had given his account of what happened at Crow Knowl, DI Patrick McIntyre turned off the DIR and leant back in his chair. He looked at Danny. 'I think we're done,' he said. 'You can go.'

'I'm very sorry about your brother,' Danny said. 'I'm sorry about both your brothers. I didn't know. How's your mum doing?'

'Since when do you give a fuck about us?' the DI said, quietly. He stared into the bottom of the plastic cup of tea he was holding. He swirled the last remains around then decided not to drink it. 'My mum is really quite upset, seeing as though you've asked, Mr Johnston. Yes, she's really quite put out by the whole situation… what with her son being murdered and all that. Plus, there's the small matter of another one of her sons committing suicide, of course. Oh yes. Then there's her husband… my fucking dad… let's not forget him. He was murdered too. Had his head just about cut off with a machete up at Kinder Scout. Is that all of it? Yeah, I think so. So, apart from all that… she's muddling through, thanks for asking.'

'I saw the articles,' Danny said. 'Just terrible. I'm very sorry. I didn't really look into it when I did my book. I was just focussing on Black Moss. What your mum did was astonishing. No wonder she can take care of herself.'

'You don't like the police,' McIntyre continued, ignoring what Danny had just said. 'I get it. But did it occur to you… just for a moment… that maybe other people want to catch these killers as much as you do? Oh… something's wrong in Oldham… it must be the cops. It's always the cops. You don't have the monopoly on virtue, Danny Johnston. There's room in the world for other, perfectly decent people, as well as you.'

Danny's solicitor Paulina spoke: 'DI McIntyre, I'm sure Danny wants to help in any way that he can. He's here of his own accord. He wants to do the right thing, don't you Danny?'

'Of course I do,' Danny nodded. 'We're all on the same side, after all, aren't we?'

'Wow. Very big of you to acknowledge that, Danny. Do you know what my brother had been doing? Spending every hour of every day trying to stop the abuse of children in Oldham. Look at this…'

The DI produced his phone and showed Danny an article from the *Manchester Evening News*:

THESE ARE THE PERVERTS WHO TRIED TO FIND VICTIMS ONLINE - INSTEAD THEY WERE LURED INTO A TRAP.

'See this Danny?' McIntyre said, jabbing at the screen with his finger. 'Sting operations to catch paedophiles… 63-year-old man meeting what he thought was a 13-year-old for sex. A guy in his 50s arranging to meet two girls of 12 at McDonalds so he could give them money. Man in his 30s arrested in Morrisons car park after sending pictures of himself to what he thought was a girl of 14. All caught by my brother posing as a kid online. He didn't even have to try that hard. They were on his fake profiles like flies on a lolly. Can you see now why he was so annoyed about you sticking your oar in? No one did more than my brother to stop this plague. So it really warms my heart to know that we are all finally on the same side.'

'Sure, I understand,' Danny said. 'It's just looked weird from my perspective… who wouldn't want paedos permanently out of the frame? Everyone's a winner, right?'

'The people doing this are murderers, Danny,' the DI stated, leaning across the table. 'Barry Mortimer hadn't been convicted of any crimes. Neither had Kabeer Sajid and Adil Aziz, the guys on the bridge. Okay, their phones painted a pretty grim picture of what they had in mind, but they had all been tortured for days before they were killed. No investigation, no report to the CPS, no court case… just straight to the toolbox and out with the claw hammers. I have two daughters, Danny. Do you think I like the idea of people like them trying to contact my kids? It turns my stomach. But the people who are killing these men aren't vigilantes. They're murderers. Last time I checked, murdering people is against the law. And we can't just ignore the law just because the victims themselves make us feel sick.'

'Okay,' Danny said, holding up his hands. 'I get it. I'm sorry. Do you know what actually happened to your brother before I found him?'

'Not yet,' McIntyre replied. 'I know he was digging about in his own time. Maybe even posing as a potential groomer online to see what he could flush out. He'd definitely gone somewhere after you'd had your little encounter at my mum's. And he definitely headed back towards Oldham. After that... we don't know. He had his phone taken off him at some stage. And his Fitbit watch.'

'So, no way of tracking his whereabouts,' Danny offered.

'Exactly. We're looking for them but... well, you know the moors around here, they could be anywhere. Whoever did this isn't daft.'

'Doesn't sound like some dickheads with an I Hate Nonces Facebook page, does it?' Danny said.

'No, it doesn't,' the DI agreed.

'I do, genuinely want to help, Detective Inspector. Can I ask a question?

The DI nodded: 'The first three victims had no criminal records, is that right?' Danny asked.

'Correct.'

'Then why target Paul Docherty? He was known to the police, served time for sex offences and was out on licence.'

'Good PR, I reckon,' the detective said. 'Keep the public onside. Offer up a known offender to show that they're the good guys. But my brother must have gotten too close to them. That's why he ended up under a plastic sheet up on Crompton Moor. It could have been you.'

'Why are you telling me this?' Danny asked. 'You've shared nothing so far.'

'Because, whether I like it or not, you're the only person the killers are in contact with,' DI McIntyre said. 'There's no other trace of them. They're like ghosts. Gives me no pleasure to say this, Danny Johnston, but it looks like I need you.'

'Fucking Nora,' Danny said with a weak smile. 'You must be desperate.'

'My brother's getting a post-mortem as we speak. Of course I'm fucking desperate.'

THIRTY-EIGHT

'In the big, long list of your all-time stupid fucking ideas, Danny,' Kate said, pacing up and down in Danny's tiny living room, 'That is, without doubt, the fucking stupidest.'

'I think that's a bit harsh,' Danny replied. 'It might work. DC McIntyre was apparently trying a similar approach.'

'And look where he is now… dead! Pretending to be a paedo and waving it about on Facebook - that's your idea of a GOOD plan, is it? If you're lucky, you'll only get battered. The more likely scenario is you'll end up dead with a claw hammer sticking out of your head out on... Lonely Skeleton Hill or something.'

'There's no such place as Lonely Skeleton Hill,' Danny pointed out. He thought for a moment. 'There isn't, is there?'

'You... are… an... idiot, Danny,' Kate said. 'That cop tried the same thing and he got himself killed. Doesn't that give you a clue that it might just be a slightly shit idea?'

'It must have worked to some degree, otherwise they wouldn't have snatched him.'

'Stunning logic, Danny,' Kate sighed, sitting down and lighting up a cigarette.

'I thought you'd quit,' Danny said, also lighting up.

'I thought you had, too. Maybe if you could quit being a total arsehole too, you'd be really getting somewhere.'

'Look, Kate. The cops are totally stuck. The public are actually supporting the killers. The internet is awash with Noncebusters and Paedopouncers - it was only a matter of time before things got out of hand, and now they well and truly have. Maybe the best way to break the deadlock is to stir things up a bit. It could really help find these vigilantes and put them behind bars.'

'Oh, so Detective Inspector McIntyre is right behind this scheme, is he?'

'Not as such…'

'Fucking Nora, Danny!' Kate exclaimed, flicking ash onto the carpet. 'No, no, no!'

'Admittedly, there's potential for things to go a little bit wrong,' Danny said. 'But it's got to be worth a go. It might even do a bit of good.'

'It might do your analytics a bit of good, more like...' Kate muttered.

'What's that supposed to mean?' Danny asked.

'You know exactly what it means,' Kate stated. 'I've seen all the money spinners suddenly popping up on your site. Didn't you used to refuse ads in death stories? Not any more it seems. Saint Danny Johnston! Defender of the oppressed! Saviour of the abused! It appears things have changed a little. You're just another clickbait bollocks bandit like everyone else.'

'Where the fuck has all this come from?'

'You're doing this for clicks,' Kate continued. 'You're no better than these paedo pile on merchants on Facebook. They don't care about child protection. They just want the online attention. But at least they're not selling ad space on the back of it. These murders are making you money. I'd have more respect for you if you admitted it.'

'I have to eat, Kate. I'll admit that. I have to light this house and put petrol in my car. Guilty as charged. If I don't get income into the site, then it'll die... and any kind of independent local scrutiny dies with it. You're a businesswoman, surely you must understand that?'

'I understand that you're going to get your head caved in if you carry on like this. And that's just not worth it. It's not worth a couple of grand of ad revenue from a double fucking glazing firm in Greenacres.'

Danny felt anger and resentment bubble up and overtake him; he stood up from his chair and shouted at Kate. 'Maybe you should worry a bit less about me and a bit more about your dad, who the whole of Oldham thinks is an old nonce... and maybe give a bit of thought to your kid, who thinks you rather carelessly let him be abducted and can barely even bring himself to look at you.'

As soon as the words had come out of Danny's mouth, he wished he could gather them up and put them back where they'd come from. Kate's face was a hurt mixture of shock and anger. She put out her cigarette into the remnants of her cup of tea. 'You're right Danny. I should definitely stop worrying about you. In fact, I'm not going to give you another fucking thought.'

'No change there, then,' Danny said, his tone shifting down several gears as he thought of a way to diffuse the situation.

Kate said nothing. She stared at Danny; she checked that her car keys were in her bag, then put the strap over her shoulder as she got to her feet. There were tears in her eyes. 'Apart from Dad, I'm your only friend. Now you've only got Dad. Congratulations. Hope you're happy, Danny Something. You stupid fuck.'

THIRTY-NINE

The Shirtless Boy and Danny were standing at the top of Crow Knowl. It seemed five times as high this time. Despite being fully aware that this was a dream, Danny could still feel the breeze coming off the moors.

Danny and The Boy seemed like friends this time. *Thank fuck for that.*

It was as if the landscape around the hill had been ironed flat. The hills and valleys looked like a two-dimensional hand-drawn map and Danny could see everything in all directions for mile after mile: there was Black Moss and next to it, Little Black Moss. He could see Hunters Hollow and Maggie Ormrod's house, with Hanging Lees just behind it. Danny had never been to the Mermaid's Pool, but he knew he could see that too, because right over there was dark oval of water with actual mermaids swimming in it. They didn't look like the mermaids he'd seen in films or cartoons though. They were grey and emaciated and their hair was greasy and matted. *Those are the worst-looking mermaids I've ever seen, absolute shockers.*

Down below Crow Knowl, Danny could see a group of men in skull face masks climbing up the hill towards them. He looked at The Shirtless Boy; he didn't seem to be too worried, but Danny was getting more panicked the closer they came. There were dozens of them, clawing their way up Crow Knowl.

No. There were hundreds. Thousands, maybe.

Danny looked at The Shirtless Boy for help. The Boy was nodding downwards towards Oldham. It was clear to Danny what he was suggesting: jump.

The gentle slopes of Crow Knowl were now sheer cliffs. Danny was really scared now, but The Shirtless Boy was adamant.

We have to jump.

So they did.

FORTY

After three days of pretending to be a paedophile on the internet, Danny's first face-to-face attempts to flush out the vigilantes didn't go quite to plan.

He'd made various fake profiles and had attempted to engage with accounts that looked like they could be the vigilantes in disguise. Different platforms generated very varied results. He found TikTok to be too time consuming; Reddit - particularly subreddits about exam advice and divorce - generated some responses but there were too many levels for him to feel like he was getting anywhere. By way of contrast, joke accounts - particularly on Instagram - like 'Oldham Incel-ectuals' and 'Memes Only Oldham High Schoolers Will Understand' were very fertile ground.

But the corner of social media that generated the best results were the places where young people were asking for things for free. He was inundated with responses. *Could one of them be the vigilantes in disguise?*

As a result of one such post, he'd arranged to meet up with a girl that he'd found remarkably easy to engage with online; the agreed meeting place was 5pm outside the Greggs in Oldham town centre. It was nestled in the familiar company of Home Bargains, Primark and McDonald's in the precinct behind Oldham Police Station.

The bakery was already closing by the time he arrived at 4.45. He was expecting a fruitless hour waiting around trying not to look suspicious before heading home. *Kate was right. I hate it when that happens. Bloody stupid idea.*

Then he heard a voice behind him; it was frail and hesitant: 'Are you Danny?'

Danny had decided to use his real first name to avoid any suspicion that he really was up to no good. *Be upfront… it'll look better later.* He'd sent emails to himself, explaining his thinking about trying to lure the vigilantes into the open that, with the hope that their date and times of sending would prove his intentions were good.

He'd also sent a good old-fashioned letter to DI Patrick McIntyre at Oldham Police station, explaining his plan, his thinking behind it and his intention to write a story about it afterwards.

He was prepared for vigilantes masquerading as young girls online to turn up. He'd even bought a small hammer from a hardware shop just in case; he could feel it banging against his hip from its resting place inside his shoulder bag. What he wasn't prepared for was the sight of a small, frightened-looking girl in an oversized sweatshirt and jogging pants. *Oh God, a real kid has turned up… She'd said online she was 'nearly 16'. She looks all of 13.*

'Have you got me phone?' the girl asked. 'I can't stop. My boyfriend is waiting for me. Have you got it or not?'

Danny had researched some of the techniques used by groomers; one was to search through social media for young people looking for something for free. In this case: a mobile phone. The girl had broken hers and didn't want her mum to find out. If someone could give her a replacement it would 'save me life' she'd posted. *It's exactly the kind of trick the vigilantes would use.*

Danny had engaged the girl in online conversation, switched over to private messaging and offered her a phone. He was surprised at how easily she'd agreed to meet him. *Maybe it's really them.* He was stunned that she'd actually turned up.

'Well?' she demanded, 'Have you got it?'

'It's Jasmine, isn't it? Or is that not your real name?'

'It is, actually. Why, are you not really called Danny?'

'I am. I didn't think you were real… that you'd really show up, I mean.'

'Well, I am real and I'm here now,' she said. 'Come on, stop messing. Me mam will batter me if she finds out.'

Danny looked at the girl. It was a warm early evening, yet she hugged herself as if she were freezing. Her hair was scraped back harshly from her head, and she wore large, hooped earrings. On her feet were Vans, but they were battered and worn with what looked like a cigarette burn hole near one of the toes. He felt stupid and embarrassed at himself over what he'd done; and he felt terribly sorry for her.

'I don't actually have one on me…' Danny explained.

'Whoah, then why get me here then, you waster?' Jasmine cried. 'You a nonceman? Is that ya game?'

'Look. Sorry. I wasn't sure if you were you… or if you'd show up or… Sorry. Maybe I could come and talk to your mum? I'm sure she'd understand.'

'Would she fook!' the girl exclaimed, as if what Danny had made the stupidest suggestion in history.

'Let's find a phone repair shop and I'll buy you one.'

The girl thought for a moment. 'No bollocks, right? If you go weird on me, I'll scream the joint down.'

'No bollocks. Promise.'

'Okay then. There's a CEX round the corner.'

They walked. Danny made a point of staying as far away from the girl as possible. They entered the CEX shop and she pointed to an iPhone in the long glass case near to the counter. Danny paid and tucked the receipt into his wallet. As he thanked the shop assistant the girl ran.

Not your finest hour that, Danny. At least it stopped her from getting a battering from her mum. For now at least.

Danny's second attempt at kicking the nest of Oldham's paedophiles was also not quite what he had hoped for.

He had thrown his net far and wide on many platforms; he'd lost count of the number of profiles he'd set up and conversations he'd initiated. But try as he might, Danny couldn't quite work out how he had managed to arrange a meeting outside the Subway outlet in Chadderton with a very nervous looking man in his late 40s called Charlie. *This man is not a vigilante. No chance. And why has he brought me flowers?*

After five minutes of standing next to each other, punctuated by the odd nod and awkward smile, Danny had said: 'Look, I know this might sound a bit weird… But you're not Charlie, are you?'

'I am actually,' the man said. He had a bunch of flowers with him and a rucksack.

'I'm Danny.'

'Really?' the man said. 'I was expecting a D.A.N.N.I.'

'Were you know? And how O.L.D is this D.A.N.N.I. you were expecting?' Danny asked. 'About F.I.F.T.E.E.N?'

The man looked scared and worried for a few moments. Then his face cleared, and a slight smile appeared: 'And how old was this C.H.A.R.L.I.E that YOU were expecting?'

'You can fuck right off now,' Danny said. 'I'm here trying to trap paedophiles… well, not paedophiles as such… What I'm really after is…look, never fucking mind what I'm doing, what's in that rucksack?'

'Never YOU fucking mind,' Charlie shouted, seeming to take genuine offence at the suggestion that he was up to no good. 'And what room have you got to talk? Hanging around Chadderton looking for… whatever it is you're looking for.'

'I think you'd better be on your way, mate,' Danny said. 'Before I call the police.'

Charlie looked as if he was about to come up with something desperately clever, but instead he gave Danny the finger and dumped the flowers in a bin outside the Subway. 'Four quid those flowers cost me,' he muttered as he walked away.

Danny watched Charlie cross the dual carriageway road that ran through Chadderton. Halfway across he gave Danny the finger again then crossed to the other side. Danny took his picture. 'Fuck off!' the man shouted as he waited for the crossing lights to change.

Charlie got into a car at the edge of the Costco car park that skirted the main road and quickly drove off. *The sooner I can go back to missing dogs and traffic delays on my website the better,* Danny thought.

Attempt number three had felt different right from the start. Instead of a takeaway or a bakery, the meeting place that 'Alice' had chosen to meet Danny was Oldham Edge, the ominous-looking lump of land that overlooked Oldham Royal Infirmary. Over the years it had been used as farmland, a quarry and even a Ministry of Defence facility thanks to its prominent position. Now it was a mix of woodland, criss-crossed pathways and abandoned shopping trolleys. The sun was already close to setting by the time Danny got there. He parked his car near to an abandoned radio station at the top of Henshaw Street. He'd been here a few years earlier promoting his book, but the building was now boarded up.

Danny made his way up the concreted MOD 'tank road' that climbed steadily up through the woods towards a radio mast at the top of the Edge. Housing estates and old mills stretched out on all sides. He could see the lights of a scrapyard below and, in the distance, the Seven Sisters tower blocks in Rochdale.

This is way too similar to the locations where the bodies were found… Windy Hill… Crompton Moor… Go back. Go back right now.

But Alice had asked him to meet her near the mast. So, the mast is where he headed. *This is the plan, isn't it? This is why you bought the phone for Jasmine and met up with Charlie, Oldham's most hopeless nonce. You wanted to flush the vigilantes out… Well, you've well and truly pulled the handle now.*

Danny lad.

As the path levelled out and more of the mast came into view, Danny saw a slight figure in the distance. There was Alice, wearing black skinny fit jeans and a hoodie. He relaxed a little. As he got closer, he saw how tiny she looked: *all spindly arms and cocktail stick legs... out here on her own, just as it's getting dark.*

Alice waved to him, then stepped into a gap between the trees that led to the base of the mast. Danny slipped a hand inside his shoulder bag and touched the rubber handle of the hammer he'd bought with him. The weight of it calmed him down a little. *Don't kid yourself. It'll be fine for waving about a bit, but it's hardly a .44 Magnum, is it?*

Danny turned into the clearing. Alice was standing directly in front of him now and pulled back her hoodie as she spoke: 'Yer in the shit now, ya fookin' wrong un,' the young man said. 'Alice' was in his early 20s with a see-through moustache and cropped hair.

Bingo!

Danny took his hand away from his hammer and reached for his phone instead: 'I think even I can take you on, you little turd,' Danny said. 'Smile for the camera. How about a few words for *Oldham Now* about being a shit vigilante?'

Danny unlocked the phone and was about to press the camera icon when the force of three people charging him from behind sent him staggering forward. He slid face down across the grass; the air was pushed out of him by three sets of knees on his back. 'Showtime lads,' he heard one of the gang shout.

The knees came off his back; he turned, and several smartphone torch lights snapped on. The glare made it difficult to see who had rushed him, but it looked like there was at least half a dozen of them and they all had scarves over their faces. It was dark now and Danny was quite willing to accept that Kate had been right: *in the big, long list of your all-time stupid fucking ideas, this is without doubt, the fucking stupidest.*

He looked around for his phone; he couldn't see it. *Fuck the phone, where's that hammer?*

The bag - with the hammer hopefully still inside it - was six feet in front of him. Danny readied himself to jump towards it, just as one of his attackers picked the bag up and threw it into the bushes.

'Right then!' a voice said from within the main group. 'Nonce target identified and subdued! Weapons at the ready, lads!'

Danny saw they all had backpacks and each of the silhouetted figures was reaching inside. He twisted around on the grass and sat up, putting his hands in the air to show he knew he was outnumbered: 'Listen, please. My name's Danny. I'm not a nonce…'

'Oh Danny,' the leader laughed. 'I have to say that 100 per cent of our subjects say those exact words. Literally! Word for word! I suspect young Alice here will disagree with you. Wouldn't you, Al?'

'I'd definitely disagree with his assessment on non-noncery, mate,' the skinny young man in the hoodie answered with a smile. 'Violently disagree, in fact.'

'Please,' Danny persisted. 'Hear me out. I've got a website…'

'Here that, lads?' the ringleader shouted. 'He's got a website. I'LL BET YOU FOOKIN' HAVE, MATE!'

Each person in the group walked towards Danny, phone in one hand, contents of their backpacks in the other. They formed a semi-circle, cutting off his escape. Behind him was the fence surrounding the transmitter at the top of the Edge. The semi-circle became a circle.

'Right then, let him have it,' the leader said.

Surrounded, Danny put up his hands to protect his head, just as six cartons of rotten milkshake were emptied onto him. 'Danny the nonce… You have been milkshaked by Nonce Upon a Time in the West of Oldham! While you're busy washing cheesy lumps of milky banana goodness out of your hair, we'll be sending these videos to the police!'

'Don't bother,' DI Patrick McIntyre said from behind the group. He was flanked by two uniformed officers. 'He's not a nonce. He's just a fucking idiot.'

FORTY-ONE

'You still smell like bin juice,' McIntyre said after Danny had used the showers at the police station.

'I think it's these clothes you've given me,' Danny replied, pulling at the baggy jumper and ragged combat trousers that he'd been given from a box stashed in a storeroom by the Duty Sergeant's desk. He gave the jumper's sleeve a sniff. 'Genuine dead bloke apparel, this is.'

'Idiots can't be choosers, Danny,' the DI said. 'If that had been the real vigilantes instead of those Nonce Upon a Time comedians, I could be scraping you off the M62 by now.'

'Well, it seemed like a good idea at the time,' Danny offered.

'Please, just stay away, Danny. We've already had one person die trying to find these murderers, we don't want another one.'

'How come you were up on Oldham Edge?' Danny asked. 'Following me? I'm not complaining. Just wondering.'

'Don't flatter yourself,' the detective said. 'We've been monitoring the Nonce Upon a Time lads for a while. We were following them, not you.'

'Oh, so you haven't seen the letter I sent you?'

'What letter?'

'Never mind. How's your mum doing?'

'She's putting a brave face on it,' McIntyre said. 'Just like she always does. But inside… that's a very different matter. Karl was her golden boy. He could do no wrong in his mum's eyes. Now he's gone, she's just stuck with me.'

'Your mum is a pretty amazing person,' Danny said.

'She is. And she seems to quite like you. Can't think why. So I don't want anyone else getting hurt. Even you.'

'You don't have to worry about me.'

'I'm not, to be honest, but every minute I spend saving your stupid arse is a minute I could spend eliminating another gang of Facebook attention seekers from the inquiry. You're really not helping, Danny. Go home. Please. When something happens that you can write about,

I'll let you know. I promise.'

'So, you're getting close to finding out who the vigilantes are?'

'Put it like this, we know who they *aren't*. They aren't milkshake marauders like the Nonce Upon a Time lot. That much we do know.'

'I could have told you that a week ago.'

'Look, you've got my number. If you get another call from the vigilantes, let me know straight away. No running about the moors on your own. No involving the likes of Kate Smithdown...'

'No chance of that…'

'…just call me straight away, understand?'

'Okay.'

Danny headed for the door. 'How's John Smithdown doing?' the DI asked.

'He's keen to clear his name, that's how he is.'

'Maybe you should concentrate on that.'

'Maybe I will.'

FORTY-TWO

6 April 1975

Maggie waited on the street corner and looked up and down the steep road; terraced houses huddled around a chip shop in one direction, more terraces and a hardware store in the other. *Come on, I haven't got all day.*

As she looked up the road, she felt a tap on her shoulder. She turned. No one there. She looked down the road. No one there either. She looked back up the road and there he was, smiling. 'Can't believe you fell for that one, Maggie Nuisance,' he said. 'Oldest trick in the book that. Tap and move. I got you, just like that. Blimey. Good job I'm here to look out for you, isn't it?'

'Spose it is,' Maggie said with a smile. Her smile got bigger when he gave her a Bar Six and a pack of Rainbow Drops. With a tilt of his head, he indicated that Maggie should follow him. She did. He placed a hand lightly on her shoulder. As they walked, a woman pushing a large, battered looking pram passed them from the opposite direction. She smiled at them and carried on. The pair walked down the street for a few yards then into a side road which petered out into a ginnell between two warehouses. Maggie began to open the Rainbow Drops. 'Hey, save them for later,' he said.

'Later? Where are we going?' She tucked the sweets onto the bib pocket of her dungarees.

'Not sure yet. Pictures, maybe?'

'I've got no money.'

'Don't worry about that,' he said. 'I've got money. Got a car too.'

'Is it one of them police panda cars?' Maggie asked.

'No,' he laughed. 'I don't use those. Too obvious. We don't want the baddies to know who we are until it's too late.'

'Oh right,' Maggie said. 'Sneaky!'

'That's right. Got to be. Baddies are sneaky, so we've got to be even sneakier. I'll take you into the police station sometime, if you like, so you can meet a few. Then you can see how bad some of them really are.'

'I'd be too frightened to do that.'

'You'd be safe. As long as you were with me.'

He stopped and crouched down until he was at her eye level. 'I worry about you, Maggie. You're out and about on your own at places like the fair. It's not safe for a girl of your age. Anything could happen. That's what I wanted to talk to you about.'

'Oh right. Am I in trouble?'

'No Maggie, you're not in trouble. Like I say, I'm worried about you. Girls like you go missing all the time. And I'm afraid the police haven't got time to look for all of them. Some of them just have to stay missing. And I don't want that to happen to you.'

'Thank you,' Maggie said quietly.

'There's no point in just taking you back to the children's home, you'll be on your toes again before I get to the end of the drive, won't you?'

'Maybe...'

'Definitely, more like. So that's why I'm making you my personal project. I'm going to make sure that nothing bad happens to you. There are some terrible people out there, Maggie. Trust me, I know. I've locked enough of them up. But I can't lock them all up. I do my best, honestly, I do. But it's just not possible. So, here's my plan. If you're going to be out and about, you're better being out and about with me rather than being on your own. Then I can protect you. What do you think?'

'I think… that's great. Thanks, Mr Smithdown!

'Call me John,' he corrected. 'I'm your friend, after all.'

FORTY-THREE

Danny pulled into Smithdown's driveway hoping to see Kate's distinctive dark blue Mercedes. Instead, there was a small Ford Fiesta that he didn't recognise. He knocked and opened the door with the key he'd had for the last two years. 'John, it's Danny,' he shouted. 'I've got the Dignitas lads with me… get your stuff, we're off to Switzerland.'

'In the front room, Danny,' Smithdown shouted back. 'You rude bastard.'

In the living room, Smithdown was in his favourite armchair. Sitting next to him on a dining room chair was Jenny Seddon. Danny saw that Jenny was holding Smithdown's hand. She smiled at him.

'Here he is,' Smithdown said. 'Oldham's biggest trouble-causer. I believe you've had a bit of a falling out with our Kate?'

'Just a touch, yes,' Danny said. 'I'm lying low at the moment. Has she cooled off a bit?'

'Not as such, lad. Not as such. I believe you've met Jenny Seddon, formerly of the Derbyshire Con-stab-u-lary.'

'I met Jennifer the volunteer at the hospital, yes. Then I got a little glimpse of Jenny Seddon Supercop outside her house. Watch your arm there, John. She'll have it up your back before you can say unnecessary force.'

'He's safe from me, Danny,' she said, patting Smithdown's hand. 'It's nice to meet you properly.'

'I'm so sorry about your son Karl,' Danny said. 'I think that under different circumstances, me and him would have got on pretty well. He couldn't let things go, could he? I get that.'

'Thank you,' Jenny said. 'That's kind. I'm sorry for all the… you know… cloak and dagger malarkey. When I spotted John at the hospital, I was worried how it would look… with the family connection to the Hanging Lees investigation. So, I thought I'd just keep an eye on him from a distance. I've been volunteering at hospitals for years. Since I retired from the police, in fact. And like a pair of old dafties, we haven't spoken properly in ages, have we, John?'

'We haven't,' he said. 'Stupid, really. After all the stuff we went through in the 80s, we just…I don't know. I thought she wouldn't want to see me after what happened to her Brian out on Kinder. I thought she blamed me.'

'I never did, John,' she replied. Both her hands were now tightly gripped around Smithdown's. 'Not once. Not ever. I know who killed my Brian. It wasn't you. You saved lives that night out on Kinder. I know you had your own battles to fight. GMP wanted you gone. You fought them and won. I left you to it. I thought I was doing the right thing. I wasn't. We were both as daft as each other.'

'That's not true, Jenny,' Smithdown said. 'You're far dafter than I am.'

'Right, well I'm sorry to break up this *Cocoon* sequel, but there's a few things I want to ask you, John. You can probably help too, Jenny.'

'I'll try,' she said.

'One thing I've learned in the last few days is that there's quite enough nonces in Oldham as it is, without adding the name John Smithdown to the list. As it happens, I'm having a little rest from the vigilante murders. So, I'm going to use my time wisely and do some more digging on Hanging Lees. I'll have another crack at some people who knew Maggie Ormrod. Find out more about her. I also need to find out more about you, John.'

'I don't like the sound of that,' Smithdown said.

Danny took out his phone and showed them the picture of Smithdown and Maggie Ormrod. 'It's definitely you, John,' Jenny said, looking at the photo. 'That's not terribly helpful, is it?'

'It is, actually,' Danny said. 'We know *who* is in the picture: John and Maggie. That means the remaining questions are… *where*, *when* and *why*. Plus, *what* the hell drove Maggie Ormrod to take her life now? Just before all this vigilante stuff kicks off. That is what's known as…'

'… a fucking coincidence,' Jenny and Smithdown said together.

'TFC. Exactly. We need to know more about this photo, more about where it was taken and why.'

'There's another "who" to add to your list, Danny,' Jenny said. That's… who took the photo.'

'And why,' agreed Danny.

'I've tried and tried,' Smithdown said. 'But I can't remember anything about that picture. It's obviously me. I accept that. But I just can't recall it being taken.'

'I brought this,' Jenny said, showing Danny a shoebox on the table next to Smithdown's armchair. 'I thought it might get his old brainbox working a bit.'

'Good idea, Jenny.' Danny looked inside the box. In it were press cuttings about the Mermaid's Pool case, along with several audio cassettes.

'Has it worked?' Danny asked.

'Not so far,' Jenny sighed. 'Why don't you take it, Danny? See if anything is of use.'

'I will. Thank you, Jenny. See, John? That's what a proper copper looks like. Watch and learn.'

'Fuck off with you,' Smithdown said.

Danny smiled at Jenny. 'The charm never fades, does it? Thanks for this. I'll take a look. I'll leave you to it.'

'I'll see you out, Danny,' Jenny said.

'Great. See you later John.'

'Danny?' the retired detective said as he headed for the door. 'You smell like a dead tramp, by the way.'

'So I believe, John. Long story. Speak to you tomorrow.'

As they got to the front door, Jenny placed a hand on Danny's arm. 'I know one person you could speak to. I didn't want to mention it in front of John. Didn't want to upset him. It'll take a while to get to him but if anyone knows what went on at Oldham Police back in the day, it'll be him.' She took a cutting from the box and showed it to Danny, placing a finger on a yellowy photo from the *Manchester Evening News*. 'Him. Speak to him. It won't be easy. But try. If anyone knows about John Smithdown's past, he does.'

FORTY-FOUR

It had taken Danny a good 20 minutes to find the cassette player he knew was stashed in a box of unwanted chargers and TV scart leads in his loft. It was an ugly red twin-deck and until he plugged it in, he wasn't entirely convinced it would actually work.

He took the audio tape from the shoebox Jenny had given him. The neat handwriting on the inlay card said:

9am Manchester Radio News, Sunday 1 April 1990.

Well, I certainly remember that date. It's the day the Strangeways riot started. The biggest British prison disturbance of the 20th century. But the trouble didn't start until lunchtime.

He put the cassette in and pressed play. The tape wobbled and wowed then settled:

"Radio Manchester News at nine, this is Beth Hall.

A policeman, hailed a hero after his part in exposing the neo-Nazi infiltration of Oldham Police, is set to return to work tomorrow after spending nearly two years on suspension.

Detective Inspector John Smithdown was told to step down from his duties over allegations that he harmed a child in his custody. But an internal Greater Manchester Police inquiry has found that there is no case to answer.

The investigation had to be put on hold until the end of the so-called 'Nazi Cops' trial. Several Oldham police officers, including Detective Constable Bob Donaldson, were finally jailed on Thursday for their part in a string of murders and racist attacks.

Danny Johnston reports..."

"What started as a murder inquiry into the disappearance of sex worker Naomi Wells in April 1988, turned into one of the biggest police scandals Manchester has ever seen.

Officers from Oldham Police were found to have conspired with neo-Nazi groups to seize power on the local council by any means possible - that included murder, kidnapping and inciting a riot. Their aim was to provoke a race war to push an extremist, racist agenda. Nine people are now serving life sentences for their parts in the plot - six were serving police officers, including Mr Smithdown's former colleague, Detective Constable Bob Donaldson.

Donaldson, along with neo-Nazi activist Tom Lennon, staged a series of murders and attacks to further their aim of generating a backlash against South Asian communities in Oldham. Their ultimate goal was grabbing political power and making money from land sales brought about by forced repatriation.

DI Smithdown is now in line for a police bravery award for his actions in exposing the plot, alongside DC Jennifer Seddon of the Derbyshire Constabulary.

After the initial arrests of DC Donaldson and several of his colleagues, Greater Manchester Police promised what was described as a 'root and branch' investigation into further links between its officers and neo-Nazi groups. So far, no other officers have been suspended and GMP describe the 'Nazi Cops' case as a one-off incident.

Danny Johnston, Manchester Radio News, at GMP Headquarters in Old Trafford."

My God, I sound about nine years old. I don't even remember doing that story. It was probably just a script shoved under my nose. Voice that up, Danny, we've got no one else to record the script, you'll have to do. The day the Strangeways riot started; the day before the boy's body was found at Back Moss. Half a lifetime ago.

FORTY-FIVE

That night, Danny did something he hadn't done for a very long time: he dreamed he was back at Strangeways Prison.

The Home Office preferred the jail to be known as Her Majesty's Prison Manchester, but no one used that name. It was and would always be called after the area of Manchester it was housed in… Strangeways.

It was dark and Danny was standing next to the perimeter fence. He could hear the prisoners inside the jail shouting; they were knocking down walls, smashing their way towards E Wing where the sex offenders were housed. They chanted as they got closer and closer: 'BEASTS! BEASTS! BEASTS, BEASTS, BEASTS!'

Two or three silhouettes could be seen, trotting nimbly across the roof of the jail towards the main rotunda. There were helicopters above and jets of water shot across the buildings as a series of fires burned brightly in the night sky. The riot was in full swing. It was 1990 but Danny wasn't young. He was middle-aged.

He saw a woman in her late 30s. Her hair, bleached white but with jet black roots, was pulled back from her face with a large elastic band. She wore an oversized black cardigan and the fingers of one of her hands were gripping the mesh of the fence and she was staring at the roof. The other hand was holding onto a boy of about ten. Danny didn't look at him. He didn't need to. He knew who it was.

'Hi,' Danny heard himself asking the woman. 'I'm sorry to bother you. I'm from Manchester Radio and I was wondering if I could ask you when you think this is all going to end.'

She didn't turn to look at Danny. 'Wouldn't you be better off asking how it all started?' she said.

'Sorry?'

'How it started,' she repeated, still looking at the jail. 'Rather than playing a stupid guessing game about when I think it will end, why not ask how it started. Why not ask about that?'

'I'm sure that will all come out once it's all over,' Danny said, slightly regretting his choice of interviewee.

'Are you sure?' the woman asked.

'Yes. I'm sure. So, when do you think this will end?'

The woman looked at Danny. Her face was so pale it looked unreal, like she was wearing stage make up. 'Not long now,' she stated as if it was the most obvious thing in the world. 'It'll soon all be over. I think so, anyway. What do you think?'

'Yes, I think so too,' Danny agreed.

Danny could hear a rattling sound; the perimeter fence was shaking. Just slightly to start with, but the rattling was getting louder and louder.

'I wasn't asking you,' the woman pointed out. 'I was asking the boy. He knows. Don't you?'

The Shirtless Boy stopped shaking the fence. Then he turned and smiled at Danny. A terrible, eyeless smile.

FORTY-SIX

Danny was led into the wigwam-shaped visitors centre at Strangeways and his fingerprints were scanned. His ID was checked - he'd spent a good 20 minutes looking for his passport that morning - and his clothes were given the once over. *No watches, sunglasses, fluorescent tops, key chains or ripped clothing; no clothes with football or gang slogans or clothes with racist or bad language on them; no diaries, bank cards or sunglasses; no see-through or revealing clothing, or crop tops that reveal the stomach. Those are the rules.*

Danny was allowed to take his passport, his locker key and £20 in cash into the main body of the jail, plus the appropriate clothing he was standing up in. Everything else was stashed in a locker.

He went through an airport-style scanner, putting his jacket and shoes into a tray. He was hand-searched - very thoroughly - got a stamp on the back of his hand like he was getting a pass out of a nightclub and then a prison search dog gave him a thorough sniffing before moving on to another visitor. His hand stamp was checked under an ultraviolet light, then he pressed his finger onto a biometric scanner before the last gates opened and Danny finally gained access to the visitors' hall.

It was large and relatively new looking; there were tables with chairs attached to them that were bolted to the floor. On the walls were examples of prisoners' art. There was a canteen and a shop as well as a children's play area; no children today though, that was only at weekends.

Danny sat and waited at one of the tables. He nodded to a middle-aged couple on the next table. 'First time is it?' the man asked him. Danny nodded. 'How are you liking it so far?'

'Not the best hotel I've ever been to,' Danny replied. 'The security's a bit over the top, isn't it?'

'You'll get used to it,' the man laughed.

I bloody hope not, thought Danny.

The prisoners arrived; dressed in various combinations of jeans, jogging trousers, plain t-shirts and sweatshirts, their pale, dejected-looking faces lit up just a little when they saw their loved ones. One face, however, remained defiantly unchanged - that of John Smithdown's former colleague, ex-Detective Constable Bob Donaldson.

He walked slowly but steadily towards Danny's table. He compared what he saw in front of him with the faded pictures he'd studied from Jenny Seddon's box of cuttings. For a man in his 80s he moved and looked reasonably well. His face was gaunt, pinched and expressionless; he'd lost his hair on top, but it was long at the back and sides, and he was wearing large, black-rimmed glasses.

Donaldson sat down: 'Tea with two sugars, a couple of Mars bars and a comfort pack,' Donaldson stated.

Danny looked at him. 'Chop chop, I haven't got all day, you know,' Donaldson said, as if Danny was a child having to be shown the most basic of tasks. Then he did something that Danny didn't like one little bit - he winked and smiled.

Danny did as he was asked and returned a few minutes later.

'The comfort pack gets delivered to you later, I believe,' Danny said.

'It does indeed,' the old man muttered. 'A few sweet treats and home comforts. I'll be thinking of you when I open it later.'

Then Donaldson opened both of the Mars Bars and ate them each in two bites. 'Tiny these are,' he complained. 'Not like they used to be. A Mars a day helps you work, rest and play. That was the old slogan. Remember that? Barely big enough to get stuck between your teeth these days.'

'Thank you for seeing me, Mr Donaldson,' Danny said, trying to keep his tone quiet and business-like. 'I know you didn't have to.'

'I was intrigued,' Donaldson said, screwing up the Mars wrappers into one, tight length then tying it into knot. 'Bored, obviously. Boredom is the *lingua franca* in here. Not a lot to occupy my time. And, as I'm sure you're aware, I've been inside for a great deal of time. But intrigued too.'

'An ex-cop inside Strangeways?' Danny said. 'I'm amazed you've lasted this long.'

'Well, you'd be surprised,' Donaldson said, putting out his hands in a friendly, open gesture. 'Yes, there has been the odd person that's taken slight offence to me being a former police officer. People can be a bit sniffy about that sort of thing in here. But there's also been plenty of others who have wanted to protect me. And it's thanks to them that I'm still here today… having a lovely chat with you.'

'What kind of people? Racists? Neo Nazis?'

'I'd prefer to think of them as like-minded souls. Anyway, the first ten years inside were… tricky. Yes, that's fair to say. Challenging they were… on a day-to-day basis. I was stabbed on three separate occasions in one year. Three times, eh? That's persistence for you. But after that, things calmed down a little. I've had no bother for a long time. We've got our own little bit of the jail, you know, us senior citizens. Our own little slice of OAP paradise in H Wing. It's a bit different to the rest of Strangeways. It's like an old folks' home. Less stairs, but more toilets. Ha ha! The staff, the gen pop… that's the wider prison population to you… they just leave us to it. They don't really bother with us. We're invisible. What do they think we're going to do… start a riot?'

'That's been done,' Danny pointed out. 'Prison riots are a bit like Mars bars. Better in the old days.'

'True. Very true. So, I got your message and approved your visit via the Unilink system. And here we are. So… what do you want?'

'I wanted to ask you about John Smithdown,' Danny said.

'John Boy! Is he still with us?'

'Yes, he is. Very much so. A great dad, a wonderful grandad, and a fantastic friend… a proper, decorated police hero too. He's loved Mr Donaldson. In fact, he's all the things you're not.'

'Less of the attitude, lad, if you don't mind.'

'You're a racist murderer, Mr Donaldson. You'll forgive me if I don't treat you like Nelson Mandela.'

Donaldson slurped his tea. 'What do you want, Mr Danny Johnston?'

'I sent you a picture in advance,' Danny said. 'Did it clear security?'

Donaldson produced a folded piece of paper. It was a printout of the picture showing John Smithdown with his arm around Maggie Ormrod. Donaldson waved it at Danny then placed it on the table.

'Who took that picture?' Danny asked.

Donaldson barely glimpsed at it. 'I did,' he smiled. 'I remember it well.'

'What can you tell me about it?'

Donaldson looked again. 'It was taken at Oldham nick. Mid-70s by the look of it. All shiny and new it was, look how white the walls are. John was showing this young girl around and he wanted a snap taking. He asked me to take it. So… I took it. In those days we got the police photographic unit to develop all our pics for free; perk of the job, if you like.'

'Did you know Maggie, the girl in the picture?'

'Didn't know she was called Maggie until you told me just then,' Donaldson replied.

'You're in prison, not on a desert island, Mr Donaldson. You have access to news.'

'News doesn't really interest me, Danny Johnston. Very one-sided in my experience.'

'Maggie Ormrod. Ex-care home kid. I've been trying to trace her records, but everywhere I go, her file is missing. Or there's been a fire. Funny that. She killed herself out at Hanging Lees reservoir the other week. She left a note saying she'd been abused as a child. I want to know who did it to her. John Smithdown says it wasn't him. And I believe him.'

'Do you, now? Well, John asked me to take that picture, so I did. That's all I know. He seemed to like showing people around. Mainly kids. Waifs and strays, that sort. I never pried. Perhaps he thought taking them around the police station and showing them the cells was better than giving them a clip round the ear. Personally, I've always been a big fan of a good clip round the ear, but there you go. What's your interest?'

'I'm interested because John Smithdown is my friend,' Danny said. 'And I want to make sure I've covered every possibility when it comes to investigating the real story behind this picture. Even coming here to see you.'

'No one's stopping you from leaving, lad. You know where the door is. Don't forget to shut it on your way out.'

Danny stood up and searched for his locker key. 'Kate's doing well, by the way… John's daughter. You remember Kate. The one you tried to kill in the 80s. That Kate.'

For the first time since he had entered the visitors' area, Danny provoked a real reaction from Bob Donaldson. His grey face flushed and he bared his uniform, false-looking teeth.

'Yeah, sold off her businesses for a fat load of cash,' Danny continued. 'Lady of leisure now. She's just like her dad, though… a proper hero. She saved my arse out at Black Moss a few years back, I can tell you.'

'Black Moss, eh?' said Donaldson. He was smiling again now. 'There are some real secrets out there, Danny Johnston, believe you me. If only those moors could talk.'

'Maybe they can, Mr Donaldson,' Danny said. He snatched the photo from the table and put it in his pocket. 'Have a nice life.'

FORTY-SEVEN

6 April 1975

'I've never seen an AH-AH film before,' Maggie said as they found a seat in the semi-darkness of the cinema.

'Double A,' he said. 'It's called a Double A film. And I should think not, you're supposed to be fourteen to see one. They only let you in because you're with me.'

He took off his overcoat, folded it several times and placed it on Maggie's seat. She looked at him, puzzled. 'Sit on it… It'll make you little a bit taller,' he whispered, tapping the side of his nose as if he was passing on a vital piece of information she could use again at a later date.

She smiled and sat down: 'It's not gunna be dead scary, is it?'

'No. I don't think so. Not really. Maybe bits of it.'

The familiar brassy stabs of the Pearl and Dean music blasted across the speaker, signalling the start of the pre-film advertisements. 'I love this tune,' Maggie said, jigging in her seat. 'It makes me happy. Pa-Pa Pa-Pa Pa-Pa Pa-Pa Pa Pa Paaaar…'

'Shhh. Not so loud. Here, have one of these.' He pulled out three packets of Payne's Poppets and shook them. The small, rectangular packets made a satisfying little chik chik sound as the small, round chocolates rattled around. 'Orange, toffee or mint?'

'I like toffee,' Maggie said. 'And I like the orange ones too. I like all of em.'

'Well, you might as well have them all, then,' he said with a sigh.

'Ta very much,' she said in a loud, excited voice.

He put a finger to his lips to indicate she was being too loud again. 'Do you know why they sell these in cinemas?' he asked, handing her all three of the pocket-sized boxes of Payne's Poppets.

'I 'spose cos they're right tasty.'

'Well, yes. There is that. But there's another reason… listen.'

He cupped a hand to his ear. All around them were the sounds of people eating snacks in the cinema. Cellophane-wrapped packets of sweets were being tugged open; boiled sweets were being unwrapped, crisps were being munched and Butterkist popcorn bags were being dug into and crunched.

The policeman took one of the packets from Maggie's lap and popped open the hatch at the corner of the box. He took hold of Maggie's hand and tipped several of the chocolates into her hand. 'See? No noise…These are the best kind because they're dead quiet.'

He smiled, took one of the sweets from Maggie's hand and popped it onto his mouth.

FORTY-EIGHT

Danny looked at the poster he had made. The two faces of Maggie Ormrod looked back at him: Maggie as an adult holding her neighbour's cat, and Maggie as a young girl at Oldham Police station. He'd cut John Smithdown out of the 1970s photo, then put both of the pictures of Maggie side by side above the text he'd written:

DID YOU KNOW MAGGIE ORMROD?

MAGGIE WAS IN CHILDRENS' HOMES AROUND OLDHAM IN THE 1970S.

SHE LIVED ON DENSHAW ROAD CLOSE TO HANGING LEES RESERVOIR.

SHE WORKED AS A CLEANER

.

DID YOU KNOW HER – PARTICULARLY WHEN SHE WAS A GIRL?

CONTACT DANNY JOHNSTON AT OLDHAM NOW
danny@oldhamnow.net
www.oldhamnow.net

Danny had already been to Hanging Lees Reservoir, taping posters to the car park sign that housed a map to the footpaths and waterways of the Piethorne Valley. He'd also attached one to the ornate metal gate at Hanging Lees itself, just yards from where Maggie's body was found. They seemed to be the logical places to put them.

But something pulled at him. Partly it was the dreams he'd been having, the terrible visions of The Shirtless Boy. But some of it was Bob Donaldson's reaction back at Strangeways. *Winding him up about what a loser he was, that seemed to make him drop his guard a little… There are some secrets out there, Danny Johnston, believe you me. Fuck me, some real secrets. If only those moors could talk… that's what he said.*

Danny took his remaining posters and drove over to Black Moss Reservoir.

He pulled into the car park at Brun Clough and headed up the path that formed the Pennine Way. Danny was fond of pointing out to people that it had been a journalist who'd come up with the idea of the Pennine Way, the 268-mile path that connected the Peak District with the Scottish borders. *Tom Stephenson… he wrote an article about the idea in the Daily Herald in 1935. Thirty years later it was opened. See, journalists are good for something.*

Standing on the paved footpath that led past Redbrook Reservoir and onto Black Moss, he remembered being on the same spot in 1990, trying to interview a very reluctant DI John Smithdown. He remembered how cold he'd been in his thin shirt and cheap jacket. He remembered the way the two uniformed officers had let the sheet slip in the wind, revealing the puffy white body of a little boy dressed in a pair of shorts. And he remembered the piece he'd filed for Manchester Radio.

"A child's body has been found close to a reservoir on the outskirts of Oldham. The grim discovery was made in the early hours of this morning. Murder squad detectives have sealed off the area close to the main A62 road at Diggle. From the scene Danny Johnston has this exclusive report.

The body of the child, thought to be about nine years old, was found at the edge of Black Moss Reservoir a few miles outside of Diggle. Officers are now sealing off the scene. Detective Inspector John Smithdown is in charge of the operation… 'At approximately 5.30 am this morning the body of a juvenile male was discovered by a man out walking his dog. The area is currently being sealed off and a fingertip search of the scene will commence shortly. The age and identity of the juvenile male are not yet known, and I have no further details to give at this present moment in time.'

Forensic teams have arrived at the scene, and murder squad officers are now overseeing the removal of the child's body before a postmortem examination can reveal the cause of his death.

Danny Johnston, Manchester Radio News, at Black Moss Reservoir."

Danny taped a poster to the gate which led to the reservoir itself, took a photo of it and walked down the slope. The mini beach at the water's edge looked smaller than he remembered. The day was bright and the sky a clear blue, but Black Moss stubbornly refused to shift from its favoured tone of dull, peaty grey. Danny looked around; there was nothing to attach any more posters to. No trees, no signposts, no information boards. Nothing. Just a cold slab of water called Black Moss.

The light moorland wind moved the surface of the water in a series of tight zig-zags. Danny looked around; he saw someone across the other side of the water. A lone figure in a light brown anorak. No one else.

He'd always loved the bleakness of the moors, the nothingness that allowed you to fill in your own version of beauty. But today the very emptiness that normally drew him in made him feel uneasy and unwelcome.

Danny found a rock and used it to weigh down his remaining posters on the path that stretched across the flat, front end of the reservoir. Then he left as quickly as he could.

FORTY-NINE

Danny sat in his at the reservoir car park, clumsily entering text and pictures into his phone. Using the photos he'd taken of his DO YOU KNOW MAGGIE ORMROD? posters, Danny pressed 'publish' on the appeal story for the *Oldham Now* website when he received a text from an unknown number. *Fuck. Here we go again.*

But the message wasn't another vigilante tip-off; it was a plea for help.

<Danny. It's Jenny. You'd better come to the hospital ASAP. Ward T4. There's trouble and you might be able to help before the police are called.>

What the fuck is that all about?

He had learned several things about Jenny Seddon in the week that he'd known her. One of them was this: she was a woman to be taken seriously. *If she thinks I can help, then I'd better get my arse down there sharpish.*

Visiting hours were just ending as Danny made his way through the last of the people who'd come to see friends and relatives. He saw Jenny standing next to the admissions desk. She raised a hand to him and then pointed to her ear, then down the corridor that ran to her left, indicating that he should keep quiet and listen.

'WILL YOU FUCKING LISTEN TO ME?' a voice screamed. 'PLEEEEEEASE? THE FUCKING PAIN! I CAN'T STAND IT ANY MORE. I MEAN IT. GIVE ME SOMETHING OR FUCKING KILL ME. I MEAN IT. I CAN'T STAND IT. PUT ME OUT OF MY FUCKING MISERY. JESUS CHRIST! I THOUGHT THIS WAS A HOSPITAL! PLEASE, WILL SOMEBODY HELP ME?'

Danny looked around the corridor corner; the shouting was coming from behind a screened-off bed. Then he heard another voice: quieter, calmer, more familiar. 'Please, mate… let's just go. Come on. Let's get you back.'

Danny put a hand on Jenny's shoulder. 'What's going on?'

'Hospital jumper,' she said.

'What?' Danny asked, as something crashed to the floor behind the curtain with a metallic clang.

'Jumpers,' she repeated over the noise. 'They go from hospital to hospital, trying to get prescribed painkillers… Putting it on that they're in terrible pain and that they're dying. He's probably already been to Fairfield or to Tameside.'

'PLEEEEASE GOD, JUST GIVE ME SOMETHING. ANYTHING. YOU PEOPLE ARE SUPPOSED TO HELP, FOR FUCK'S SAKE! I'M DYING HERE AND YOU'RE DOING NOWT!'

'I see,' Danny said, raising his voice over the din. 'That's a new one on me. Not sure how I can help though.'

The curtain was pulled back and a harassed-looking nurse in her mid-20s appeared. Through the gap Danny could see there were two young men in the cubicle. One was Josh, the aspiring journalist from Hunter's Hollow; he was doing all the shouting. The other was Jonathan Smithdown. He was doing the peace-making. The teenager made eye contact with Danny just before the curtain swished closed again.

'Oh, for fuck's sake,' Danny sighed.

'Exactly,' Jenny said. 'I recognised Jonathan from all the photos of him at Smithdown's house. If they don't leave in a minute the police will get called. And young Jonathan seems to be a bit of a bystander here. So, if you could help get them both out of here, we might avert a bit of a situation. The last thing the Smithdown family needs at the moment is for the lad to get banged up.'

'I can but try,' Danny said. 'But Josh seems pretty amped up.'

'All jumpers seem pretty amped up, Danny,' she said. 'That's the idea.'

Jenny spoke to the nurse, pointed to Danny and then at the cubicle; then she waved him over. He passed through the curtains; Josh was lying on the bed holding his sides around his lowers ribs and moaning and swearing.

'Hey, Josh,' Danny said, trying to be heard over the shouting. 'What's all the commotion?' Jenny and the nurse were standing just behind him.

'You a fucking doctor?' Josh asked, his face buried in a pillow.

'No, I'm the fucker who's going to try to stop you pair of dickheads getting arrested,' Danny said. 'Jonathan, what are you playing at?'

'Danny… shit,' Jonathan said. 'Josh, it's not a doctor, it's Danny.'

Danny expected Jonathan to be angry or defensive, or in denial. Instead, the teenager looked almost relieved that he was here. 'I didn't know he was going to go mad, Danny,' Jonathan said. 'He told me he just had bad guts. Then we got in here and he went mental.'

'Bad guts?' Danny queried. 'Well, he's definitely full of shit, Jonathan, I'll give him that. Okay, we need to knock this on the head right now.'

Danny kneeled down so his face was level with Josh's. The young man's face was knotted with apparent pain, his eyes were closed and a low howl came from his lips. 'Listen to me, Josh,' Danny said. 'You have three seconds to get your arse off this bed and out of the door. Otherwise I'll take Jonathan here back to Hunter's Hollow and leave you here. Do you know what'll happen next? Well, that woman there with the grey hair - she's called Jenny - she will push your arm so far up your back you'll be able to wave to yourself. Then she'll fucking Ninja you from here to Chadderton and back. Then she'll hand you over to the cops. Her son's a cop… so him and all his cop mates will be really rather cross with you. So they'll probably take great pleasure in kicking your kidneys out down at the local police station. If you think you're in pain now, just imagine what you'll feel like then...'

Josh looked at him. The grimace fell quickly from his face. The moaning stopped. 'What do you think?' Danny whispered. 'Back to Hunter's Hollow right now, or watching your kidneys flopping about on the cell floor of Oldham nick?'

Jonathan spoke: 'He's right, Josh. Come on, let's go. Please.'

'Listen to him, Josh,' Danny said. 'He's clearly the brains of the operation. I'll even give you a lift back if you like. Then we can let these good folks get on with helping people who are really sick. Rather than throwing pills at the likes of you… just to make you shut the fuck up.'

Josh looked at Danny and then at Jonathan. Then he leant to one side to see the expression on Jenny Seddon's face. She nodded her confirmation that everything that had just been said would definitely happen.

Josh sat up and swung his legs around to the edge of the bed: 'Can we stop for a McDonald's on the way back?' he asked.

FIFTY

'Danny, thank you so much for what you did,' Susan said as she and Ben Matlock walked Danny to his car outside the school. 'And thank Jenny from the hospital for us as well.'

'Absolutely,' Ben agreed. 'That was a tricky call, but we're so glad she made it.'

'I'll tell you what, Josh deserves a BAFTA for his acting work tonight,' Danny said. 'He pretty much convinced me he was on his way to Oldham Crematorium. A stellar performance. Hospital jumpers, eh? You learn something new every day.'

'We've tried so hard to keep Josh out of the criminal system,' Ben explained. 'He's 16, for God's sake. Another product of adult abuse. That's why he's here. He's a victim and his problems are too complex for the mainstream structure to understand. Criminal detention would probably be the end of him. You and Jenny probably saved his life tonight. I mean it.'

'What about Jonathan?' Danny asked.

'Oh, he's about to get a punishment far worse than mere incarceration,' Susan said as Kate Smithdown's car came up the Hunter's Hollow driveway. 'I wouldn't wish it on my worst enemy…'

Kate's car stopped. She got out and gave the door a very robust slam. 'Where is he, Susan?' she asked, ignoring Danny completely.

'He's inside,' Susan said. 'Me and Ben were just thanking Danny for what he did. You would have been visiting Jonathan at Oldham Police Station if it weren't for him.'

Kate still didn't look at Danny and made no response. 'Right, well I'll take you to him, Kate,' Ben said with a smile. 'He's fine. Bit shaken up, but fine. I think he's definitely learned something tonight, hasn't he Mum?'

'Oh yes. We all have, haven't we Danny?'

'Yes,' Danny agreed. 'I should do a piece about it, show the kind of stuff that hospital staff have to put up with.'

Again, Kate ignored him. 'I'll see you inside, Susan,' she said. 'Lead on, Ben.'

'You're welcome, Kate,' Danny said as Kate and Ben walked towards the main entrance.

'I'm still not taking to you, dickhead,' Kate shouted. She carried on walking.

Danny tried again: 'Kate, you'll never guess who I went to see…'

'Don't care!' she said and went through the main doors of the school.

Danny smiled awkwardly at Susan. 'That went better than I was expecting if I'm honest,' he said.

'Hate to see what things would be like if it went badly,' Susan replied. 'Can't work out who she's more annoyed with… you or Jonathan. What on earth went on between you two?'

'Just me being an insensitive arsehole,' he sighed. 'As usual. It'll all blow over. Nothing that a bit of time won't heal. About 90 years should do it.'

'Oh dear,' Susan said, rubbing Danny's arm. 'Listen, I'd better go. Thanks again for what you did. I mean it. You're a good un, Danny Johnston.'

Susan leant in, apparently to hug Danny and press her cheek against his as she had done before. Danny did the same. At the last second, she turned her head and kissed him very quickly on the lips. Danny was so shocked he stepped back sharply and almost slipped on the gravel path.

'Okaygottagobye,' Susan said, and half walked, half ran to the school's main entrance. Danny watched as she punched in the key code on the front door and went inside. Then, Susan looked back, pulled an 'Ooooh' face at him and then gave a smile and a wave. Then she was gone.

Fucking Nora.

Danny made his way back to his car; it looked very battered next to Kate's gleaming Mercedes that was parked next to it. As he dug around in his pockets for his keys, he heard a tapping sound. John Smithdown was sitting in the passenger seat of Kate's car, trying to get his attention. As Danny approached the car, the electric window slid down: 'You dirty bastard,' Smithdown said. 'I saw you.'

'I think it's fair to say it's YOU who's the dirty bastard in this scenario,' Danny pointed out. 'Spying on people in the dark… I should call the police.'

'I believe the police were narrowly avoided this evening, thanks to you and Jenny,' Smithdown said.

'Looks that way. Not that I'll get anything resembling a thank you from your daughter, though. It appears that I'm still very much on the shit list. Anyway, what are you doing, sitting here like Piffy on a rock bun?'

'I just thought I'd let Kate get on with bollocking young Jonathan. Plus, I don't care for all the stairs in there.'

'Fair enough. Not going to be pretty, is it?'

'Fucking brutal,' Smithdown said. 'What've you been up to?'

Danny wanted to tell him about his encounter with Bob Donaldson but thought better of it. Nothing that Smithdown's former colleague said during their encounter had really helped matters. In some ways, it had made things worse. *He's never coming out of Strangeways, he's got nothing to gain from lying. But, all that stuff Donaldson said about Smithdown and his waifs and strays. Grim.*

'I've been putting posters up at Hanging Lees about Maggie Ormrod,' Danny said. 'That's what I've been up to. Not everyone's on the internet. You never know. I left some at Black Moss as well.'

'Why did you do that?' Smithdown asked.

'Honestly? Not sure. It just seemed like… I don't know, a good idea.'

'Hmm… I think you're going a bit weird in your old age, Danny.'

'Coming from you, that's quite the observation. What about you?'

Smithdown didn't reply. His attention seemed to have wandered off elsewhere; he seemed to be transfixed by something in the rear-view mirror of Kate's car.

'Helloooo? Danny calling space cadet Smithdown. Are you receiving me?'

'I am, Danny. Loud and clear.' Smithdown tapped the mirror. 'I was just wondering what these fuckers are up to…'

Danny turned to see what Smithdown was looking at in the mirror. On the ridge to the east of the school was a fast-moving line of lights. From down below they looked like a shiny snake, swerving and bouncing across the edge of the moor. They were shimmering their way west towards the motorway. 'Motorbikes, John?' Danny asked.

Smithdown thought for a moment. 'Looks like it, Danny lad. Scramble bikes, maybe. Good way to get across the moors. You don't have to worry about roads and paths. You can just go straight from A to B. No messing.'

'Absolutely, John,' Danny said, following the lights as they ran parallel to the school. 'No messing. I'll speak to you later.'

Danny got into his car and drove as fast as its worn-out engine would take it. He left the road that led up to the school, clipping the stone-mounted sign on the way out with his front wing. He cut across the busy Standedge Road, then drove at high speed through the village of Diggle, winning himself a cheer from a group of teenagers outside the local chip shop for driving so fast.

The bouncing line of moorland lights was still clearly visible on his left; Danny took out his phone and managed to get a few seconds of video just before he crossed the small bridge over the Huddersfield canal with a harsh clang. *What the fuck are you lot doing?*

The village road gave way to lanes and then tracks as the hedgerows on either side of the car got closer and closer to Danny's windows. Any ambient light had now disappeared; the car's headlights were the only thing cutting through the darkness of the moors. As he passed what looked like a derelict hunting lodge Danny realised he had absolutely no idea where the track led to. *You didn't really think this through, did you?*

He looked to his left as he slowed and then came to a stop; the dancing lights had disappeared. The track ended at what looked like some abandoned reservoir workings. The moor rose steadily ahead of him and there was little by way of turning room. As he turned in his seat to start manoeuvring his way backwards out of the dead end, he saw a bank of lights behind him; the bikes were blocking his exit. *Fuck!*

He waited.

One by one, the engine noises he could hear cut out and fell silent. There were just the lights now, dazzling him so he couldn't see who was on the bikes. Then the lights were extinguished.

Danny looked left and right across the moors that surrounded him on three sides. The silent stand-off continued for another 30 seconds. 'Bollocks to this,' he said and was about to put his car into reverse when a cluster of bricks, held together by concrete, came flying towards him and crashed through his rear window, hitting the back of his seat. The headrest took most of the force but the remaining impact on the side of Danny's face was enough to make him shout out in pain.

He drove backwards as quickly as he could back up the track towards the bikes. He got within 20 feet of where he thought they were before he slid backwards into a ditch, tilting the car at a 45-degree angle as it came to a stop. The driver's side door was now blocked by the hags and broom bushes that ran alongside the track. Danny could hear the sound of shouts and laughter; he could also hear feet scrambling across the side of his car. The passenger side door was now above him; Danny looked up just as another lump of brick and concrete smashed through the window. Thousands of tiny chunks of glass showered down onto him. He covered his head with his hands to brace against the impact of the bricks and concrete he expected to follow the glass, but it didn't come. The side window was too small, and the lump had jammed in the frame.

Danny unfastened his seatbelt, twisted himself around and clambered into the back seat. Above him, one of the attackers was now jumping on the concrete block, trying to stamp it through the window frame. He looked around for something to defend himself with. There were plenty of takeaway cartons, empty cans of coke and bits of paper, but not much else. The best he could find was a can of de-icer spray.

He climbed up the back set and managed to push open the rear door that was now facing the starless night sky. Danny leant through his car's door frame and rammed the end of the de-icer tin into the shin of the biker who was standing on his car. A highly satisfying scream resulted, and the attacker fell forwards, hit his face on the side of the car and then bounced into the ditch on the other side of the path.

Danny pulled himself through the open car door and ran into the dense gorse that surrounded the path. Just as he got clear, a shower of half bricks and concrete lumps rat-a-tatted onto his car, breaking the remaining windows and wing mirrors and peppering the bushes around him like gunfire. He lay on the ground and waited for a few beats before moving forwards on his elbows. The jaggy gorse thorns pulled and pinched at him as he crawled along the damp ground. He could hear random, indistinct shouts and instructions all around him; the biker he hit with the can was still screaming.

Danny worked his way away from his car on his belly before turning left; he was now moving parallel to the path, trying to get behind his attackers as they swarmed around his car. The sound of his car being comprehensively trashed grew louder, then suddenly stopped. There was silence for a few seconds, then a few shouts. Danny sensed the bushes behind him moving with increasing energy. Then the gorse shook either side of him. And then stopped. Everything was still. *They've sussed me out. Fuck.*

Danny found a piece of brick and a small chunk of concrete. He took them in his hands, tapped them together for good luck - *ridiculous thing to do* - and got to his knees. *Time to find out if you really are one of the world's worst fighters, Danny lad.*

Danny then stood up and shouted, 'FUCKING COME ON THEN!' Just as he did this the track and surrounding moor was lit up by two powerful beams of light coming from down the track. Danny was blinded by the light but could hear shouts and commands, plus the sound of revving engines.

Then the lights dipped to a more manageable level, allowing him to see what was going on. There was now a Land Rover parked near to where his car had gone into the ditch. Susan got out of the driver's side; Kate put her head out of the passenger window. Both looked at him as if he'd just crash landed from another planet.

Danny, his face dirty and scratched, was standing waist-high in a gorse bush with lumps of brick and concrete in each hand. His eyes were wide with fear and confusion.

'Oi, Rambo,' Kate shouted. 'What the fuck are you doing?'

FIFTY-ONE

'Oh, that's nice,' Danny said, sipping on the mug of hot chocolate that Susan had given him.

'How come he's got little marshmallows in his?' Kate asked looking at her mug with a sigh. 'He fell into a ditch; he didn't storm the beach at Normandy.'

'Come on now, Kate,' Susan said, pulling up a chair and sitting next to Danny. 'Anyone would think you're letting the fact that you're still pissed off with Danny effect your normally very high levels of human compassion.'

'Yeah, Kate,' Danny agreed, giving the marshmallows a little stir with his spoon. 'Anyway, I fell into a bush. It was my car that went into the ditch.'

'Mard arse…' Kate muttered.

'So did you get any idea of who it was, Danny?' Ben Matlock said, leaning against the wall of the school meeting room.

'No really, it was either totally dark or it was blindingly light from the headlights of the motorbikes. Either way you couldn't see anything. So… no idea at all, I'm afraid.'

'So, you reckon they were on motorbikes?' Ben asked.

'Sounded like it, yes,' Danny confirmed.

'Mum?' Ben asked. 'Did you see them?'

'I must confess I didn't actually see anyone,' Susan said. 'I heard something that sounded quite like motorbikes. Scramble bikes are quite common on the moors, we all know that.'

'What about you Kate?' Ben continued. 'You were there with Mum.'

Kate nodded towards Danny: 'I saw Jason Statham there shouting his head off. That's about it. There could have been motorbikes. Or it might have been the sound of Danny reversing up the track at a hundred miles an hour. Not sure. Didn't see any kind of gang, though. Certainly nothing like the vigilantes we saw out at the M62 bridge. Sorry.'

'I saw them,' Smithdown pointed out. 'Looked like five or six lads on bikes to me.'

'From the car park, Dad…' Kate pointed out. 'That's bloody miles away, that is.'

'I know what I saw, Kate,' Smithdown said. 'And if Danny says they attacked him that's good enough for me.'

'Absolutely,' Susan said. 'I'm sure Danny is right. We just didn't see what he saw, that's all.'

Jonathan Smithdown appeared at the doorway: 'Hi. Is everything okay?'

'It's all fine, Jonathan,' Ben Matlock said. 'Danny had a bit of car trouble out on the moors. We're just sorting out getting it towed away.'

'Oh, right… you look a bit messed up, Danny.'

'I just fell on my arse, Jonathan,' Danny said. 'Nothing that a cup of hot chocolate won't sort out.'

'Yes, Susan's doing a grand job of warming Danny up,' Smithdown said. Susan narrowed her eyes at the ex-detective and shook her head. She couldn't stop herself from smiling, though.

'Can I make a suggestion?' Susan said. 'Kate, you've barely had a chance to see Jonathan yet. I'm sure you've still got plenty more to say to him after tonight's other little escapade. Ben, you need to have a proper session with Josh as well. We need to know if he managed to get any pills from anywhere else. How about we have a quick word now, then let them both sleep it off. Then we can reconvene in the morning when we're all a bit calmer… how about that?'

'Sure,' agreed Kate, finishing her hot chocolate. 'Seems sensible. Danny, you stay here with Dad, then let's get home. I suppose you'll be needing a lift?'

'I suppose I will,' Danny agreed. 'If only I knew someone nice who'd help me out in my moment of difficulty…'

'Now, now,' Susan said with a smile. 'Play nice you two. Come on Ben, let's get this over with. Lovely to see you, Mr Smithdown. Take care.'

'You too, love,' Smithdown said with a wink. 'You'll need a good rest after all tonight's excitement, won't she Danny?'

'I'm sure she can handle it, John,' Danny said, not rising to the bait.

'Absolutely, Mr Smithdown,' Susan agreed. 'Night, Danny. Thanks again for what you did for Jonathan and Josh.'

Susan placed a hand on Danny's shoulder as she stood up. Then she led Kate and Ben out of the room, giving Danny a smile as she left.

Danny and Smithdown were left alone in the room. There was silence for a few moments. 'Not a fucking word, John Smithdown.'

'I'm sure I don't know what you mean, Danny,' the old man said.

'It WAS the vigilantes,' Danny said. 'I know it was. It's weird, though. One minute they're inviting me along to their little parties, next thing they're attacking me. Something's changed.'

'He's a funny bugger, that Ben,' Smithdown observed. 'He seemed very keen to know what you did and didn't see. Proper nosey.'

'Yeah, I noticed that too,' Danny agreed. 'Kate and Susan seemed to get the same treatment too.'

'Oh, and one other thing,' Smithdown added. 'There's one aspect of this that no one seems to have noticed yet.'

'What's that?'

'That you're a dirty little bastard.'

'Thanks for that, John. Much appreciated.'

FIFTY-TWO

'VIGILANTE BIKERS' ATTACK *OLDHAM NOW* REPORTER
Danny Johnston - Oldham Now

A motorbike gang, thought to be connected to the killings of several men in recent weeks, attacked *Oldham Now* reporter Danny Johnston during the night.

The gang were spotted at around midnight on moorland close to Diggle. Video footage shows at least six bikers heading over the moors towards the M62. They then carried out the attack on a track close to the disused firing range near Diggle Reservoir. They used bricks and stones to smash in the car's windows. The vehicle ended up in a ditch next to the track and is due to be removed this morning.

Motorbikes have been heard close to the scene of all the recent killings. Barry Mortimer, Kabeer Sajid, Adil Aziz and Paul Docherty were all killed by vigilantes claiming they were ridding the area of paedophiles.

Oldham police officer Detective Constable Karl McIntyre also died at the hands of the gang; it's thought he got close to discovering the gang's identities and was killed to keep him quiet.

Since DC McIntyre's death there have been no more killings, but murder squad detectives - led by Mr McIntyre's bother Detective Inspector Patrick McIntyre - seem no closer to catching the gang.

Did you see anything suspicious on the moors last night? Please contact Danny Johnston at *Oldham Now* if you have any information. Email: danny@oldhamnow.net

FIFTY-THREE

That night, Danny saw The Shirtless Boy skimming towards him across an icy slab of dark reservoir water.

Danny wasn't sure if he was at Hanging Lees or Black Moss; either way it was a bizarre, elongated version of one of the reservoirs he'd seen earlier that day. It was longer, wider and deeper looking. It looked so deep he felt it was trying to pull him in. It tugged at his clothes and skin like it had a gravitational force.

Come on, Danny. Join us. Just a quick dip. It'll make you feel so much better.

The Shirtless Boy's toes just touched the surface of the water as he moved closer and closer to the sandy bank where Danny was standing.

Sandy bank? It's a beach. Manchester has everything apart from a beach. That's what they say. It's clearly not true…

The Boy came near to Danny then moved away in an elegant arc across the water. Danny realised that he was now following The Boy, floating across the surface behind him like an upright bird. They travelled for hours. Or maybe seconds.

Danny blinked then looked around. They weren't at the reservoir anymore; they were in the doorway of a tiny bedsitting room. It felt cold and damp, much more so than out on the moors.

The Shirtless Boy stepped inside and waved a hand, inviting Danny to join him.

In the corner of the room a woman was nursing a baby. Her back was turned so Danny couldn't see her face. The baby was crying but it wasn't the kind of noise you'd expect a baby to make; it was a horrible metallic sound, like an aluminium can being ripped in two.

Skrawk.

Skrawk.

Skrawk.

Then the tearing sound stopped. All was still in the room. The Shirtless Boy's hand was outstretched, as if to say… *come on, step inside.*

Danny didn't want to. He was happier where he was. Reluctantly, he took one small step. He was almost clear of the door frame.

Skrawk.

Skrawk.

Skrawk.

He couldn't bear the noise anymore and closed his eyes. When he opened them, he was above the water again. He hovered for a moment, then dropped into the darkness.

FIFTY-FOUR

The next morning Danny rolled over in bed to answer his phone. DI Patrick McIntyre's number came up on Danny's phone. *He's unlikely to be pleased.* 'Hi, Patrick. You don't mind if I call you, Patrick, do you? Don't shout at me. I'm very sore. Please remember, I'm the victim here.'

'You're a pain in the arse, Danny,' the DI said. 'That's what you are. When were you planning to report what happened last night to us? Or was it more important to get the hits on your website first?'

'There's no way I'm going to sit on a video that shows the very gang that your lot seems unable to track down,' Danny said. 'I did you lot a favour; every news outlet in the country is carrying the story. I should be charging you for acting as your Press Officer.'

'Yeah,' the detective agreed, sarcastically. 'Every news outlet in the country. Which means that I'll be getting calls from Weymouth to Wick from nutters who think they know something, when what I really need is proper information from around here. Still, as long as it drives traffic to your site, Danny. That's the main thing, isn't it?'

'Is there a wider reason for your call, or is it just to question my journalistic ethics? There's a bottle of paracetamol in the cupboard that's got my name on it.'

'Did you film anything else last night?' the DI asked.

'No. What's on the site is all I have. That's literally every second of it.'

'Is there anything else that you saw or heard that might help us? You must have gotten pretty close to them.'

'Well, they got pretty close to me is probably a fairer way to put it,' Danny pointed out. 'It was all pretty chaotic.'

The detective pressed Danny for more: 'Anything at all, Danny. Anything unusual. Anything that struck you as out of place.'

Danny thought for a moment. He debated whether to mention something that had been on his mind. 'Maybe. Possibly. I'm not sure.'

'Anything, Danny. No matter how small or weird.'

'Well speaking of small and weird… I did actually hit one of them. With a can of de-icer. I know, proper Crouching Tiger Hidden Dragon stuff.'

'What about it?'

'It's just that… he went down like a sack of spuds. I barely touched him, and I still managed to knock him clean off his feet. I'm literally the least hard person in Oldham and I took him out with minimal effort. Plus, he… screamed.'

'How do you mean?'

'I mean… he really screamed. Proper high-pitched stuff.'

'Okay. That is a bit weird. But you never know, it might come in useful. Can you send me the full clip please? For evidence. Include any shaky stuff at the beginning and the end too. We'll overlook the whole driving at high speed through Diggle while using your phone stuff. For now.'

'That's very decent of you,' Danny said. 'Give me your email and I'll WeTransfer it to you now.'

McIntyre gave Danny his GMP email. 'Okay, thanks. Oh and Danny… Let me know when anything else happens that might be of help to us. You remember us, right? Oldham Police. The ones that are apparently NO CLOSER TO CATCHING THE GANG according to your piece. No fucking wonder, is it? Maybe we will actually catch them if we get a bit more co-operation from the likes of you. Just a crazy thought.'

'Okay. Will do. It was a spur of the moment thing; I spotted them and just sort of went for it. It wasn't like before… they didn't contact me. I don't actually think they'll be contacting me again anytime soon. I seem to have been dropped from their Christmas list, for some reason. Maybe I've served my purpose. Not sure.'

'Just let us know, Danny. That's all I ask.'

Danny thought about mentioning his visit to Strangeways to see Bob Donaldson. *Think I'll keep that to myself for the time being.* 'I'll keep you up to date at all times, Detective Inspector,' he said. 'Guaranteed.'

FIFTY-FIVE

Danny's afternoon wasn't the most exciting he'd ever spent. Painkillers, ignoring requests for interviews from other news organisations and being kept waiting on the phone - that was the main thrust of it. *They never show people on hold to insurance companies in films, do they? There are crashes and mayhem and all that, but you never see people listening to light jazz whilst being told, 'you are currently 49th in the queue... your call is very important to us,' after their car's been trashed by the bad guys. Never happens.*

He put his landline on speakerphone, took another couple of painkillers and listened to the voicemail messages on his mobile:

'Hi Danny, it's Mike from *Granada Reports*. We were at Strangeways together, remember? Those were the days mate! Can you give me a call please? It's about the vigilantes, obviously. Love to get your eyewitness account to go with the video. Cheers. Bye.'
<*Message deleted*>

'Danny it's Carrie O'Connor from Sky. Been trying you since the murder presser. My editor is going to kill me if we don't get you on. He knows we're mates! We are still mates, aren't we? Ha ha! Anyway, please call. Thanks.'
<*Message deleted*>

'Danny, it's James from GB News. Really keen to speak to you about those vigilantes. Our viewers are 100 per cent behind them, no surprise there! Anyway, would really like to get you on air to debate with one of our tame Lefties about why killing paedos is actually the way forward. It'll be brilliant. Give me a call, ASAP. Cheers.'
<*Message deleted*>

'Alright, dickhead. It's Kate here, in case you've deleted me from your contacts list. Or you've forgotten what I sound like. I don't care either

way, but I'm just seeing if you're alive and stuff. If you are then… fine. Well done. That video's taken off, hasn't it? Your analytics will be going bingo bango bongo, won't they? Anyhow, glad you're not dead, assuming you're not dead, that is. Call me if you like. Not bothered, obviously. Bye.'
<*Message saved*>

'Danny, it's Susan. Just checking in and seeing how you are. Bit sore I imagine. Nothing that a bit more hot chocolate with marshmallows won't sort out, eh? Anyway, give me a call and I'll come round and see you if you like. Okay? Give me a call. Bye.'
<*Message saved*>

'Danny, it's Susan again. Sorry. I was just thinking… hope you didn't mind that I gave you a little extra goodbye last night. Did Mr Smithdown see us? Anyway, hope you didn't mind. I thought it was nice. Give me a call. Bye. Again.'
<*Message saved*>

'Danny… Hiya. Yes. It's Joy Pritchard, Maggie's neighbour. Well, not anymore obviously. Anyway… you know what I mean. If you're passing, give me a knock. Something a bit weird is going on here, thought you'd want to know. Ok. Bye.'
<*Message saved*>

<*You have no new messages*>

FIFTY-SIX

Danny looked out of the rear first floor window of Joy Pritchard's house and into Maggie Ormrod's garden. Amid the tangle of overgrown bushes and discarded household goods, a figure in a beige coat was sitting on an upturned beer crate. It was raining and they had what appeared to be a plastic carrier bag on their head to keep them dry.

'How long has he been there?' Danny whispered, realising almost straight away that he probably didn't need to whisper.

'Half an hour or so,' Joy said. 'It's the fourth time they've been in Maggie's garden in the last day or so. It's a she, by the way.'

'Oh right. Have you spoken to her?'

'The first time I saw her I knocked on the window and she left straight away. Second time, I opened the window and said hello - same result. Off she went. Third time I went down to see if she was okay. She spotted me from the path around the back and made off. So, no… I've not actually spoken to her yet.'

'She must want something, otherwise she wouldn't keep coming back.'

'Well, it's clearly not me she wants,' Joy pointed out. 'Maybe it's someone else. Maybe it's you.'

Danny looked at Joy then back down at the woman in the garden. 'How do you get to Maggie's garden?'

'There's a ginnel at the end of the terraces. Walk down there and it'll take you round the back.'

'Okay, I'll give it a go.'

'Danny?' Joy said. 'Take care, alright?'

'It's a woman with a bag on her head sitting on a crate,' he said. 'How dangerous can it be?'

'I don't know, just take care, okay?'

The rain made the ginnel cobbles slippery underfoot as Danny made his way through the back of the terraced houses. Each had a small backyard; the narrow alley separated each house's yard from a series of tiny, gated gardens. Most were modern and neat, with pricey-looking outdoor furniture and fire pits. But not Maggie's. Her garden looked messy and out of place. Danny could imagine some of the neighbours looking down their noses at Maggie and her raggle taggle patch of unkempt grass. Thinking about it made him angry.

Danny stood at the gate and waited. The woman hadn't moved. Danny saw the crate she was sitting on was clearly from a pub; it had a Skol lager logo on it. 'You okay?' he asked. No answer. 'Did you know Maggie? This was her house. I'm Danny, by the way. I've been trying to find out more about her. Do you think you could help me?'

Danny noticed he was speaking in a loud voice and saying his words LIKE THIS AS IF THE PERSON COULDN'T UNDERSTAND HIM. *Don't do that.*

'Yeah… I knew Maggie,' she said. Her voice was quiet with a West Yorkshire accent, more pronounced than its Oldham equivalent. 'You're that journalist fellah, aren't you? I'm not deaf, by the way. I'm wet, but I'm not deaf.'

'Why don't you come in?' Danny suggested. 'Joy next door will make us a brew. She's nice. We can get in out of the rain. What do you think?'

'I think I like it out here,' the woman said. 'I don't like inside. I prefer outside. Maggie was the same. She didn't like being shut in. If there was a chance to get herself out and about, she was away.'

She turned to Danny and smiled. She looked thin and exhausted; the bag on her head was from Kwik Save. *I thought Kwik Save had gone out of business years ago.*

'You're Danny Johnston, aren't you? You used to be on that Manchester Radio years and years ago. MAN-CHEST-AH RAY-DEEE-OOOH… FIRST WITH NEWS! Funny how you remember stuff like that. Can't remember what I had for tea last night, but I can remember your radio station's daft jingles.'

'Yeah, they sort of worm their way into your brain, don't they? What's your name?'

'Alma. Alma Jane Richards… care of the Greenacres Children's Home, Oldham.'

The woman shuffled slightly on the crate and moved to the right. She patted the space she'd vacated. The rain was easing now, barely spitting, so she took the bag from her head, folded it and put it in the pocket of her coat.

Danny did as he was asked. The two sat for a moment in silence. 'What was Maggie like?' he asked. 'I never met her. I feel like I know her a bit. But not enough.'

'She was nice,' Alma said. 'A bit older than me. She was like our big sister. She looked out for us younger ones.'

'In the care home? I tried to find the records but every time I tried the files were missing or there'd been a fire and the paperwork had been destroyed.'

'Yeah, funny that, isn't it?' Alma smiled. 'All these… what do they call them? Agencies! All these agencies that are supposed to look after kids. They often do the opposite, don't they? Different now though. Better. That's why she liked doing cleaning work at kids' homes and that. Sort of comforted her. Knowing things had changed. She loved that one up past Diggle.'

'Which one?' Danny asked.

'Hunter's Hollow,' Alma said. 'Said that the things they did for the kids there was amazing. Taking them rock climbing and quad biking and all that. Amazing place, that's what she said.'

'Maggie worked at Hunter's Hollow? I know people there. They never said anything.'

Alma was adamant: 'Well, she did. On and off. And she loved it.'

The rain had stopped now. The crate felt wet under the seat of Danny's trousers. 'When they found her at Hanging Lees, Maggie had left a note,' he said. 'She named someone she said had harmed her when she was young.'

'Harmed her?' Alma laughed. 'Ha! That's a good one. Very polite talk, that is, Danny Johnston. Harmed her… that's brilliant. There's that other one they use these days, isn't there? Groomed. It sounds quite nice, doesn't it? Like he was brushing her hair or something. Groomed? Abused her… raped her… got her pregnant… got rid of her kid… abandoned her… drove her to kill herself out on them moors. Yeah. He harmed her alright. That fucking bastard John Smithdown.'

'Smithdown… that was his name?'

'She used to talk about him all the time. Like he was her boyfriend or something. He'd come and pick her up and the people at the care home would just let him. Sick.'

'And it was definitely John Smithdown?'

'Definitely. She told me all about it.'

Danny took out his phone and showed Alma the photo of Maggie

Ormrod with John Smithdown. 'The man in this photo… is this him?'

She looked at the screen. 'I have no idea who that is, at all. Is he one of Smithdown's mates?'

'No, it's him. John Smithdown. The police found this picture in Maggie's house. It's Smithdown. I know him.'

'No idea who that is, but it isn't John Smithdown,' Alma said, emphatically.

Danny pulled a newspaper clipping from his pocket: 'What about this man. This picture is from 1988. Do you recognise him?'

Alma looked at the story: 'Yeah. THAT'S John Smithdown. I'd recognise the slimy twat anywhere.'

'Come inside, Alma,' Danny said. 'Please. And tell me everything you know.'

Inside, Danny introduced Alma to Joy. They put her wet coat over a radiator and gave her tea and toast.

Then Alma Jane Richards - formerly care of the Greenacres Children's Home - told them everything she knew about Maggie Ormrod.

Danny listened to what she said. Then, finally, Danny understood. And then Danny wept.

FIFTY-SEVEN

16 April 1975

Maggie sang along to the theme song at the end of the TV programme: 'B… O… B.O.Y.S… boys to entertain yoooo!'

The policeman switched off the television set and pointed to his watch. 'Look at the time, Maggie! It's way past your curfew. The people at Greenacres will be going mad. You'll get in big trouble if you go back now. I knew I shouldn't have let you talk me into watching another programme.'

'Well, you should have told me what time it was, John!' she said, indignantly. 'Why is it always my fault?'

'I don't know Maggie Nuisance,' he said, leaning across the sofa to tickle her. 'Why IS it always your fault?'

'Gerroff!' she screamed, laughing so much she could barely speak. 'I'll scream, gerroff!'

'Go on then,' he said. 'Scream all you like. I dare you.'

She looked at him for a moment; then let out a scream so loud it hurt her own ears. She put a hand to her mouth, embarrassed at what she'd done.

'It's fine. You can't disturb the neighbours here. I haven't got any.'

He got up and stood at the window. The curtains were open, and the sun had set across the moors. The wind scraped at the windows, giving them a playful rattle. 'That's the beauty of this house. Nobody either side. Nobody at the front, nobody at the back either. Just the moors. We can't bother anyone, and no one can bother us.'

'But what about the home?' Maggie asked. 'If I get in trouble again, I'll get shipped off to Borstal.'

The man stood up and paced around the front room, apparently deep in thought. For a moment it looked like he had an idea, but then he shook his head, dismissed it and returned to pacing the floor. Maggie tried to say something, but he shushed her to stop his train of thought being disturbed. Then he clicked his fingers. 'I've got it,' he said. 'You can stay here tonight. I'll take you back in the morning and we'll tell them you were being chased by some older kids and hid because you were so frightened. I found you and brought you back. I'll tell them it wasn't your fault and that I'll get the kids that did it. How about that?'

'Great,' Maggie said. 'Yeah. If that's okay?'

'Of course,' he replied, reassuringly. 'Not a problem. So, it's settled. You can stay here tonight.'

FIFTY-EIGHT

John Smithdown was watching *Pointless* on the TV when Danny ran up his driveway, banged on his window and then let himself into the house.

'What's up with you?' Smithdown asked as Danny came into the room. 'Have you been crying?'

'I'm so sorry, John,' Danny said and knelt beside the old man's armchair. 'I mean it, I'm sorry.'

Danny's face was already wet with tears; he started crying again. 'Come on, lad,' Smithdown said. 'Whatever it is that's upset you, it can't be as bad as all this.'

'It is, John. I have to tell you… I thought you might have done it. I thought you might have hurt Maggie Ormrod. I hate myself for saying it, but it's true. I definitely thought it. I'm sorry for doubting you, even for a second. After everything you've done for me as well. Now I know you didn't do it, and I can prove it.'

'Well, that's great then… isn't it?'

'But now everything is coming crashing down. It's like I've been digging and digging all this time and now everything has caved in on me all at once. Black Moss, Mermaid's Pool, Hanging Lees, the whole stinking lot.'

Danny was now crying so hard he couldn't speak. Smithdown seemed unsure of what to do; he went to put a hand on Danny's shoulder. Then he seemed to change his mind and held his hand instead. Initially that made things worse; Danny cried even harder. Slowly, he calmed down and the tears lessened.

'That's better, Danny,' Smithdown said. 'Simmer down.'

Danny wiped his face on his sleeve. 'Fucking Nora,' Danny said. 'Look at the state of me. What a mess. Sorry. But I don't know what to do, John. It's too much to take in. There's so much to sort out, so much to put right. I don't know where to start.'

'Now you know what it's like being a policeman, Danny. So much shit to deal with and not enough shovels.'

Danny had regained his composure by now: 'So, how did you manage it, then?'

'An old boss of mine used to say: save a life today, change a life tomorrow.'

'Sounds like the kind of thing they'd put on a poster up at Hunter's Hollow,' Danny said, still sniffing and rubbing at his eyes.

'Yes, I used to think it was corny old shite, but he was spot on. Like getting you and your sister out of that house when you were kids. That was the priority. The other stuff can wait. The other stuff happened BECAUSE we prioritised what was important. Same with this. I know I didn't harm Maggie Ormrod. Now you do too. But sorting that can wait until tomorrow. It sounds like there's shit that needs shovelling before that.'

Danny laughed and wiped the last of his tears away: 'I think that's fair to say, John.'

'Then never mind about me,' Smithdown said. 'Get your shovel out.'

FIFTY-NINE

Danny had called Susan Matlock several times already, but thanks to the poor phone signal at the school, every attempt so far had gone straight to voicemail. On the fourth go, he got through: 'Hi, Susan, it's Danny.'

'I know, you daftie,' she laughed. 'I've got one of those up-to-date phones where the caller's name appears. Very modern here, you know… apart from our 1980s phone signal.'

'Yeah, of course. Listen, I wanted to ask you something about Maggie Ormrod, the woman that was found up at Hanging Lees. Why didn't you tell me she'd worked at Hunter's Hollow?'

Susan's tone changed; the good-natured cheeriness slipped away a little: 'Not being funny Danny, but I assumed you knew. I didn't want to talk about it in front of Kate for obvious reasons… all that stuff with her dad. And to be honest, I only met her once or twice. She tended to be on site really early. She was nice, though. I remember that. It was so sad what happened.'

'Did you ever talk to her?' Danny asked.

'Just to say hello, mainly.'

'That's it?'

Susan paused. Danny waited. 'She did ask me about the work we did at the school. It was literally while she was cleaning one of the classrooms. She seemed quite interested.'

'In what way?'

'Well, she asked me a question that I get asked a lot. The question I'm asked more than any other, in fact.'

'Which is?'

'She asked me… what should someone do if they'd been hurt by someone in the past?'

'And what did you tell her?'

'I told her what I tell everyone; that it's important to hold them to account for what they did and to get justice.'

'Justice?'

'Justice, yes. Always. It's the bedrock of everything we do here. Is everything okay, Danny.'

'Sure. Everything's fine. One more thing… Why was Maggie let go from her job?'

'I'm not sure I should say,' Susan replied.

'Please. It's important.'

Danny heard Susan let out a long breath. Then she spoke: 'She'd been buying booze for some of the pupils. She was letting them drink it at her house too. That's just not acceptable, especially as some of the kids have addiction issues. We had to let her go.'

'I see.'

'Danny, where are you now?' she asked.

'I'm at home, Susan. Why?'

'I was going to come round and see you. Make sure you're okay.'

'I'm fine. Pretty tired, though. And sore too. I'm going to get an early night.'

'Sure. We can speak tomorrow, yeah?'

'Definitely. Bye, Susan.'

Danny hung up and tightened the fasteners on his jacket to keep out the cold moorland breeze that was pushing its way across the valley. He watched and waited in his position on the ridge opposite Hunter's Hollow School. Fifteen minutes later he saw a line of bikes appear on a ridge to the north. Their lights dipped in and out of the curved landscape until they reached the hills to the right of the school. Then the bikers turned off their lights and travelled the last mile in darkness. Then they went out of sight behind the final ridge that curved around the back of the school. Danny heard the engines stop one by one. A few minutes later a line of five bikers walked down into the hollow behind the school, helmets in their hands. The hills behind acted like a natural amplifier and Danny could hear them laughing and chatting; he was too far away to make out any faces. A sixth person was clearly having too much fun to stop; they circled around the group and then did a wheelie across the top of the hill. For the first time Danny got a good look at the transportation the group was using to zip across the moors. *Not motorbikes at all. Quad bikes. Kids on fucking quad bikes.*

The lone quad biker got a telling off from someone; the gang waited until he put his bike away over the ridge and joined the group. Lights came on at the back of the school as they entered through the rear doors.

Danny pulled out his phone again and called up a stored number: 'Detective Inspector McIntyre…? Danny Johnstone here. Are you still keen to catch those vigilantes? Thought so. Well, get your boots on. I think I've found the little fuckers. Oh, and John Smithdown's innocent. And what's more, I can prove it.'

SIXTY

'Where's the back up?' Danny asked as he and DI McIntyre took a wide route on foot to the right of the school. 'Not that it isn't a pleasure to see you, but I was expecting back up. You know… big lads from the Tactical Aid Unit with body armour and guns. Where the fuck are they?'

Danny's mind was tumbling with everything he now knew. But he was trying to maintain some level of normality in front of the detective as they half walked, half ran up a steep path hemmed in by a dry-stone wall and an ancient-looking hedgerow. The wall provided cover for them as they passed the school; it was dark now and the pew-pew-pew sound of moorland curlews punctuated their steps.

'The Tactical Aid lads will be in the pub, if they've got any sense,' the DI replied, stepping nimbly over a stile and then a small stream that crossed their path as their route eased its way up the moors. 'I'm only here out of the kindness of my heart, Danny. That sort of stuff takes time. And money. And paperwork. I'd need to get an operational order, not to mention a risk assessment. All we've got to go on at the moment is you seeing some kids on quad bikes near the school.'

'It's a bit more than that,' Danny insisted. 'I know fuck all about motorbikes, but I know the sound I heard out on the moors after the murders; and it sounded just like those quads. The bikers that attacked me seemed small and light. I knocked one over and I barely tried. Kids, Patrick. They're just kids. And I think that arrogant twat Ben Matlock knows all about what's going on.'

'Let's just calm down a little, Danny,' the detective said. 'Let's just have a look over this ridge and then take it from there. Okay?'

'Sure. Okay. I've got something to tell you about Maggie Ormrod too that'll do your nut in. I've already texted Kate. She's going to freak out.'

'Danny! One thing at a time, please. Let's stick with the job in hand. Kate's son, Jonathan might be one of them… you know that don't you?'

'Yes, I do,' Danny said, reaching out a hand to steady himself as the land around them got steeper and steeper. 'I'm trying not to think about it.'

They crested the brow of the hill and lay on their bellies; the quad bikes were there; half a dozen of them had been stashed under a corrugated iron shelter. Beyond that was a battered caravan; it looked like a 1970s model, long with mouldy-looking net curtains and moss growing up the brown and white side panels. 'Oh shit, I hate them,' Danny said, his voice dropping to a whisper. 'Fucking abandoned caravans. There's literally nothing creepier in the world than rancid old, abandoned caravans out in the middle of nowhere.'

'Oh yes there is something creepier… look,' McIntyre said. 'An abandoned caravan in the middle of nowhere with a light on inside.'

The curtains were closed and there were newspapers stuck to the insides of the windows, but a few thin strips of light could be seen between the sheets. Danny rolled onto his back. 'Caravans with bit of light coming from inside. Fucking Nora. They're the worst kind!'

'We can go back if you like,' McIntyre said. 'God forbid that you get freaked out by the sight of a manky old caravan with a light on. Get your big boy pants on, Danny and let's go and check it out.'

The pair got up and walked down the other side of the hill, keeping low as they crossed the field towards the caravan. They stopped outside the door and listened. All they could hear was the sound of the moors.

McIntyre took out his phone and used the torch to examine the door. Two u-shaped clamps had been screwed into the panels on either side of it and a plank of wood had been slotted into them, barricading the door. 'I don't think it's to keep people out,' the DI pointed out to Danny. 'I reckon it's to keep someone in.'

'Oh, that's welcome news,' Danny said. 'Just what I was hoping for, a scary caravan with something locked inside. I suppose we'd better go in then, hadn't we?'

'I suppose we had.'

Danny looked around; the orangey glow of lights from the school gently lit the edge of the hill behind them. He could hear cattle in the distance, but they were definitely alone. 'Fucking Nora,' Danny muttered. 'Absolutely Fucking Bloody Nora...'

He gently lifted the plank that was keeping the door closed. The caravan wasn't level and it tilted slightly in their direction, so when the door came free it swung open towards them, taking both men by surprise. They stepped back and waited. There was silence apart from the squeaking of the door as it swung to and fro.

'You big mard arse,' the DI said. 'In you go.'

Danny took out his phone, swiped on the torch and stepped inside; *why am I going in first?* The caravan smelled of beer and stale sweat. Most of the fixtures and fittings had been ripped out and the floor was littered with empty lager cans. In the small kitchen area there was a bunch of flowers standing upside down in the sink. Further inside a few cushions and an old car seat could be seen on the floor. Then they saw the light that they'd spotted from outside. It was coming from the rear bedroom; there was also a tikka-tikka-tikka-tikka sound coming from the other side of the door.

The two men glanced at each other and then looked at the door.

Tikka-tikka-tikka-tikka.

Without a word being exchanged they both began to look around for some form of weapon. DI McIntyre kicked over some takeaway containers and discovered a stave of wood the size of a cricket bat; the best Danny could find was an old milk bottle.

'Really?' the DI whispered. 'Is that all you can find?'

'It's either that or the bunch of flowers,' Danny replied. 'Come on, are we going into this bedroom or what?'

They stood close to the door with their improvised weapons raised; the detective pulled at the magnetic catch and the door swung open.

The tikka-tikka-tikka-tikka noise got a little louder.

In the middle of the caravan's bedroom was a topless man taped to a chair. There was blood smeared across his chest and arms; several of his fingers were pointing in the wrong directions and were clearly broken. His mouth was covered with gaffer tape and a pair of headphones had been taped to his head. They were attached via a curly lead to an old cassette player. The song that was being played had clearly been set at a deafening volume; the sound of the drums could be heard leaking from the headphones from across the room: tikka-tikka-tikka-tikka.

Danny pulled at the tape and loosened it enough to free the headphones: 'FUCKOFFANDDIE!' could be heard before DI McIntyre stopped the cassette. The man looked up and made eye contact with Danny; there was a pleading look in his eyes. 'Oh, for fuck's sake,' Danny sighed, lowering his milk bottle. 'Not you.'

'Do you know this guy?' the detective asked. He dug around in his pocket and then used the serrated edge of his car keys to saw at the tape around the back of the man's head.

'Yeah, I'm afraid I do,' Danny replied. 'It's Charlie, at least that's what he told me his name was. He's officially the stupidest nonce in the whole of Oldham. We had a hot date outside the Subway in Chadderton the other week.' Danny helped the DI remove the tape from the man's mouth. 'Still going with the whole flowers thing, Charlie? Classy. Who did this to you?'

Charlie opened his mouth; he made a moaning sound and two of his teeth fell out. 'Kidsss,' he slurred. 'Fucking kidsss.'

'We need to get him out of here,' the DI said. 'Those kids could come back at any time.'

'There's plenty of people out there who'd say we should leave him here,' Danny said.

'Well, I suppose right now is the perfect time for you to decide which side you're on, isn't it?' the detective responded, pointing his car keys at Danny. 'Are you the kind of person who turns a blind eye and lets someone be tortured and murdered because they disgust you? Or are you genuinely trying to put an end to this? It's as simple as that. Decide, Danny. Because I can't carry this fucker on my own and I'm getting a bit tired of you sitting on the fence. You wanted to get the vigilantes. Now's your chance. Or was this just a story to you? A bit of clickbait for your website? Because I'm a police officer, and I don't have a choice. I have to protect this man whether I like him or not.'

'Alright, Captain Self-Righteous, keep your halo on,' Danny said. 'What about if we bust the door off and use it as a stretcher?'

'Perfect. Let's do it.'

The two men went to the bedroom door. They put down their weapons; Danny held the bottom and DI McIntyre grabbed the top. They braced themselves. 'I get it,' Danny said in a whisper. 'I know you're right. But me and my sister… We were both done over when we were kids. Passed around like sweets. It fucked up our lives. She died last year. Cancer. This shit is hard. Really hard.'

'I know, Danny,' the detective said. 'I'm sorry. Nobody would like to change the past more than me. But I can't. All I can do is deal with what's happening right now… and right now we need to get this door off these hinges so we can get that nonce out of this caravan. Okay?'

'Okay. How come you're about 20 years younger than me, yet about 20 years better at dealing with this shit than I am?'

'Absolutely no idea, Danny. Ask my mum. Right. Are you ready?

After three…'

On three, the two men pulled at the door; it came away in one go but the effort put both of them on their backsides. As they got to their feet the caravan flooded with light from three powerful head torches. Ben Matlock entered with a hammer in his hand; with him were two teenage pupils, Josh and Carly. They had hammers too. Danny noticed that the teenage girl who'd asked him how much he earned during his talk, was limping and one side of her face was puffy and bruised. The three faced off against Danny and the detective with just four or five yards of caravan floor between them.

'Detective Inspector McIntyre, meet Ben,' Danny said. 'He's the nasty bastard who's been getting these kids to do his dirty work. Ben, meet Detective Inspector McIntyre. He's the man who's going to arrest you… Something I'm very much looking forward to. And this is Carly… That leg must be proper sore. Nothing worse than a can of de-icer right in the shin, is there Carly? And finally, here's Josh; pill popper and hospital jumper extraordinaire. Is that how Ben gets you to do stuff, Josh… by limiting your pills? That's lovely, that is.'

'Ha ha!' Ben said. 'Brilliant! Let me have a turn, this is fun: Josh and Carly, you've already met Danny. He's the self-righteous hypocrite who makes money from writing stories about all the nasty things that happen in life. But unlike us, he isn't prepared to actually do anything to try to stop them. He's all talk and no action.'

'They're kids, Ben,' Danny pleaded. 'Vulnerable, damaged kids. They need to be helped, not filled with vengeance and hate. You've groomed them.' He nodded towards, Charlie, who was moaning and crying behind them. 'You're as bad as him over there. Maybe worse.'

Ben ignored him and carried on with his introductions: 'Now then Ben… Carly… this is Detective Inspector McIntyre. You've already met his brother, out at Crow Knowl. That didn't end well, did it? Look at him… he's more interested in saving that sick fucker Charlie who tried to nonce on Carly than he is in protecting the children of Oldham. I've said it before and I'll say it again: the law doesn't care about kids. The law only cares about making sure that Charlie the Paedo's precious rights aren't violated. That's why we have to do what we do.'

'Oh, shut the fuck up,' McIntyre said, picking up one end of the bedroom door. 'I'm not listening to this shite. I fancy our chances here, Danny. We'll make light work of these three and then get on our way. Because what are we dealing with here? One pill head, one girl with a gammy leg and one BIG MOUTHED TWAT THAT'S ABOUT TO

GET THIS DOOR IN HIS FUCKING FACE.'

Danny took hold of the other end of the door and steadied himself. The two men bent their knees, ready to charge across the caravan. There was silence for a few moments, then Danny heard a banging noise on the side of the caravan. It got louder and more frequent; it started to their left and moved to the right. The banging was all around them now, the sound of metal clanging on the outside panels on all sides. DI McIntyre reached out and pulled away several sheets of newspaper that were taped to the window nearest to him. Danny did the same on his side. The caravan was surrounded by Hunter's Hollow pupils; they all had hammers and were banging them on the outside of the caravan. Then the banging stopped.

Susan Matlock stepped into the caravan. Charlie, still strapped to the chair behind Danny and the DI, began to cry and moan and plead even louder. He shook his head and begged for mercy through his broken teeth. 'Not her. Please. Not her!'

'Oh, Danny…' Susan said with a disappointed smile. 'It shouldn't have turned out like this. Makes me very sad, it really does. We should all be on the same side. You, me, the police, the kids. All fighting the good fight against the common enemy. I honestly believed that you'd join us. I read your book and thought… this guy is one of us.'

'So that's why you sent me the tip offs about the bodies?' Danny said. 'Fucking hell, Susan, couldn't you just film them in a car park and stick it on Facebook like everyone else? Surely naming and shaming is a pretty good deterrent?'

'If doing shit like that was such a good deterrent, why doesn't it seem to deter them?' Susan snapped. 'They just keep on coming. Wave after wave of online predators. Then it's down to the likes of me and Ben to pick up the pieces after the abuse has already happened. Mopping up the mess isn't the way forward. I've been doing that for years. I've been through all the social care systems there are - worked in every single one of them - and none of them do any good. None of them… no matter how hard people like me try. And what's more, coppers like your friend here have looked down their noses at us for years. Do-gooders... Hippies... Tree huggers. I'm sick of it. So, we tried a different method. And this one very clearly works. Online grooming incidents in Oldham have almost entirely stopped. Amazing! And why? Because the predators are in hiding. They're the ones living in fear. Makes a nice change. All apart from that prick behind you, of course. He was too stupid to listen to the warnings. Which is why he's here to face a little bit of instant justice.'

'This is no way to help children, Ms Matlock,' DI McIntyre said. He looked at Josh and Carly. 'They've already been abused. That's bad enough. Now you've turned them into murderers.'

Carly laughed and shook her head: 'He just doesn't get it, does he? It'd be funny if it wasn't so pathetic.'

'You're so wrong, Detective Inspector,' Josh said. 'We're not murderers, we're warriors. Me, Carly and the others are doing this so that young people in the future can be safe. And the best way to keep kids safe is to go to the source of the danger and cut it off. And that's exactly what we're doing.'

'What about my brother?' the detective said, firmly. 'Did you all have a meeting and just decide that he should be cut off too?'

'That was very unfortunate,' Susan admitted. 'But we are at *war*, Mr McIntyre. You and your brother had your chance to fight it and you lost. You can't stop this, and you know it. So, now you need to stay out of our way. I'm afraid your brother didn't do that. I'm sorry. But this is more important.'

'Was Maggie Ormrod in the way too?' asked Danny.

For the first time, Susan's resolve seemed to falter. 'Maggie was another victim. Abused by someone she trusted when she was just a child. More proof that we can't trust the so-called authorities. I told you the truth about my dealings with her, Danny, I really did. I told her that it's important to hold abusers responsible for what they did and to get justice. Taking her life was the way she chose to do that. She held her abuser accountable for her life and her death. She's a heroine.'

'Christ Almighty, Susan,' Danny said. 'This is madness. You can't seriously think that you can keep all this secret and just bury it, can you?'

'Depends how far you're prepared to dig, Danny,' Ben Matlock said with a smile. 'The moors around here can be very accommodating.'

Susan held up her hand as if she was in a classroom silencing her pupils: 'Okay… I'm done with this. Look. Danny… DI McIntyre. Let's be practical here. There's too many of us. If you want to fight us, fine. Have a go… smash a few kids' heads in with your stupid bit of caravan door. But you'll lose anyway. This is over.'

Danny looked at Charlie and then shook his head: 'We can't let you take him, Susan. I hate myself for saying it, but we can't.' Danny picked up his milk bottle again, while still holding onto the corner of the door. He looked at DI McIntyre. 'It's wrong.'

Then half a dozen more teenagers with hammers stepped inside the caravan. 'Well, that's disappointing to hear, Danny,' she sighed. 'Very disappointing indeed. I'd expect that kind of nonsense from Detective Inspector Dickhead over there, but not you. Oh well.'

She turned to face her pupils: 'Take them,' Susan said. Then she pointed her hammer at Charlie: 'Then we'll rip that fucker apart.'

'I'm telling you now, I'm shit at this,' Danny whispered to DI McIntyre; he felt slightly foolish holding the milk bottle above his head.

'I'll go for Ben, you go for Susan,' the detective said. 'Maybe the kids will take fright and run. Maybe not. Worth a go.'

'You want me to bottle her, is that what you're saying?' Danny asked.

'Fine. You take Ben. He'll knock you into next Friday but at least you won't have the indignity of Susan kicking your arse.'

'Fucking Nora,' Danny muttered. 'We'd best take a run up, I suppose.' He looked around; there was hardly any space. They'd edged backwards so far that they were almost pressed against Charlie. Danny could feel the injured man's bloodied, wet skin against the back of his hand. *Even if we did just step aside and let them take him, they'll kill us anyway.*

Fuck it.

Danny and McIntyre readied themselves to dash forwards just as the whole caravan lurched violently to the left, accompanied by a metallic crashing sound. The front end, where Susan and Ben were standing, crumpled inwards and sent them and the pupils violently across to the opposite wall. The outer shell of the caravan tore open; Danny heard the sound of an engine revving and then the caravan spun sideways for a second time. It was now facing the opposite way and the back end of the caravan had been completely sheared off. Danny could see that the damage had been caused by the school's Land Rover; Jonathan Smithdown was at the wheel. Danny and Jonathan looked at each other for a moment; then he gave the teenager the thumbs up. 'Fucking nice one,' he mouthed to him.

Danny couldn't see Susan, Ben and the other pupils; it appeared they'd been knocked out of the caravan with the impact. 'Right,' said McIntyre, grabbing the back of Charlie's seat with his left hand and tipping him backwards. 'We haven't got time to untie him - grab the chair legs and let's take this twat out of here as he is.'

Danny did as he was asked, and the two men half-carried and half-dragged Charlie through the hole in the end of the caravan. The detective was clearly struggling with the weight; then Danny noticed that McIntyre's right arm appeared to be the wrong way round; it was bent outwards and there was blood and bone visible around the DI's wrist. 'That's going to be a bit sore in the morning,' Danny pointed out.

He got no answer; McIntyre's eyes were unfocused, and he looked like he was struggling to breathe. *Don't pass out you bastard, I need you to be conscious.*

They managed to get Charlie out of the caravan; Jonathan pulled the Land Rover close to them, nearly hitting Danny in the process. 'I didn't know you could drive, Jonathan,' Danny said.

'I can't, really,' the teenager said, stepping out of the vehicle just as McIntyre let go of the chair and dropped Charlie on his back. There was shouting and screaming all around them. Some of the pupils were running back to the school, but others were regrouping and pointing at them. Danny started pulling at the gaffer tape that was securing Charlie to the chair.

'Jonathan… you help the policeman and I'll get the paedo,' Danny shouted. 'There's a sentence I didn't think I'd be saying when I got up this morning.'

Jonathan helped McIntyre get to his feet and then pushed and pulled him onto the back seat of the car. The detective immediately keeled over and lay flat across the seats. Danny was still struggling with the tape; the more he pulled, the tighter it seemed to get. He looked up and saw half a dozen pupils coming towards him.

'Right fuck this,' Danny said. 'Jonathan, open up the boot. Then grab the chair legs. We'll just chuck him in as he is.'

The pair opened the rear of the car; they got Charlie as far as the lip of the boot before Jonathan lost his footing in the muddy ground and let go of the chair. Charlie let out a cry as he fell on his side. The pupils were getting closer to them now. 'Danny, please,' Jonathan cried. 'Leave him and let's just go. Trust me. I know them. We need to get out of here right now.'

'No,' Danny stated. 'Grab the chair legs and get him in. He's a prick, I know. But we can't leave him. They'll tear him apart. I mean, fucking literally tear him apart.'

'Fucking Nora,' Jonathan said and grabbed the chair legs again. This time, Charlie went into the back of the Land Rover with one lift. He was face down in the boot, but he was in. 'Probably best if I drive,' Danny said as they ran to the front of the vehicle. They slammed the doors closed. The pupils were nearly on them. Danny recognised some of their faces from his talk; Josh and Carly were at the front of the pack. 'Jonathan, have you got your phone?' Danny said. 'Call the police. Now.'

'There's no signal,' Jonathan cried. 'We need to be out of this valley and away from the school.'

Josh then appeared at the driver's side window and smashed it in with his hammer; Danny was peppered with tiny cubes of glass as he shoved the gear stick into reverse. He heard a bang at the rear. *That could have been a kid hitting the car with a hammer… or I could have hit a kid. Hard to tell.*

Danny had never driven a Land Rover before and struggled with the gears; he finally managed it and reversed up the hill behind the school at high speed. The further up the slope he got, the faster he seemed to be going. 'Signal, Jonathan?' Danny shouted. 'Come on, there must me a signal!'

'No, nothing!' the teenager said. 'Shit. Keep going higher.'

Danny saw the dry-stone wall at the top of the field getting closer and closer. 'I'm running out of field, mate. There must be something.'

'Nothing! Still no signal!'

'Typical fucking Oldham,' Danny said. 'It's like a Third World country.'

They reached the top of the field and Danny stopped. The wall was five or six feet high and there was no gate or break in the stones. The pupils were lined up in front of them now.

'Did you know?' Danny asked quietly, watching the teenagers as they walked towards them.

'What the fuck are you talking about?' Jonathan shouted. 'We need to go, now!'

'Did you know what Susan and Ben were doing?'

'No!' Jonathan cried. 'Well, not really. I mean, a bit, I suppose… but I don't KNOW know, if you know what I mean. Josh was talking about it at the hospital. Ranting about how we had to stop people harming kids, take them out and all that.'

'You seemed pretty happy to leave Charlie behind.'

'I wasn't… *happy*. I was just… I don't know. It's fucking complicated, Danny. You must know that better than anyone.'

'Yes,' Danny admitted. 'I suppose I do.'

'Now, can we go, please!' Jonathan cried. 'Go around them, past the school and head for the main gate.'

Danny put the car into first gear and shot off down the hill. He did his best to avoid the pupils as several hammers came flying at them. One cracked the windscreen making it difficult for Danny to see. He heard a heavy clunk to his left and the vehicle lurched briefly upwards. *Was that a rock in the field or a kid? I don't give a fuck, to be honest.*

They passed the caravan and saw Susan Matlock lying on the ground; her face was covered in blood. 'Looks like Susan will be calling in sick tomorrow,' Danny muttered as the Land Rover went up the hill on the other side of the valley and then headed down the other side towards the main school building. As they passed the side entrance, two more hammers hit the rear windscreen; the first cracked it, the second smashed it in. In the back, Charlie moaned as the glass covered him. Some of the glass hit DI McIntyre too, but he didn't make a sound.

'Any signal?' Danny shouted as the moorland wind came blasting through the car.

'No. Wait, yes. No, it's gone again.'

The car sped through the school car park and out onto the main drive towards the exit. A sign said:

THANK YOU FOR VISITING HUNTER'S HOLLOW SCHOOL. THANK YOU FOR BELIEVING IN US!

Twenty yards from the main road Danny saw a car heading towards the entrance from the main road. It was Kate's blue Mercedes.

'Yes!' Danny cried. 'It's your mum! God love her! Now we're talking.'

Danny waved at Kate through his broken window as they both approached the narrow exit at the same time. Danny waved at her to move back but instead Kate pulled her car across the drive and blocked it. 'Kate, shift yourself, we need to go,' Danny shouted as the Land Rover came to a halt. He looked around. Several pupils were coming down the school drive towards them on quad bikes.

'Kate, stop dicking about and move your arse!' Danny shouted.

Kate stepped out of the car. She looked at Danny. There were tears in her eyes as she shook her head.

'Kate, please. Jonathan's in the car. Come on!'

'Jonathan will be fine,' she said, hugging herself from the chill air. 'You've decided which side you're on, Danny. So have I.'

'FUCKING NORA!' Danny shouted. He banged his fist onto the

steering wheel. He looked around and saw that the lead quad biker was close to them now. It was Ben Matlock; he came to a skidding stop with a hammer held high over his head and was about to throw it at Danny. 'FUCKING FUCKING NORA!' Danny shouted. He jammed the Land Rover into reverse and backed up sharply, straight into Ben's quad bike.

Danny saw the bike fly to the right and Matlock go to the left. He drove forwards again, right up to Kate's car. 'Move yourself, Kate.'

She shook her head. 'You stood by and fucking let them do it, Kate,' Danny shouted. 'You fucking knew what was going on and you did nowt.'

'Not at first,' she said. 'I suspected, but I didn't know. We had to do *something* to stop them. Nothing else works, Danny. Stupid videos on the internet don't make a difference. You can't name and shame someone who's not ashamed of what they're doing.'

'But you can't just kill people just because you hate them, Kate. It'll never end.'

'You should have helped us, Danny. That's why Susan gave you all those stories. To get you onboard. You didn't mind what they were doing when you were making money out of it, did you?'

'What they're doing is sick, Kate. It infected poor Maggie Ormrod's mind and look what happened to her. Look how it pulled in your dad too. Nothing good has come from this. Your Jonathan can see this is wrong and he's just a kid. Yet somehow, you can't. Now move your car or I'll ram it out of the way.'

Kate stood her ground. A group of quad bikers were now grouped behind the Land Rover, unsure of what to do. Susan Matlock was walking up the drive towards her son. He was lying by the drive and wasn't moving. 'What are you waiting for, you stupid fucking kids,' she screamed. 'Stop him!'

'Fuck this,' Danny said. Danny banged the Land Rover into reverse, accelerated hard and smashed it straight into Kate's car.

'Danny!' Jonathan cried. 'Mind my mum, please!'

'I'll do my best,' Danny said, reversing again. He smashed into the car twice more until he'd battered Kate's Mercedes halfway across the road and there was enough space for the Land Rover to get by. Kate and Danny looked at each other as they passed; then he drove as fast as he could away from Hunter's Hollow School. Behind them, Danny could hear her screaming: 'Jonathan, please. Come back! I'm so sorry. Please.'

They were 100 yards down the road when Danny heard Jonathan's voice next to him: 'Hello? Yes! Police, please…'

SIXTY-ONE

CHARGES MADE OVER 'VIGILANTE' KILLINGS

Danny Johnston - Oldham Now

A mother and son have been charged with a series of murders after police were called to an award-winning school on the outskirts of Oldham.

Emergency crews found what eyewitnesses describe as a 'scene of carnage' at the Hunter's Hollow School near Denshaw. Many of those arrested required hospital treatment before they were taken in for questioning.

Susan Matlock, aged 47, and her son Ben, 25, have both been charged with multiple counts of murder. The charges follow the deaths of Barry Mortimer, Kabeer Sajid, Adil Aziz and Paul Docherty in alleged 'vigilante' killings.

The Matlocks have also been charged with the murder of Detective Constable Karl McIntyre. His body was discovered on Crow Knowl on Crompton Moor, accompanied by a note apologising for his death. He's the brother of Detective Inspector Patrick McIntyre who was also badly injured during the events at Hunter's Hollow. He's currently in the Royal Oldham Hospital but is expected to make a full recovery.

The Matlocks also face kidnapping, false imprisonment and grievous bodily harm charges in relation to another person, Charles Morris of Chadderton. Mr Morris also sustained serious injuries at Hunter's Hollow; it's alleged he'd been tortured. He's now in hospital but his injuries aren't thought to be life-threatening.

Nineteen other people face conspiracy charges in connection with the incidents; they can't be named for legal reasons because of their ages.

Another person, local businesswoman Kate Smithdown (52) has also been charged with conspiracy. She's been released on police bail on the understanding that she doesn't contact anyone connected with the school or members of her own family.

Susan and Ben Matlock have both been remanded in custody and will appear before Oldham Magistrates tomorrow morning. The teenagers connected with the case have all been taken into the care of Oldham Social Services and are being held in secure units across the town.

SIXTY-TWO

'Painkillers are all well and good,' Danny said, looking at the metal rods and pins that were clustered in and around DI Patrick McIntyre's arm. 'But there's only one thing that will really get you on the mend. And that's these fellahs.'

Danny put a box of Wine Gums onto the cabinet next to the detective's hospital bed and made a dramatic hand gesture towards them, like a magician drawing his audience's attention to a thing of great wonder.

'Thank you very much, Danny,' McIntyre said. 'If my arm didn't feel like an elephant was sitting on it, I'd give you a great big manly hug.'

'Speaking of your horrifically mangled arm, young Jonathan asked me to say hello,' Danny added. 'And to say sorry, of course. Sorry for driving into the caravan and breaking your arm in 97 places and all that. He's concerned he's going to be charged with assaulting a police officer. I told him not to worry about it.'

'That's very Christian of you,' McIntyre said. 'How's he doing?'

'All things considered, not bad,' Danny replied. He smiled at Jenny as she approached with her drinks' trolly. She handed him a cup of Vimto and a Tunnock's Teacake. 'Me and him are staying at Smithdown's house for the time being. Until we get things sorted out.'

'You, Smithdown and Johnathan all under the same roof,' Jenny laughed. 'What's it like looking after that pair, Danny?'

'It's not easy,' Danny replied with a shake of his head. 'He's moody, answers back all the time and plays his music way too loud. Jonathan can be a pain in the arse as well.'

'Very funny,' Jenny said. 'That poor boy. He's been through so much. He's lucky to have you as a friend, Danny. Anyway, I need to get on. Can't have people thinking I'm giving my son preferential treatment, can I? You take care, Danny. Don't take any nonsense from this one.'

'I won't, Jenny.' He gave her a hug. She smelled of Vimto. Just for a moment, Danny thought he might cry. *Not everyone's a bad un.* It was as if Jenny could sense it, so she held him just a few moments longer.

'I mean it,' she whispered. 'Take care, Danny. People forget how much you've been through too.'

'Thank you, Jenny. I will.'

Danny watched as she went out of the ward, then took a seat next to DI McIntyre's bed. 'She's lovely, your mum.'

'She could still knock the shit out of you, though,' the detective replied.

'I know, but who doesn't appreciate a highly protective mum? Wish I'd had one.'

'Some mums can take being protective a bit too far though, can't they?' McIntyre pointed out. 'Is Kate sticking to her bail conditions?'

'So far, yes,' Danny said. 'I think it's only a matter of time until she tries to contact Jonathan though. It's just the way she is. I think she genuinely believes she was doing the right thing. I bet the courts might disagree with her, though.'

'And how's Smithdown doing?' McIntyre asked.

'He's putting his stoic, old school Oldham face on things but I think he's pretty devastated that Kate could side with what was going on at Hunter's Hollow. I don't blame him – I am too.'

McIntyre scratched at the small area of skin on his hand that wasn't covered by plaster, bandages and steel rods. 'You were going to tell me about how you could prove Smithdown was innocent,' he said. 'You know, before I got my arm twisted backwards by a kid who can't drive.'

'I've found a friend of Maggie's who was in a care home at Greenacres with her. She'll give a statement confirming that it wasn't Smithdown who abused her.'

'Then what are you doing here? Get her down to Oldham Police Station sharpish.'

'I will,' Danny said. 'Definitely. But there's something I need to do first.'

SIXTY-THREE

'No care package?' Bob Donaldson asked as he sat down opposite Danny in the Strangeways visitors' area.

'No, Mr Donaldson,' Danny replied. He gripped his hands together under the table. They were shaking. 'No care package, I'm afraid. Not today.'

'Hardly worth coming then, was it?' he stated. 'I hear Kate Smithdown's been a bit of a naughty girl. Very disappointing. You can't be taking the law into your own hands, I always say. It's just not right.'

'Well, it's a good job you're here to provide us all with a bit of moral guidance, Mr Donaldson.'

'Have you come all this way just to take the piss, Danny Johnston? Wish I hadn't okayed your visit request now, to be honest.'

'Well I for one am very glad you did,' Danny said.

'Why's that then?'

'I met Alma Richards the other day. Do you know her?'

'I don't, I'm afraid,' Donaldson said. 'Is that it?'

'She was in a care home out at Greenacres with Maggie Ormrod. She certainly remembers you. For some reason, she thought your name was John… John Smithdown. I showed her a photo of you, and she identified you as the person that was always taking Maggie out of the care home back in the 70s. Treating her to the pictures, giving her money… all of that. They didn't call it grooming in those days, did they? But that was exactly what you were doing. You took your time too. No rushing, nice and steady. You've got to cover your tracks too, haven't you? Making sure her files all went missing; you even took that photo of Smithdown and Maggie, didn't you? When you were giving her a tour of the police station. Even then, all those years ago, you were covering your arse. Just in case.'

Donaldson stared at Danny. He didn't move. He just listened.

'Alma told me how you got Maggie pregnant,' Danny said, leaning in. 'Raped her then kept her and the kid hidden away in some ratty bedsit in Royton. By the time Maggie was old enough to realise how wrong the situation was, it was too late.'

'It's good stuff this, Danny Johnston,' Donaldson observed. 'Riveting. Do go on.'

'Sitting in here after you'd been done for the Mermaid's Pool murders, you knew you had to get rid of the kid, didn't you? Did you get some of your skinhead mates to snatch the lad? Doing it at the start of the Strangeways riot was the perfect cover, wasn't it? Being in here, you would have known trouble was brewing. I wouldn't be surprised if you actually started it. You arranged to have that kid given to Jan Cave and Beth Hall. And they tortured him and killed him. Then they dumped him out at Black Moss. You handed that kid over to them like a piece of meat. That poor little lad, face down in the sand at Black Moss. All these years and I never knew his name. Now I do. Alma told me. Robbie Ormrod. His name was Robbie Ormrod. Maggie's son. *Your* son.'

Though the visitor's room was noisy, there was total silence between the two men. Donaldson continued to stare at Danny. Then he clutched his chest and grimaced in agony. Danny flinched and jumped to his feet. Then Donaldson's face changed to a smile. 'Ooh, you got me. You're so fucking clever… you got me,' he laughed. 'You're right! So… fucking… what. Nobody gave a shit about the kid then. Nobody gives a shit about him now. You and John Smithdown on your high horses. Fuck the pair of you.'

'It's always been you, hasn't it?' Danny said, raising his voice. One of the guards glanced in his direction. 'Every truly terrible thing that's happened in Oldham for decades has your stink attached to it. Black Moss, the Mermaid's Pool, Hanging Lees. All covered in Bob Donaldson's shit. Even while you were in here you were still infecting the whole town with it. Well not any more. You're done.'

'It's not like the films this, you know,' Donaldson said, jabbing at the table with his finger. 'This is real life. You can't suddenly whip out your phone and show me you were recording the conversation the whole time. That's the beauty of this place. No phones allowed. It's on the list, along with see-through clothing and crop tops that reveal the stomach. No phones. You can't prove anything, Danny Johnston. And even if you could, what's the worst that could happen? I'm never getting out of Strangeways. I'm in here until I die. Good luck with making things worse for me than they already are. There's literally fuck all you can do to me.'

Danny was quiet for a moment. He thought about Maggie Ormrod, lying next to Hanging Lees Reservoir. He thought about the deaths at the Mermaid's Pool and how Oldham had come close to a race war thanks to Bob Donaldson. And he thought about little Robbie Ormrod, lying face down in the sand on the edge of Black Moss in 1990.

Then he thought about standing outside Strangeways during the riot in 1990. He remembered hearing the mainstream prisoners breaking down walls to get to E Wing, where the sex offenders were. From the perimeter fence he had listened to the prisoners shouting as they smashed their way towards the section of the jail where the lowest of the low were housed. They chanted as they got closer and closer: 'BEASTS! BEASTS! BEASTS, BEASTS, BEASTS!'

One remand prisoner in E Wing had later died after getting an horrific beating from the mainstream prisoners. Danny even remembered his name. Derek White. Beaten to death because he was in E Wing. Where the sex offenders were.

Bob Donaldson wasn't in the sex offenders wing. Because as far as the prison was concerned, he wasn't a sex offender.

'You're wrong, Mr Donaldson. There is something I can do.'

'Oh, fuck off, you self-righteous prick,' the old man said.

'Goodbye Mr Donaldson.'

Danny stood up, put a foot onto his seat and got up onto the table. He looked across at the other visitors. And the prisoners. He could see that he'd caught the attention of the guards immediately. They shouted at him to get down.

He didn't have much time. 'HEY!' he shouted. 'LISTEN! LISTEN TO ME! THIS MAN IS A PAEDOPHILE.' He pointed down at Donaldson. 'HE GROOMED A YOUNG GIRL CALLED MAGGIE ORMROD AND RAPED HER. HE RAPED A LITTLE GIRL AND SHE HAD A KID. A BOY CALLED ROBBIE. WHEN HE THOUGHT HE WAS GOING TO GET FOUND OUT HE ORGANISED FOR ROBBIE TO BE KILLED. THIS MAN, RIGHT HERE. HE'S A CHILD RAPIST. HE'S CALLED BOB DONALDSON. AND HE'S IN H WING.'

Danny heard someone shout: 'Control and restraint!' The guards dragged him from the table, and he was pulled firmly to the floor. Three guards were on his legs and arms immediately; they pushed the left side of his face firmly onto the floor. 'We're going to keep your head down, so you don't hurt yourself or bite one of us,' one prison officer said. 'Then we're taking you out of here. Please don't struggle, understand?'

Danny confirmed that he understood; from his position on the floor he still was facing Bob Donaldson and could still talk. 'It's one thing to be an ex-cop in prison, Bobby lad,' he shouted. 'But it's quite another to be a paedophile. A child raping, murdering fucking paedophile.'

The prison officers picked him up and carried him away, headfirst towards the exit. As he was transported through the visitor's area, Danny carried on shouting as loud as he could: 'BOB DONALDSON! H WING!'

Danny was at the door now: 'BEAST!' he cried. 'BEAST! BEAST! BEAST, BEAST, BEAST!'

SIXTY-FOUR

That night, Danny dreamed about The Shirtless Boy.

Robbie Ormrod.

The two were standing on a metal walkway. Robbie had no shirt on. As ever. Danny gave him a parcel wrapped in brown paper, tied up with string. The boy opened it, excitedly. It was a V-necked jumper; the kind that gave the impression the wearer was sporting another top underneath it. Danny remembered wearing them when he was a kid.

Despite Robbie having no facial features, Danny knew the boy was pleased with it; he put it on and looked at it admiringly. Then Danny took the boy by the hand, and they headed along the walkway.

They were at Strangeways… *inside* Strangeways.

The prison was a ruin. Danny had seen footage of the jail after the riot in a documentary on Granada TV. The riot had clearly ended, and the jail looked empty. Toilet paper hung down from the balconies like streamers; rubble and rubbish filled the safety netting that hung below the balconies; the walls were covered in graffiti. Danny and Robbie stopped to look at one of the paint-daubed walls. Someone had written:

WE WONDER WHY?

Still holding hands, the pair walked on. At the end of the walkway a slit of light could be seen from under one of the cell doors. They stood outside and Robbie looked up expectantly at Danny.

I don't know what you want. Tell me.

Robbie nodded towards Danny's pocket. For the first time Danny noticed that there was something heavy there. He reached in; it was a key. A large, metal key. Danny handed it to Robbie; he took it and put it into the cell door. It took both hands for the boy to turn the lock. There was a satisfying loud *thunk* when the mechanism shifted.

A strip of moonlight stretched across the walkway as the cell door swung open. Bob Donaldson was asleep in his bed.

Danny and Robbie looked at him and then at each other.

Robbie put a finger to his face where his lips should have been, then waved his hand at Danny to say goodbye.

Bye Robbie.

Then the boy stepped inside and closed the cell door.

SIXTY-FIVE

KILLER COP FOUND DEAD IN STRANGEWAYS

Danny Johnston - Oldham Now

Bob Donaldson, the former police detective who was behind the Oldham race riots of the 1980s, has been found dead in his cell at Strangeways Jail.

Donaldson, who was 84, was given a 'life-means-life' sentence for his part in a brutal string of murders that were part of a plot to kickstart a race war in Oldham.

The former Detective Constable conspired with neo-Nazi groups to stage a series of murders and racist attacks in Oldham in 1988. Among his victims was Oldham Councillor Sharmeen Chowdhury, who was burned to death at the Mermaid's Pool beauty spot in neighbouring Derbyshire. Mountain rescue volunteer Brian McIntyre also died at the same spot, along with Oldham woman Naomi Wells.

Donaldson's co-conspirator, racist murderer Tom Lennon, also died in prison in 1993. He was stabbed to death, the victim of an apparent revenge attack. The cause of Bob Donaldson's death isn't yet known.

Meanwhile, Donaldson's former colleague, retired detective John Smithdown, has been cleared of any wrongdoing in connection with the recent death of Oldham woman Maggie Ormrod. She's believed to have taken her own life at Hanging Lees Reservoir; a note left at the scene said she'd been abused as a child by an Oldham police officer. That officer is now known to have been Bob Donaldson.

SIXTY-SIX

Danny tucked the sandwiches he'd made into a rucksack, added a water bottle and some fruit and zipped it up. 'Ready?' he asked Jonathan.

'Ready,' the teenager replied. 'See you later, Grandad.' He leant in and kissed John Smithdown on the head.

'See you in a bit, lad,' Smithdown said. 'Take care out on those moors.'

'See you John,' Danny said. He also moved in to kiss the ex-detective.

'Fuck off, Danny, you weirdo,' Smithdown said, swatting him away.

'We'll make a metrosexual of you yet, mate,' Danny said. 'Right, got the flowers, Jonathan?'

'I have,' the teenager said. 'I've taken all the cellophane off them too. There's enough rubbish out on the moors without us adding to it.'

'That is very true,' Danny agreed. 'Jenny, are you sure you won't come with us? You know the hills better than anyone.'

Jenny Seddon came through from the kitchen with mugs of tea for herself and Smithdown. 'No, I'll stop here and look after His Lordship,' she said. 'But I wonder if you would do me a favour?' She went to her shoulder bag and pulled out two small bunches of tulips. They'd been tied together with a natural raffia ribbon. She gave them to Jonathan. 'Danny will know where to place them,' she said.

'Yes, I do, Jenny,' Danny confirmed. 'It'll be an honour.'

Danny and Jonathan drove away from Smithdown's house and headed up Huddersfield Road towards Black Moss Reservoir. Jonathan had Jenny's box of newspaper cuttings on his lap and was leafing through them as they went.

As he drove, Danny could clearly remember the directions he'd been given in 1990 when he'd been sent out to Black Moss when all the good reporters were busy covering the Strangeways riot:

Stop at Brun Clough Reservoir car park. There's a Pennine Way sign on your right. Walk the PW path until you reach another reservoir, (Redbook). The next one is Black Moss Reservoir, with Little Black Moss next to it. Look for a beach and police activity.

After they'd parked up, Danny and Jonathan set off down the windy Pennine Way path. The gravel soon gave way to paving slabs, which rocked and squelched under their feet; the ground below was soaked through with water. The path forked right at the first reservoir and then headed upwards, following the soft, rolling flow of the moorland. The slabs that formed the path were drier here, the slope of the route allowing the moisture to drain off the watershed. Danny looked right; down through the valleys he could see the growing skyscrapers of Manchester. He looked left; over there were the neighbouring moors of Yorkshire.

Even after all these years he was still surprised by the sheer unrelenting *nothingness* of the area. It was like the world had been horizontally cut in two - sky at the top, moor at the bottom, with nothing to provide any form of relief from the two themes. *Not even a tree. Not one. In any direction. Bleak.*

As they crested the hill, Danny could see a second reservoir; the wind pushed tiny, quick waves across the surface of the water. Danny saw a dark, yellowy strip that separated the mossy moorland from the reservoir. Next to the reservoir - there was no other word for it - was a beach.

They stood quietly for a while, then Jonathan took out two bunches of flowers. Danny laid them on the sand close to the water's edge; one for his old friend from Manchester Radio, Gary Keenan, the other for Robbie Ormrod. 'How old would Robbie have been now?' Jonathan asked.

'I've never thought of it like that,' Danny said. 'My God, he'd be about 40. Old enough to be your dad.'

'Fucking Nora, as Grandad would say,' Jonathan replied.

Danny smiled. 'Yes, he probably would say that, wouldn't he?'

The pair stood still for a few moments. Then Jonathan spoke: 'Let's go, shall we? Lots to do.'

They retraced their steps, returned to Danny's car, then headed south past Bury and Ashton and then through Glossop before cutting through the village of Hayfield. Smithdown had told Danny that in the 80s, the local mountain rescue team had been based in an old stable building behind a pub. It still was, and Danny pointed it out to Jonathan as they drove through the village and up Kinder Road.

They parked up at Bowden Bridge next to the plaque that marked the start of the Kinder Scout Mass Trespass in 1932. Danny explained to the teenager how young ramblers and communists had taken it upon themselves to organise a mass invasion of the moors around Kinder Scout in 1932, a place that they were forbidden to walk on by moneyed landowners.

Then they took out a bunch of Jenny's flowers and placed them in the rocks below the plaque. Danny told Jonathan about Jordan McIntyre and how he'd taken his own life here in 1998, ten years after the murder of his father. For the second time that day they took a moment to think about what had happened at this spot. Then, once again, they moved on.

Danny and Jonathan headed up a cobbled path, past Kinder Reservoir and across the moors towards a walled plantation of trees. They saw scorch marks on the rocks from the fire that had been set there in 1988. Jonathan read out a cutting from the *Manchester Evening News* that detailed the bravery award that his grandad had received for his actions that night. Danny pointed out that Jenny Seddon of the Derbyshire Constabulary had also received one.

'Grandad says it's pronounced Con-stab-u-lary,' Jonathan said.

'If that's what he says, then it must be true,' Danny agreed.

They passed through the plantation and over a steep brow; in front of them was the Mermaid's Pool. It seemed strangely unimpressive; brown and shallow-looking, with a few rocks and reed banks scattered around the perimeter. It was about 40 feet long and less than 20 feet wide in the middle. It was uneven, shaped not unlike a map of Ireland. Behind the pool, the ground rose up sharply to meet the edge of the Kinder plateau above. Blue dragonflies flitted and swooped around the water's edge.

Jonathan found another cutting that told of how Councillor Sharmeen Chowdhury had been murdered here, set on fire by a racist gang led by Bob Donaldson and Tom Lennon. Jonathan got upset after reading it and took a walk around the water's edge to recover. They left flowers at the place where her body had been found and moved on.

Then they walked under the edge of Kinder Scout and went to bottom of Red Brook, the ravine that stretched up to the lip of the Kinder plateau high above them. They left two bunches of flowers;

one for Naomi Wells, who'd sacrificed her life to save her daughter here in 1988 and another for Jenny's partner Brian McIntyre.

Having read the cuttings in Jenny's box, Jonathan convinced Danny to make another, unplanned stop. They called in at a florist and left flowers at the boating lake of Alexandra Park in Oldham town centre. 'They're for all the people killed and hurt in the race riots in 1988,' Jonathan said. 'We shouldn't forget them.'

'You're right,' Danny said as they stood next to the boating house next to the lake. 'As usual.'

Finally, they returned to John Smithdown's house to pick up the retired detective. Jenny made sure Smithdown was wrapped up warm but declined their offer to come too. 'It should just be you three, I reckon,' she said. 'I'll see you when you get back.'

There was no way Smithdown could have walked to Black Moss, and the Mermaid's Pool would have been totally impossible. But Hanging Lees had a wide path running up to it and Danny was able to drive right up to the reservoir, despite annoying some of the walkers who were crossing the Piethorne Valley.

When they got there, Jonathan handed his grandfather the last bunch of flowers and Smithdown attached them to the metal gate at Hanging Lees. He tucked it between a fish and a dragonfly on the ornate metalwork. 'Maggie Ormrod, that poor woman,' Smithdown said. 'She had no chance, did she, lads? Right from the start. No chance at all.'

'We'll come back again another time, Grandad,' Jonathan said. 'With more flowers. We won't forget her.'

'That's a lovely thought, lad,' Smithdown said, cupping Jonathan's face with his hands. The old man looked across the water. 'What are you going to do then, Danny?' Smithdown asked. 'Your website has gone a bit quiet. There's been nothing new since your story about Bob. What's the plan?'

'My heart's not in it anymore,' Danny said. 'Not in the way it works now, anyway. Making money off people dying, writing stuff that's just designed to get clicks and put eyes on adverts. It seems wrong. Maybe I'll turn *Oldham Now* into a subscription service. Charge people a few quid a month. That way I can write longer, more in depth stuff, not just snappy headlines about death and destruction. Proper stories that could make a real difference. I'd like to investigate hospital jumping, those addicts going from hospital to hospital blagging pills. That kind of thing.'

Danny looked across at Jonathan: 'Maybe I could take an apprentice on, who knows?'

'I'd rather he got a proper job than be a journalist,' Smithdown said with a wink. 'That's a job for dickheads, that is.'

The wind was gathering now. It moved the surface of the reservoir left and right. The sky was blue but the reservoir was stubbornly grey. 'Hanging Lees…' Danny said. 'Who the fuck calls a reservoir Hanging Lees? It sounds like a Nick Cave song, doesn't it? *The Ballad of Hanging Lees.*'

'Who's Nick Cave, Grandad?' Jonathan asked.

'I don't bloody know,' Smithdown said. 'One of those modern singers I suppose. Sounds a bit depressing.'

'Right,' said Danny. 'Let's get ourselves off home.'

'Can we go to the chippy on the way back?' Jonathan asked.

'That sounds like a great idea, what do you say John?'

'It's a resounding yes from me, Danny,' the ex-detective said. 'Steak pudding, chips, peas and gravy please. You're buying. Jonathan, call Jenny and see what she fancies.'

Danny took one last look at the dark, choppy waters of Hanging Lees. 'Fucking reservoirs,' he said. 'They creep me out.'

'They're just lumps of water, Danny. They can't do anyone any harm. It's people that do that.'

'Maybe. But I'll tell you what, John. I'm never going near a reservoir ever again.'

THE END

Books in the Manc Noir series…

- *Black Moss*
- *The Mermaid's Pool*
- *The Ballad of Hanging Lees*

Author's Note

The events of this book are fictional, but like all the stories in the Manc Noir series, they are based on fact. In 2021 the National Society for the Prevention of Cruelty to Children (NSPCC) carried out freedom of information requests on police forces in England and Wales. They found that online grooming crimes recorded by police jumped by around 70% in the last three years reaching an all-time high in 2021.

There were 5,441 Sexual Communication With a Child offences recorded between April 2020 and March 2021, an increase of around 70% from recorded crimes in 2017/18.

Almost half of the offences used Facebook-owned apps, including Instagram, WhatsApp and Messenger.

Instagram was the most common site used, flagged by police in 32% of instances where the platform used was known.

Snapchat was used in over a quarter of offences, meaning the big four platforms were used in 74% of instances where the platform used was known.

Andy Burrows, Head of Child Safety Online Policy at the NSPCC, said: 'Year after year tech firms' failings result in more children being groomed and record levels of sexual abuse. To respond to the size and complexity of the threat, the Government must put child protection front and centre of legislation.'

Acknowledgements

For the title of this book, I need to thank Jake Lucas-Nolan: 'Dad, you're collecting weird reservoir names, right? I've found one called Hanging Lees…' David Prior of *Altrincham Today*, a pioneer of hyper local news, helped me with the realities of running a news operation like *Oldham Now*. David doesn't run adverts in stories where people have died. See, journalists can be good guys too.

Police Coroners Officer Emma Campbell advised me on the crime scene stuff. She was about to go on maternity leave when she was helping me and was still messaging me when she went into labour. That's dedication for you.

Maureen Carnighan, OU Distance Learning Co-Ordinator for HMP Manchester (Strangeways) and Amy Jenner of Partners of Prisoners were very patient and helped me with the up-to-date procedures for visiting prisons. Strangeways Prison Officer Russ Kenyon was a great help, explaining exactly what would happen if a visitor started making a nuisance of themselves, like Danny does at the end of the book.

Thank you also to Matt Keyes for making sure the vibe was right and that the book stayed true to Oldham.

The Map of Manc Noir is by Lucy Milburn. Check out her work on Instagram at @lucymilburnart.

Thanks to everyone who gave me their time for all the books in the Manc Noir series, especially Nicola Graham, former Detective Constable with Greater Manchester Police who was there for all three. We've been through a lot together.

About The Author

David Nolan is a journalist and television producer and the author of Manc Noir books *Black Moss* and *The Mermaid's Pool*. His true-life crime book *Tell the Truth and Shame the Devil*, which followed the largest historic abuse case ever mounted by Greater Manchester Police, was the basis for the multi award-winning Radio 4 documentary *The Abuse Trial*. David has also written music biographies about Tony Wilson, Ed Sheeran and The 1975. His book about the infamous Sex Pistols gig at the Lesser Free Trade Hall in Manchester in 1976, *I Swear I Was There*, was called 'one of the greatest rock stories ever told,' by *GQ* magazine. His writing has also appeared in *The Mirror*, *The Mail*, the *Manchester Evening News* and the *NME*.

More books from Fahrenheit Press

Black Moss by David Nolan

In April 1990, as rioters took over Strangeways prison in Manchester, someone killed a little boy at Black Moss.

And no one cared.

No one except Danny Johnston, an inexperienced radio reporter trying to make a name for himself.

More than a quarter of a century later, Danny returns to his home city to revisit the murder that's always haunted him.

If Danny can find out what really happened to the boy, maybe he can cure the emptiness he's felt inside since he too was a child.

But finding out the truth might just be the worst idea Danny Johnston has ever had.

"As one would expect from a writer with the skill and experience of David Nolan, this haunting book deals with very difficult issues in an incredibly sympathetic manner while at the same time throwing a light onto one of the most complicated and shaming areas of our society - the failure to protect those who are the most vulnerable."

The Mermaid's Pool by David Nolan

Detective Inspector John Smithdown is a good man with some bad things to deal with.

It's 1988 and ecstasy is flooding the streets of Manchester. The Second Summer of Love is here.

Tell that to the locals on DI Smithdown's patch.

Over one weekend, Smithdown is faced with a missing single-mum, machete wielding gangs in Oldham, simmering racial tensions across communities and a mutilated body found at the edge of a remote lake with a mythical reputation.

People say bad things happen at the Mermaid's Pool. They're dead right.

David Nolan – author of Black Moss - brings you a second helping of Manc Noir. Things just got even darker.

'Manchester is a location that's been underused in fiction but David Nolan is keen to claim it - this is Manc Noir" - Northern Soul Magazine

The Beloved Children by Tina Jackson

Three young women; Chrysanthemum, Rose & Orage are thrown together on the stage of Fankes' Theatre during the closing days of the Second World War performing as The Three Graces.

It's there they come under the spell of wardrobe mistresses Dolores and Janna – a chance encounter that will guide and change all of their fates forever.

Set in the dying days of vaudeville theatre and laced with mysticism, fortune tellers, ghosts, and evocative descriptions of the closing days of the War - The Beloved Children will literally make you laugh out loud and perhaps even shed the odd tear.

The Beloved Children is wise, funny, heart-breaking, joyous, poignant, and entirely entirely enthralling.

"There is some really atmospheric storytelling and joyful language at play here, with Jackson as an entertaining mistress of ceremonies." - Ben East, The Observer

Blood & Cinders by DDC Morgan

London 1949. Speedway fever runs high.

Its stars are the working class heroes of a Blitz-torn city emerging from the ravages of war. With cash in their wallets and hoards of adoring fans, these dirt-track chancers enjoy a life of speed, celebrity and sex.

But as Bermondsey Bullets defend their league title, they are rocked by the death of star rider Des Fenton in a mid-race smash.

It's the start of a new and dangerous chapter for stadium security boss Reg Calloway, as he's dragged into the dark side of life at the track, with echoes of his own troubled wartime past.

"DDC Morgan perfectly captures the sheer raw excitement of speedway's glory days..."